SAUNA SEDUCTION

'Oh God,' he muttered, and pulled her towards him; she found herself sitting sideways on his lap, her hands round his neck and her mouth opening under his. He stroked the bare skin on her back, making her arch towards him; he broke the kiss just long enough to untangle her arms from round his neck and slide the straps of her swimming costume over her shoulders.

'I don't care if anyone comes in,' he said hoarsely. 'I need you too much. I need to see you, Carolyn. I need to touch you, to taste you.'

He pushed the costume down to bare her breasts, then bent his head to bury his face in the creamy globes . . .

Days of Desire

Evelyn D'Arcy

NEW ENGLISH LIBRARY
Hodder and Stoughton

Typeset by Hewer Text Limited, Edinburgh
Printed and bound in Great Britain by
Clays Ltd, St Ives plc
Hodder and Stoughton

A division of Hodder Headline PLC
338 Euston Road
London NW1 3BH

For Nicola

ONE

Carolyn drove along the A11, her windscreen wipers on full pelt. What the hell was she doing, driving from Norwich to deepest Cambridgeshire at six p.m. on a Friday evening in torrential rain? There were all sorts of things she could have done instead – maybe gone to London to stay with friends, or painted her bathroom, or spent the weekend indulging herself by lazing in bed with a good book and a tub of expensive vanilla ice-cream . . .

She sighed. Who the hell was she kidding? She was doing her friend Mandy a favour, yes – agreeing to run her writing course, that weekend, as Mandy had been laid up with the flu – but Mandy was also doing her just as much a favour. Spending the weekend working would help to take Carolyn's mind off things. At least she would be busy, instead of doing what she had done the previous weekend: spending the whole time mooching round, feeling miserable and replaying events over and over and over again in her mind, wondering where she'd gone so wrong.

She turned up the volume on her car stereo, and scowled in irritation as the opening notes of the next track flooded through the vehicle's interior: *This Ain't A Love Song*. She wished suddenly that she hadn't borrowed the Bon Jovi tape from Mandy. The last thing she needed, right at that moment, was to listen to slushy rock ballads about relationships breaking up. She jabbed at the eject button and retuned the stereo to Radio Three. At least classical music was safe. It wouldn't make her think about Rupert. He had disliked classical music, not sharing her love of cello concertos, so she had only ever played contemporary music in his company.

Rupert. No, she wasn't going to think about him. She wasn't going to think about what had happened, his cruel words that had cut her to the quick. She forced herself to focus on the weekend ahead of her instead, and on the course. Carolyn had originally trained as a journalist, but she had always had a slight hankering to teach. Although she had enjoyed her job, she had always felt that she didn't quite suit office life; she had been happiest when she had been helping to train new entrants to the firm.

In the end, she had been headhunted by Write Right, a local creative-writing school. It had turned out to be the perfect job for her. She had recently been promoted to the position of Director of New Courses, but she still taught personally a couple of the programmes. She ran the ones on the principles of copywriting and journalism; if the school was short-handed, she ran the PR course as well. She didn't usually teach creative writing – that was her friend Amanda Wedderburn's department – but as Mandy had gone down with an especially virulent strain of flu, one that had robbed her of her voice and left her with an almost continual hacking cough, she had asked Carolyn to step in on this particular course.

Carolyn couldn't restrain a smile. She had expected it to be the usual course about romance writing or short stories so she'd thought she would be dealing mainly with character, conflict and plot. But Mandy had put her straight. *This* course was about writing erotica for women, with an all-female group.

Her smile faded. Erotica. She wasn't sure that she could teach it. If Mandy had asked her a couple of weeks before, she would have been fine. She would have had no doubts; she would even have enjoyed the thought of it. But after Rupert's accusations . . . Again, she shook herself. That was a forbidden topic of thought. Rupert wasn't worth even thinking about. She knew that. So why the hell couldn't she get him out of her head?

A black sports car came up close behind her then overtook, cutting in narrowly in front of her. Annoyed, she gave the driver a V-sign. She was hardly crawling along. She was doing seventy, at the top end of the speed limit. And, considering how wet and slippery the roads were and how heavily the rain was coming down, she was probably driving too fast as it was. 'Boy racer,' she snarled at the sports car's tail lights. 'Arsehole.'

Yelling made her feel slightly better, and she let her mind drift back again to the course. It was a residential weekend course; she had run a few residential courses before, but not at this particular location. Heywood Hall. It was deep in Fenland, and was apparently an old manor house with a moat. *It would be the perfect place for a course on writing historical novels*, she thought. Or romance. And probably erotica, too.

If the place was as lush as Mandy said that it was, the environment would certainly help her get across the points about a story's setting. She only hoped that Mandy's information was accurate. Carolyn had taken a course before at a place that had sounded marvellous but hadn't lived up to the brochure's claims. Yes, it had been an old hall, and it had looked marvellous from the outside, all golden stone and red ivy; but the poky bedrooms had had hard mattresses and narrow beds that would have been more suited to a student Hall of Residence than to a hotel. None of the rooms had even had a washbasin, let alone an *en suite* bathroom, and they hadn't had a phone or an alarm clock, either.

The food had had more in common with school dinners than

with a good restaurant, featuring mothball-flavoured mashed potato and lumpy custard, and the teaching facilities had been diabolical. Carolyn had been prepared for the usual high-tech facilities – where she could attach her laptop to an overhead projector and run her presentation through it – but she had brought some old-fashioned overhead projector slides with her, just in case. She had learned the hard way that it was always safer to have a back-up, in case there was a glitch with the equipment. In the end, she had discovered that there wasn't even a flip chart for her to write on, let alone an overhead projector. There had been only a whiteboard, with pens that hadn't worked properly. Luckily, she'd had a spare set of pens with her, so all hadn't been lost.

The course delegates had taken it all in good part, and Carolyn had made sure that half the cost of their course had been refunded, to make up for the poor facilities. Write Right had never used that venue again, and she'd written a very sharp letter to the management – who had completely ignored it. Heywood Hall was an unknown quantity; she only hoped that it would be up to scratch. If it turned out to be anything like that bloody hotel in Warwickshire . . .

Her car skidded slightly on the wet road, then began to judder. She knew that the A11 was the main Norwich-to-London road, and that this particular stretch had recently been resurfaced – so it wasn't as if it was like the usual back roads in Norfolk, full of potholes and bumps that tested the suspension in every car. 'Oh, hell,' she groaned, annoyed. There was only one thing that it could be. A puncture.

She was at Roudham Heath, just outside Thetford Chase. *At least*, she thought gratefully, *I can pull off at the side of the road and do something about my flat tyre, without worrying about where the next lay-by is or whether another car might plough into me.* She slowed down, indicated left, and pulled off onto the Heath, not far from where Peddar's Way, the ancient track that led to the coast on the other side of Norfolk, crossed it. It was officially a picnic space, but the weather had put paid to anyone's idea of eating alfresco. The place was completely deserted. Even the hot-dog stand was closed.

She took her umbrella from the floor on the passenger side and climbed out of the car. The umbrella wasn't much protection against the rain, which was driven hard by the wind; by the time she had walked round to the other side of the car and confirmed that her front tyre was indeed flat, she was completely soaked. She got back into the car, throwing her umbrella on the floor in a fit of temper. Changing a tyre wasn't a job she relished at the best of times, but doing it in torrential rain was near enough impossible. She also had a nasty feeling that, as she had never taken off these particular wheel-nuts before, she would have problems.

The last thing that she wanted to do was to spend hours struggling to change the wheel, failing, and then being very late for the course. Still, she had upgraded her car insurance to include a roadside-rescue facility: it was just about to become active. She opened her handbag, taking out her mobile phone, and turned it on. It beeped twice – and turned itself off. Carolyn frowned, her blue eyes narrowing, and switched it on again. Again, there were two beeps, and again the phone switched itself off. She realized with horror that the battery was flat – she had forgotten to charge it up, the previous night. Probably because she'd been too busy brooding about bloody Rupert.

'Oh, fuck!' she said loudly. This meant that she couldn't phone the AA to come and rescue her. She couldn't phone Heywood Hall either, to warn everyone that she was going to be late. Roudham Heath was several miles from the edge of

Thetford, and the nearest garage had to be at least six miles away – well over an hour's walk even in the best of conditions, and it would be still more miserable in the rain. Part of her was tempted to thump the steering wheel, then lay her head on her hands and burst into tears. Though she knew that that wouldn't solve a thing. She had to go it alone, and hope that she could undo the wheel-nuts.

This time, when she got out of the car, she didn't bother putting up her umbrella. There was no point. Instead, she went to the boot, took out the jack, spanners and spare tyre, and went round to the front of the car again. She knelt down on the ground, not fussed by the fact that her knees would be covered with mud. She would have to change her wet clothes as soon as she got to Heywood Hall anyway, so a little mud wouldn't make any difference. She fitted the jack without any problems, then removed the hubcap and fitted the spanner to one of the wheel-nuts. It didn't budge. She tried again; still it didn't budge. 'Undo, you bloody thing, undo!' she growled at it; she pushed harder, but *still* it wouldn't budge. It was stuck fast, and she didn't have the brute strength to shift it.

'Need a hand?'

Carolyn looked up in shock. She had been so busy concentrating on trying to remove the wheel-nut that she hadn't seen the car pull up behind her, or the driver get out. She froze. For all she knew, he could be a maniac. It was every woman's worst nightmare, breaking down or having a problem with the car when she was on her own, miles from anywhere – and there had been more than enough cases reported in the papers about female motorists who'd broken down and then been raped or murdered by the person who'd offered to help.

On the other hand, this man didn't look like a maniac. He was tall, with dark hair brushed back from his face and cornflower-blue eyes, and he was wearing an expensively-cut dark suit. From her position at his feet, Carolyn could also see that his shoes were handmade and highly polished. She risked a quick glance at his car. It was a black and shiny BMW, with a personalized number plate: it looked like a new and very high-spec model. A man like this wasn't some social deviant who'd prey on vulnerable women. This was a genuine offer of help help that she needed, very badly. Pride didn't come into it.

She raked a hand through her wet dark hair, pulling it back from her face, and stood up. 'Thanks. It's just my luck to get a puncture, and the battery in my mobile's flat, so I couldn't call the AA to come and help me.'

'Sod's law,' he agreed.

He had a nice voice, too: slightly upper-class, well-spoken, with a flicker of humour round the edges. Despite her fury at the situation, particularly as it could have been so easily avoided, she found herself smiling at him.

'Here, let me.' He held out his hand; Carolyn gave him the spanner and he crouched down.

'What about your suit?' she asked, feeling suddenly guilty. With the amount of rain around them, there was no way that he could avoid being splashed with mud.

He shrugged. 'There are such things as dry cleaners.' From anyone else it would have been a put-down but, from the look on his face, he was merely passing a comment to say that it didn't matter, trying to make her feel better.

She watched him in silence as he undid the wheel-nuts, then changed the wheel efficiently. He had nice hands, she thought. The hands of someone who was more used to an office job – but was practical with it. She could imagine those hands undoing her shirt, stroking her skin, and . . .

She forced the thought away. Christ, what was wrong with

7

her? She had just split up with Rupert, her lover of twelve months, and here she was, fantasizing about the first man she met. A man whom she didn't even know was available. *Don't say that I'm turning into one of those desperate women who'll fling herself at anything in trousers rather than be alone*, she thought grimly.

Though this man *was* extremely attractive. He was the proverbial tall, dark and handsome stranger. His car should have been white, not black: the knight on the white charger, rescuing the damsel in distress. She smiled to herself, catching her thoughts. How ridiculous. And yet it was an irresistible comparison.

He lowered the jack again, straightened up, and smiled at her. 'All done. Though you'll need to get your spare sorted out over the weekend.'

'Yes. Thanks.' She smiled back at him. When he had been bent over the wheel, his face partly hidden from her; she hadn't realized just how attractive his mouth was, with a full lower lip that promised a deep sensuality. A generous mouth, one that she could so easily imagine trailing over her skin, starting innocuously on her cheek and travelling down, caressing her jaw, moving over her throat and the hollows of her collarbones, then drifting down still further, gliding over her breasts and tantalizing her nipples with his lips and his tongue . . .

Again, she jerked herself away from the thought. This was ridiculous. For all she knew, he was married – or, at least, very firmly part of a couple – and anyway, why the hell would he be interested in someone like her? She was average-looking: of average height, with dark hair worn in a glossy bob, blue eyes and fair skin. She wasn't fashionably thin, though she wasn't overweight, either. Just average. Her face wasn't ugly but neither was she the stunning kind who could attract second glances, even if she wore make-up. She could have melted into any crowd with ease. Carolyn Saunders was, quite simply, ordinary – and she knew it.

He put the punctured tyre into her boot, then replaced the jack and spanners and closed the boot for her. She held out her hand. 'Thank you. I don't think that I could have done it on my own.'

He took her hand, shaking it. 'Yes, it was pretty stiff.'

She couldn't help flushing as the *double entendre* hit her and she glanced automatically at his groin. She was furious with herself for being so adolescent, particularly as she knew that her high colour – on her usually fair skin – was very, very obvious. 'Mm.' She didn't trust herself to speak.

It was probably just her imagination. Of course he wasn't aroused. Of course his cock wasn't stiff and engorged from the way he had been fantasizing about her. He had just been a good Samaritan, stopping to help a fellow motorist who was obviously stranded. The bulge at his groin was – oh, something in his trouser pocket, that was all.

She didn't dare to meet his eyes. She felt too ashamed of herself, of the sudden rush of desire flowing through her body. This was crazy. Utterly crazy. And yet, at the same time, it was irresistible. There was a kind of current running between them, a current of pure raw sexual attraction. Her whole body was aware of him, of the way his body moved when he breathed. It made her blood pound hard in her veins; it made her nipples harden and her sex begin to pool. She wanted him. She wanted him badly.

He looked at her for a moment, then rubbed his hands on his trousers, wiping the dirt and grease from them before taking her chin between his thumb and forefinger. Carolyn froze. This wasn't happening. He wasn't touching her. He wasn't going to— Then she stopped thinking as he bent his head and touched his mouth to hers. It felt as good as she had imagined, his mouth soft and warm against hers; she couldn't help responding, sliding her hands round his neck and pressing against him, opening her mouth beneath his.

A detached part of her brain said that she should stop, that very second. She didn't even know his name, for God's sake, and she was letting him kiss her intimately. He was sliding his tongue into her mouth, squeezing her buttocks and moulding her body against his so that she could feel his erection pressing against her pubis. Any moment now, he would start to peel her wet clothing from her skin – and they were at the side of the road. Anyone who pulled off even just a little way onto the Heath would see them. Anyone who glanced to the side of the road could see them. She was letting him make a public spectacle of her. She should stop, right then. She was no exhibitionist, and everyone knew that you didn't make love with a stranger, not even a perfect one, not in this day and age. Not if you valued your health.

But the sensible side of her wasn't strong enough to stop her body responding. She pressed against him; the combination of her arousal and the coolness of the rain had made her nipples so hard that they almost hurt. When she pressed against his chest, the friction on her nipples felt incredibly good. It made her want him to touch her more intimately. She wanted him to undo her shirt, take off her bra, and expose her naked body to the elements. She wanted him to suck her nipples, caress her breasts and stroke her skin, until her sex was hot and puffy and ready for him to penetrate her.

As if in a kind of dream, she registered that he had eased one hand between their bodies and was doing precisely that: undressing her and caressing her bared flesh. Her wet shirt had stuck to her skin, revealing the lacy pattern of her bra, the generous curves of her breasts and the very obviously erect state of her nipples. But he, too, obviously wanted to feel her skin to skin. His hands felt smooth and good against her body as he finished undoing her shirt and peeled back the wet, clinging material, exposing her bra.

He held her away from him for a moment, looking at her; then, slowly, he dipped one forefinger under the edge of her bra and pulled one cup down to expose her breast. Carolyn tipped her head back and closed her eyes, delighting in the feel of the rain on her skin. It was raining harder and she felt as though she were standing beneath some kind of gigantic cosmic shower. The cold water bounced off her skin, the little needle-like jets of water hardening her nipples still further; the man standing before her made a small noise of pleasure at the sight and repeated his action with the other cup of her bra, pulling it down to expose her creamy skin, her taut and dusky-rose nipple.

Carolyn suddenly didn't care that virtually anyone who might drive past could see them. It didn't matter any more. It wasn't important. What *was* important was the way that he was touching her, his fingertips brushing the sensitive undersides of her breasts. And then, to her mingled delight and relief, she felt him cup those breasts, rubbing his thumb over the hard peaks of flesh. She arched her back, lifting her ribcage at the same time; then he began to kiss his way down her throat, his breath warm and sensual against her rain-soaked skin.

His lips drifted lower, lower; at last she felt his mouth close over one nipple, and he began to suck on the hard peak of flesh, using the tip of his tongue to stimulate it even more. She slid her hands into his hair, massaging his scalp with her fingertips and urging him on. His sucking grew harder, fiercer; she could feel his teeth graze the sensitive tissues of her nipple, keeping just the right side of the pleasure–pain barrier. He switched to the other breast; she rocked against him, wanting more. She wanted him to use his mouth over the whole of her body; she wanted him to lick her like a cat. She wanted him to arouse her to screaming pitch with his lips and his tongue and his hands.

The next thing she knew, he had walked her back to the bonnet of his car and had gently pressed her backwards so that she was lying supine on the shiny metal. He began to bunch her straight dark skirt upwards. She lifted her buttocks slightly, letting him push the hem of her skirt up to her waist to reveal her thighs and her groin. She knew that she was behaving like a whore, but she didn't care. Blood was racing round her body, her heart was pounding, and she wanted to feel him inside her. She wanted him to make her come.

She was wearing tights, the fashionable opaque kind; she wished that she was wearing something more sensual. She should have been wearing sheer black silk stockings attached to a lacy suspender belt, or maybe even the hold-up type with black lacy welts that would give a tantalizing glimpse of her creamy thighs. As it was, she was dressed more like the professional tutor she was, not the sensualist she wanted to be.

He said nothing, and she felt him tug at the waistband of her tights as if to roll them down; then she heard a hissing sound, and realized that he had somehow managed to *rip* the tights, opening the seam all the way down to give him access to her crotch. Her quim felt warm and wet with excitement. Soon, soon, he would touch her. He would push the gusset of her knickers to one side, part her labia, and dabble his fingertips in her musky wetness. He wouldn't need to go down on her to lubricate her: she was already wet and slippery, ready to receive him. And she wanted him. She wanted him so badly. She wanted him to fill her.

Would he be shocked if she spoke her thoughts aloud? *I want you to fuck me.* Part of her wanted to do it, to be wild and rebellious and demanding; but part of her held back. Speaking might shatter the spell: and she couldn't bear it if he stopped now. She needed what he was going to do to her. She couldn't drive the thirty-odd miles between the Heath and Heywood Hall with her nipples hard, her quim unsatisfied, and her belly a tight coil of frustration, waiting until she could fling herself onto her bed in her hotel room and masturbate herself to a raging climax. She wanted to come, right now.

She opened her eyes; he was looking at her, and there was a dark slash of red across each cheekbone. She smiled in satisfaction. He was as turned on by this as she was. He, too, loved the spice, the danger of making love with a complete stranger – someone whose name he didn't know and probably never would. Someone he would never meet again. A brief encounter of the best kind. She widened the gap between her thighs, tipping her pelvis up. There was a flash of lightning and a loud crack of thunder; she nearly laughed aloud, in triumph and amusement and sheer glory. This was the stuff of fantasy – letting a complete stranger fuck her over the bonnet of his car, in the middle of a thunderstorm, her skin exposed to the elements. Except that this wasn't fantasy. This was really happening.

He pushed the gusset of her knickers to one side, and she spread her thighs wider, giving him access to her sex. He slid one finger down her quim, parting her labia and feeling how warm and wet and puffy her intimate flesh was. He slid one finger into her, and she closed her eyes again, tipping her head back and making a small noise of pleasure in the back of her throat. She didn't care that she wasn't lying on a bed, with her head on a feather pillow; the hardness of the car bonnet and the slight warmth from the engine felt so good, in such contrast with the coldness of the rain and the softness of water on her skin.

He sought her clitoris with his thumb, finding the hard bud of flesh and teasing it from its hood. Carolyn moaned again as he began to work on her clitoris, rubbing it lightly in a figure-of-eight pattern and then increasing the pressure, almost jabbing at the apex. She let her mind go into free fall and lifted her hands to her breasts, squeezing her nipples and enjoying the sensations running riot through her body. Tomorrow, maybe, she would deal with her emotions, deal with the guilt. Right now, all she wanted was pleasure – more and more pleasure. She wanted him to bring her to a shrieking climax, and then another. She wanted him to make her body come alive, echo the tumult of the storm.

He continued to rub her, plunging his finger in and out of her moist channel at the same time; neither of them spoke, but she knew without having to ask – or even look at him – that he was as turned on as she was. The sight of the woman lying on the bonnet of his car, abandoning herself to pleasure, was a sight that very few men could have resisted. She continued rubbing her nipples, plucking at them and opening her mouth in an 'Oh' of ecstasy; then her climax ripped through her, taking her by surprise. Thunder continued to crash round them, and she yelled out, giving herself up to her climax. Her internal muscles clutched sharply around his finger; she shuddered, and then was still.

A few moments later she opened her eyes, and flushed when she realized what a state of undress she was in. She looked lewd and wanton, whereas he was still fully clothed and, apart from being a bit wet, was quite pristine, not even his tie slightly out of place.

Before she could make a protest and restore order to her clothing, he took her hands, drawing her upright again; then he placed her fingers on the buttons of his shirt. He bent his head and kissed her again, his tongue pushing into her mouth; the action reminded her of what she'd wanted only moments before – for him to fill her, stretch her, with his cock. Renewed lust fanned within her and she began to undo the buttons of his shirt, sliding her hands over the wiry hair on his chest as she exposed his skin. He removed his tie, throwing it negligently onto the bonnet, and helped her to push his shirt from his shoulders. Then her hands dropped down to the buckle of his belt, undoing it with difficulty. He helped her to undo the button of his trousers, and then she slid the zip downwards.

He was still kissing her deeply, but she heard the moan of pleasure in the back of his throat as she burrowed under the waistband of his boxer shorts and curled her fingers round his cock. He was gratifyingly large, she thought, his cock long and thick. She couldn't resist squeezing it gently, moving her hands up and down; he thrust his pelvis towards her, and she laughed inside. *Fuck you, Rupert*, she thought. *I'm not what you say I am.*

She leaned back on the bonnet, pushing his boxer shorts down to reveal his cock as she did so. She spread her legs wide and he pushed the gusset of her knickers to one side. He curled his fingers round hers, guiding her hand until the tip of his cock fitted the entrance of her sex. Then he gently removed her hand and pushed.

He broke the kiss, and she cried out in bliss as he slid deep inside her, up to the hilt. It felt so good, so very, very good. It was exactly what she wanted, what she needed: to be filled and stretched by a thick hard cock, to be taken by a man who knew exactly what to do to give her pleasure. She met his eyes and smiled back at him; he began to move, thrusting very slowly and very deeply. She wrapped her legs round his waist, pressing her heels on his buttocks to pull him even deeper inside her, and he rocked back and forth, moving his hips in small circles to change the angle of his penetration and increase the pleasure for both of them.

She lifted herself slightly, pushing back at him, and his control snapped. He cupped her exposed breasts, squeezing them and rubbing her nipples between his thumbs and forefingers; she closed her eyes and gave herself up to the maelstrom of emotions within her. It had been years since she had experienced sex this good – if ever. She couldn't stop a moan of lust bubbling from her; the sound only served to encourage him, and he jammed his mouth over hers, kissing her fiercely again and still paying attention to her breasts.

She eased one hand between their bodies, resting the heel of her palm on her mons veneris and locating her clitoris with her middle finger. She adopted a rhythm that matched the way he thrust into her, rubbing the engorged bud of flesh rapidly. Neither of them now cared that they could be seen from the road; most of the drivers would be concentrating on their driving in any case, hardly able to see through their windscreens in the torrential rain.

Carolyn had never felt so alive. She had never done anything like this before, even when she'd been drunk – and it felt good. The power of the storm seemed to pulse within her and, coupled with the warmth of the car engine below her and the way her rescuer was pumping into her . . . *Yes*, she thought. *Yes. This is what I was born for. Mutual pleasure, no strings.*

Her orgasm began to ripple through her body, flowing up from the soles of her feet and causing her thighs to tremble, then snaking in her gut and exploding. Yet he didn't stop. He kept thrusting into her, taking her to a higher peak. When she felt his balls lift and tighten, and then his body tensing against her, she cried out into his mouth. She felt his cock throb deep within her; the way her internal muscles rippled round its hardness lengthened his orgasm, so that his whole body seemed to flow into hers.

They remained locked together for what could only have been moments, although it felt like a lifetime; finally, he withdrew from her. He opened his mouth as if to say something; she sat up quickly, placing a finger on his open mouth and shaking her head. She didn't want him to speak, to spoil what had happened by apologizing. She wanted to remember this forever, an episode of lust and longing and desire, untainted by any of the usual platitudes.

He looked surprised but acquiesced, saying nothing. He restored order to his clothing, pulling up his boxer shorts and trousers and buttoning his shirt, tucking it in before zipping up his flies and refastening his belt. He didn't bother putting on his tie again; instead, he gave a wry grimace and squeezed the water from it.

His good humour made her smile. She pulled up the cups of her bra, then did up her shirt, pulling her skirt back down to its normal position and tucking her shirt into it. She smiled at him then. 'Thank you,' she said softly, and walked away to her own car.

She was completely soaked; she had nothing to put on the seat to protect it from her damp clothing, but she didn't care. He remained there, watching her as she started the car; when she glanced in the mirror as she pulled back onto the dual carriageway, she could see him sitting on the bonnet of his car, just staring at her as if he couldn't quite believe what had just happened.

Well, their paths would never cross again. It didn't matter that they hadn't exchanged names or anything like that. They had enjoyed each other's bodies, and that was all there was to it. She felt a brief pang of regret – it was the kind of lovemaking that she would have enjoyed repeating – but it was too late to do anything about it now.

TWO

Ten miles further down the road, Carolyn began to shiver in her wet clothes. She rolled her eyes, cross with herself. How could she have been so bloody stupid? Apart from the risk she had just taken, making love with the stranger who had come to her rescue, she had probably also managed to catch a chill, getting soaked to the skin like that and then driving to the hotel without changing and drying herself off. If she ended up losing her voice, like Mandy had, it would be a disaster for the course. It wasn't fair of her to let people down like that. She switched the car heater to full and hoped that she'd be at Heywood Hall quickly enough to climb out of her wet things and have a hot shower and a hot drink, in the hope of avoiding a chill.

She still couldn't quite believe what had just happened. She had made love with a complete stranger, in a place where anyone could have seen her, in the middle of a thunderstorm – a thunderstorm that was still raging across the sky. She had spread her legs for him; she had exposed herself and touched herself for him; and she had let him make her come – more than once. It wasn't the way that the quiet and professional Carolyn Saunders usually behaved.

Her friend Mandy had no scruples about one-night stands, saying that it was her body and, if she chose to enjoy using it, that was her privilege. But Carolyn had always needed more than just physical attraction between her and a potential lover.

She preferred to know him better, before they went to bed together; and there had to be some potential in the relationship. Brief encounters weren't enough for her.

She frowned. Rupert had called her a power-crazy bitch – and frigid. Well, she'd certainly proved that she wasn't the latter. A frigid woman wouldn't have been able to have one orgasm, let alone several.

Although she felt slightly ashamed of her behaviour, she still couldn't keep a smile from crossing her face as she thought about what had happened on Roudham Heath. Yes, it had been good. The handsome stranger's body had felt fantastic as it had surged into hers. Maybe Mandy had a point about one-night stands, after all. That way, you didn't have all the emotional baggage weighing you down when you made love. You could just enjoy your lover's body, your lover's skill, as you touched and kissed and caressed each other to a climax, without having to worry about what would happen afterwards. No strings, no ties, no regrets.

Rupert wouldn't see it that way. At least, not where a woman was concerned. She had the nasty feeling that Rupert would have been quite happy to have a no-strings fling with a woman; though he would have despised that woman as cheap afterwards. Carolyn's lips tightened. He had it both ways. In his eyes, if a woman enjoyed herself and really let go, she was louche; if she remained tense or didn't perform loudly enough for him, she was frigid. 'Bastard,' she growled softly. 'I had no chance.'

Rupert. Tall, blond-haired, blue-eyed and handsome Rupert, with his perfect bone-structure and charming smile. He was an amateur actor by evening – though, of course, he was just waiting to be discovered by a talent scout and swept off to the big time in the West End or Hollywood – and an office clerk by day. He had resented the fact that Carolyn was successful in her career and earned her living doing something that she enjoyed. *And*, she thought wryly, *he had resented the fact that she earned a lot more than he did, despite the fact that she put in more hours than he did, and had taken professional exams.*

She earned good money, yes, but she knew that she deserved it. Rupert had made no attempt to do well for himself in his day job, saying that what he did in the evening was more important than working in an office. But instead of recognizing that the flip side of that attitude meant that he would be passed over for promotion in his day job, in favour of someone who was prepared to do that little bit more than he was, he resented the fact that he hadn't done as well as he thought he should have done.

She sighed. It should have been over between them months ago. They hadn't been getting on well together for a long while. There had been a time when she had enjoyed going to see him in a production, buying tickets every night to support him. But recently she had begun to be irritated by the drain on her spare time. Seeing the play once was enough for her, unless it happened to be a particular favourite of hers. She wasn't theatrically trained and couldn't see the subtle differences between each night's production, which annoyed him when he quizzed her about his performance afterwards and she couldn't say whether his phrasing in a certain scene had been better than the previous night's version. Though if she made an excuse not to go, he sulked. Either way, she couldn't win.

And he hated it if she had to run a course at the weekend. Rupert always expected that she would be there to do whatever he wanted, if he wasn't rehearsing or performing in a matinée. She grimaced. Moving in together hadn't made things better. If anything, the downhill slide had become steeper afterwards.

Rupert had expected her to take on more than her fair share of the housework, saying that he was busy in the evenings – despite the fact that she, too, was often busy, setting up new courses or marking assignments. They'd compromised by hiring a cleaning woman – whom Carolyn had paid – and living more or less on ready meals from Marks and Spencer's during the week.

Mandy had never liked Rupert, calling him 'Mr Narcissus'. She had suggested once that Carolyn should hold a fancy dress party for her birthday, and get Rupert to dress as a daffodil – ostensibly because of the colour of his hair, but really because the flower reflected his vanity. Carolyn had protested that Rupert wasn't like that, but she hadn't been able to stop laughing at the same time. Mandy had had a point.

Her blue eyes narrowed. Just why the hell had she let it go on for so long? Why hadn't she ended it, instead of waiting for the humiliation of Rupert himself ending it? And the way he'd ended it . . .

Her fingers tightened on the steering wheel and her knuckles whitened. It still made her feel angry and hurt to think about it. She had decided to make a real effort and make a fuss of Rupert in the first night of his new production. She had finished work early, working through her lunch hour to make sure that everything she needed to do for the current course was up to date. Then she'd cooked him a special dinner from scratch, rather than nipping into Marks and Spencer's food department. She'd made mushrooms in cream sauce, followed by salmon en croûte and lemon brûlée. All his favourites. She had even bought champagne, saying that they should celebrate after the performance – because Rupert always preferred to be stone-cold sober before going on stage.

The first night had gone well, the actors returning for three ovations. She had been there in the front row, applauding loudly. They'd had a drink with the cast after the final curtain; then they had gone back to their Victorian terrace. Rupert had been quiet in the car but she had put it down to the fact that he was drained after a battle with first-night nerves. He never admitted it but she knew that he suffered from stage fright on the first night.

She had opened the champagne when they got in, pouring them both a glass and proposing a toast to his latest success. He had drunk deeply, draining the glass virtually in one gulp, and poured himself another. And another. Then he had reached for her.

He had touched her face, his fingers brushing so very lightly across her skin. 'Carolyn.'

She had recognized his tone of voice instantly. It meant that Rupert was in the mood for making love. Considering that they hadn't made love for nearly a fortnight – either he had been out late and she had been asleep when he had come home, or he had claimed to feel too tired and stressed-out from rehearsals – she had been a little surprised. But she had been relieved at the same time. She had been beginning to think that he was having an affair, and she had grown tired of relieving her frustrations with her own right hand when he was absent or asleep.

'Carolyn.' His pupils had dilated, making his bright blue eyes seem almost navy. Carolyn had felt suddenly nervous. She and Rupert had been getting on particularly badly during the previous week, and she hadn't been a hundred per cent sure that she really wanted to make love with him, right then. On the other hand, she had thought that this might be Rupert's way of making his peace with her, appreciating the effort she had made with his meal and attending the first night, so she couldn't afford to knock him back. She had smiled at him, hoping that he wouldn't notice the strain in her eyes. He had smiled back, then stood up, drawing her to her feet.

She still hadn't been able to rid herself of the thought that Rupert was playing a part – the part of the great seducer. And when he was acting, he expected to be appreciated. She had closed her eyes, hoping that Rupert would take it for arousal, rather than the mixture of worry and slight distaste that it really was.

Slowly, he had cupped her face, tracing her jawline. Then he had stooped slightly, fitting his mouth to hers. She had opened her mouth beneath his automatically, knowing that it was what he expected; he had given a sigh of pleasure, and pulled her into his arms, stroking her buttocks and deepening the kiss.

Carolyn had fought the sudden urge to push him away. This wasn't fair. This was her lover of twelve months. She loved him – didn't she? So why couldn't she respond to him in the way he wanted, be warm and pliant and sexy? She had forced herself to respond. Knowing that it was disloyal, and feeling guilty – though knowing at the same time that this was the only way she could do it – she had started imagining that it wasn't Rupert in front of her. She had made believe that she was in the arms of another man – a nameless man, a mixture of the actors she'd fancied over the years, in her favourite roles. A man with David Duchovny's mouth, as Fox Mulder, sensitive and vulnerable and irresistibly sexy. He had Richard Burton's beautiful and sensuous eyes, as Cleopatra's lover Antony; Kenneth Branagh's physique, as Frankenstein; the bright, sparkling mind of Sam Neill, as the irascible scientist in *Jurassic Park*; and Gary Oldman's sheer sensuality, the brooding and sensual power of Ludwig van Beethoven in *Immortal Beloved*.

She had found herself relaxing then, and had made no protest when Rupert began unbuttoning her fitted shirt, pushing the soft silky material from her shoulders. He had unclasped her bra, dropping it on top of her shirt, and then cupped her breasts in his hands, squeezing them. She had itched for him to touch her in the way she really wanted, stroking the soft undersides with the pads of his fingertips and outlining her areolae, teasing her nipples into hardness. Yet she had remained silent, knowing better than to criticize him. Rupert didn't appreciate his sexual performance being appraised in anything less than a favourable light; even a suggestion of trying something different could be taken as criticism, rather than just trying something new. So Carolyn had kept most of her desires and fantasies to herself.

He had undone the zip of her tailored black trousers, pushing them down over her hips so that the garment slid in a rustle to the floor; as was expected of her, Carolyn had kicked off her shoes and stepped out of the trousers. Then he had hooked his thumbs into the waistband of her knickers, drawing them down, too. She had waited, expecting him to part her legs and bury his face in her quim; but he hadn't. He had stood up, and held her slightly away from him. 'Touch yourself.'

She had opened her eyes in surprise and shock. 'What?'

'Touch yourself,' he had repeated.

Her pupils had dilated. This had been the last thing she had expected. And yes, although she had often masturbated, particularly over the previous few months when their sex life had started to go downhill, she really didn't feel comfortable doing it in front of Rupert. She had never really felt comfortable masturbating in front of anyone else. It was something private, the one time when she could really let herself go, with no thought of the consequences. If Rupert saw her abandoned to pleasure, he would know that she had been faking it for weeks with him – and that would lead to a row, something she wanted desperately to avoid.

'Touch yourself,' he had said again. There had been a faint air of menace in his tone and she had frozen, not sure what to do. She hadn't wanted a fight with him; on the other hand, she hadn't felt like being a picture show for him.

But that had been exactly what he wanted. He had turned her round, then flung himself on the sofa and poured himself some more champagne. 'I want to see you touch yourself, make yourself come. I want you to perform for me,' he had added, as if his words really hadn't been clear enough. Again, Carolyn had had the uncomfortable feeling that Rupert was playing a part. Mickey Rourke in *9½ Weeks*, perhaps, the lover demanding that his woman went further, further, pushing her sexual boundaries to the limit.

She had lifted her chin. 'No.'

'What?' His eyes had narrowed.

'You heard.'

Then he had switched from sexual dictator to being charming. His face had been full of hurt incomprehension. 'Carolyn. Darling. I've had a good night. I want to celebrate by making love with you. But I want you to have pleasure, too. I want to watch you come – and then make love with you, all night.'

Carolyn had been tempted to mention the fact that they both had to go to work in the morning, but it really wasn't worth the hassle. In the end, she had done exactly what he wanted. Again, she had pretended that her dream lover was in front of her, sprawled on the sofa and sipping champagne as he watched her – champagne that he would share with her later. Champagne that maybe he would dribble onto her skin, licking it off again. Then she had slid one hand across her ribcage, cupping her breast and stroking the soft under-side. She had traced her areola with her middle finger, teasing the rosy nipple into hardness; she had felt the soft flesh pucker beneath her fingertips as she became aroused.

She had done the same with her other breast, then pushed both breasts together and up slightly, deepening her cleavage. Then she had tipped her head back and allowed one hand to drift very smoothly over her abdomen, until the heel of her palm had been resting against her mound of Venus. In her mind, her dream lover had smiled in appreciation, his tongue moistening his sensitive lower lip. Though, in her mind, her lover hadn't *ordered* her to perform for him. It had been *her* idea, a game where he would have to stay as still as he could, and she would be trying to tempt him away from the sofa, to touch her.

Still focusing on her dream lover, she had parted her labia with her index and ring fingers, letting her middle finger stroke slowly along her musky divide. She had curled her middle finger up again, then straightened it, skating along her silky intimate flesh. She had repeated the action again and again, until her flesh had grown moist and slippery to the touch. Then she had plunged her middle finger deep into her moist channel, parting her legs in a way more likely to give her easier access. Her thumb had settled on her clitoris, rotating the hard bud of flesh; she had worked herself swiftly then, imagining that her dream lover had been unable to resist her. He had dropped to his knees and crawled over to her, pushing her hand away and using his own hands and lips and tongue to pleasure her . . .

She had brought herself to a shuddering climax with the lover of her dreams; and then she had felt Rupert's body against hers. While she had been pleasuring herself, he had removed his clothes too, and she could feel his smooth skin sliding against hers as he'd pulled her into his arms, kissing her deeply. She had felt slightly guilty, but she had still had her dream lover in mind as Rupert drew her down to the floor, pushing her onto her back and then parting her legs. He had thrust into her without any preliminaries; and he had come quickly afterwards. Too quickly for her: she hadn't climaxed. Again. And she hadn't been thinking fast enough to fake it, either.

That's when the row had started. Rupert had rolled from her, his eyes like hard blue chips as he stared accusingly at her. Carolyn had remained silent, not knowing quite what to say; Rupert had been the one to break the silence, scowling. 'You didn't come, did you?'

Carolyn had winced. 'I . . .'

'Don't try to deny it. And you were thinking about someone else, weren't you?'

Her instant flush had betrayed her. 'No.'

'Don't lie to me.'

'I'm not.' It wasn't strictly a lie. Her dream lover didn't exist. He was an amalgamation of several people, people she'd never meet in a million years. Mr Fantasy.

'You've been seeing someone else, haven't you?'

She had shaken her head. 'Of course I haven't.' That, at least, had been true.

His eyes had narrowed. 'Well, you haven't been very interested in my work lately. There *has* to be someone else.'

She sighed. 'Look, Rupert. I've been busy at work. You know I've got more responsibilities now.'

'Yes, and a huge pay rise to go with it.' His lip had curled.

She had known that it would be a bone of contention between them, even before she had been promoted. Rupert's ego couldn't handle the fact that she earned more than he did. 'Rupert—'

He had interrupted her sharply. 'You're more interested in your bloody career than you are in me. And we hardly ever have sex now – you're always too tired, or you've got a headache, or there's some other excuse. I'm beginning to think that you're frigid, as well as a power-crazy bitch. Well, I've had more than enough of it.'

His words had been so unexpected that Carolyn had reeled. 'Rupert . . .'

But he had already been on his feet, dressing swiftly. He'd left the room without another word, ignoring her question about where he was going and slamming the door hard behind him.

The next day, Carolyn had returned home to find a note from him, saying that he had had enough and he had moved out, taking his things with him. He had taken quite a few of hers, too, including some of her favourite CDs and some of her books. That's when she had discovered that Rupert hadn't just moved out – he had moved in with one of the women in the amateur dramatic group. His row with her had all been a pretext, to save himself from the guilt of admitting that it was he who was having an affair.

Carolyn's hands tightened on the steering wheel. She was still furious about it. But the worst thing was, his words had gone home. She had started to wonder whether it had been true. *Was* she a power-crazy bitch? She *had* risen rapidly through the writing school, and they had recently promoted her to director of new courses. To get on in any company nowadays, you had to be focused. Everyone knew that. But had she nurtured her career at the expense of her relationship? Was she really more interested in work than in sex?

She had been so upset about it that she hadn't even been able to talk to Mandy about it. Mandy had noticed that she'd been a bit quiet, and had taken her out for a drink after work, plying her with more than enough wine to loosen her tongue. Though Carolyn hadn't been able to admit to her real worry. She hadn't told Mandy that Rupert had moved out, either. She'd made some feeble excuse about pressures of work, and they'd both known that she'd been lying. And that's when Mandy had persuaded her to tell the truth.

'Come on, Caro.' Mandy's brown eyes glittered with sympathy. 'I know that there's something wrong – and it isn't work, either. You love your job, and you thrive on pressure.'

Carolyn sighed. 'Okay. If you must know, Rupert and I have split up.'

'Oh.' Mandy digested the news, torn between feeling sympathetic towards Carolyn and relieved that her friend was no longer with the obnoxious Rupert. 'Look, we can't really talk here.' She waved a hand at the wine bar. It was dark and cosy, the brass lamps and dark green soft furnishings giving the place a confidential air – although there were several groups of people dotted round the various tables. It was all too easy for someone to overhear them. 'Let's go back to my place. There's some wine in the fridge and some chocolate in the cupboard: I think that's what you need, right now.'

She drained her glass; Carolyn followed suit and stood up, leaving the wine bar with her friend. They walked back to Mandy's flat in near silence: when they were inside, Mandy kicked off her shoes, went to the fridge, and extracted a bottle of Chardonnay. She poured two glasses, handing one to Carolyn, then delved in a cupboard and extracted a large bar of chocolate before ushering Carolyn through to the sitting room. She put a light-jazz CD in the player, keeping the volume low, and flung herself on the sofa. 'Right. Tell me what happened – and I mean *all* of it.'

Carolyn crumbled then, and told Mandy the whole story – including Rupert's assertions that she was a power-crazy bitch and frigid.

Mandy raked an indignant hand through her cropped blonde hair. 'That's ridiculous, and you know it. You're not power-crazy at all. You're one of the least political people I know.' She scowled. 'Just because he's a failure – look at all the years he's been working in amateur dramatics, waiting to be discovered, and he's still there, waiting. Not to mention how he's still an office junior in his day job. Rupert thinks that he's God's gift to the world, and the only way he can make himself feel better is to put you down. Don't take any notice of a word he said, Caro. It's all complete bollocks. Mr Inadequate was just trying to make himself feel better at your expense.'

Mandy was even more incensed when Carolyn told her that Rupert had moved in with someone else. 'Bastard! Well, Caro, you're well rid of him. I know you loved him, but he was a complete jerk. He wasn't good enough for you, and he was more in love with himself than with anyone else. I'll give it a month, and he'll be bored with his totty. He'll come crawling back to you then.'

Carolyn pursed her lips. 'Well, I don't think I want him back.'

'Good. I'll remind you of that, when he rings you up and does his Mr Charming act. I bet he'll send you roses, and write you bad slushy poems on scented paper – that sort of thing.' Carolyn suppressed a grin. Mandy really had Rupert off pat. That had been exactly the sort of thing he'd done soon after they'd first met. 'And as for you being frigid, that's a load of crap, too. You're not frigid in the slightest.'

Carolyn sipped her wine. 'All the same, the last few times we made love, I *did* have to fake it.'

'And why do you think that it's your fault?' Mandy widened

her eyes. 'Hasn't it occurred to you that he might be an inadequate lover, as well as an inadequate person?'

'Well, it *used* to work between us. It's just been the past few months. That's why I thought maybe he had a point – it's been ever since I've got that promotion.'

'As I said, he's Mr Inadequate, and the only way he can handle the fact that you're better than he is, is to be nasty to you and make you feel bad. That's how bullies work.' Mandy spread her hands. 'Caro, what does it take to prove to you that it wasn't your fault?'

Carolyn sighed. 'As they say, it takes two to tango.'

Mandy sipped her wine. 'Even so, it's not your fault, Caro. It's his.'

Carolyn smiled. Her friend's loyalty was more than appreciated. 'Mm.'

'I mean it, Caro.' Mandy put her glass on the floor. 'And I'll prove it to you, if you like.'

'Prove it to me?' Carolyn repeated.

Mandy nodded and stood up, walking towards Carolyn. She reached out to take Carolyn's hands, pulling her friend to her feet. 'Like this,' she said softly, stroking Carolyn's face.

Carolyn's eyes widened. If Mandy was suggesting what she thought she was suggesting . . . Part of her was frightened. She'd never made love with another woman. She hadn't thought that Mandy swung both ways, either. Maybe she didn't know her friend as well as she thought she did.

Gently, Mandy rubbed the tip of her nose against Carolyn's, then brushed her lips against her friend's. The caress was light, non-threatening, and Carolyn felt herself relax. Everything was going to be fine. 'No strings,' Mandy said quietly. 'This is strictly a one-off, but I can't let you go on thinking that you're the one with the problem, when you're not. It's not fair.' She paused. 'Look, if it bothers you that I'm female, just pretend I'm Harrison Ford or someone like that. But go with the flow. I'll prove that you're not frigid, Caro. Not in the slightest.' She traced Carolyn's lower lip with her forefinger. 'Your mouth's a perfect Cupid's bow. Your lips are so soft, and the way they curve . . . You were just made for kissing, Carolyn. You probably don't realize it, but you just ooze sensuality.'

Carolyn arched an eyebrow. 'Since when? I'm perfectly ordinary, Mandy.'

'Oh no, you're not. I've seen the way some of the students look at you, Caro. When you're lecturing, you're animated, and I've seen the look in their eyes. They're wondering what it would be like if you were saying other words to them, what it would be like to feel your mouth moving on theirs. Like this.' Again, Mandy brushed her lips gently against Carolyn's. This time, Carolyn opened her mouth, letting Mandy nibble at her lower lips and then slide her tongue inside her mouth.

A shiver of desire rippled through Carolyn. She'd never seen her friend as a potential lover. Drinking companion, yes. A woman she could talk to, laugh with, shop with – but make love with? Part of her froze. She'd never been attracted to another woman in a sexual sense. This wasn't her scene. But then again, as Mandy had said, she could always close her eyes and pretend that her new lover was Harrison Ford . . .

And then she stopped thinking as Mandy slid her hands down Carolyn's sides, moulding her curves and stroking her buttocks. Slowly, Mandy untucked her shirt, then undid the buttons and slid the soft silk from her shoulders. Carolyn felt a kick of desire in her stomach as Mandy unzipped her skirt and pushed it down over her hips. Then Mandy hooked her thumbs into the waistband of Carolyn's black opaque tights, rolling them down and removing her knickers at the same time.

Carolyn stepped out of the garments, and then Mandy undid her bra. When she was naked, Mandy held her at arm's length. 'Beautiful,' she pronounced. 'I don't think that any man could resist you, Caro. You're lovely. Soft and warm and curvy and . . . Mm.'

Carolyn flushed. 'I'm just ordinary, Mandy,' she said again.

Mandy shook her head, then led her out of the sitting room, pushing her bedroom door open. She released Carolyn's hands and drew the curtains, before coming back to switch on the light. 'Look,' she said, leading Carolyn over to the cheval mirror. She stood behind Carolyn. 'Look at yourself. Your body's lovely. Your skin's so pale, in such sharp contrast to your hair. You're pretty, too, though I know you don't think so. Your face is a perfect oval, and your eyes are a beautiful colour. And then there's your kissable mouth.'

She slid her hands round Carolyn's waist. 'And here – you're all warm and soft and curving and feminine. Not one of these mannish women with washboard stomachs.' She let her hands brush upwards, her fingers moving in tiny erotic circles over Carolyn's skin. Then she cupped her friend's breasts, pushing them up and together slightly to deepen the cleavage. 'And here. Here, you're irresistible. Your breasts are perfect. Any man would want to touch them.' Mandy splayed her fingers wide, then closed her ring and middle fingers, squeezing Carolyn's hardening nipples. 'And you're so responsive.' She squeezed slightly harder, and Carolyn couldn't help arching her back.

'See?' Mandy breathed softly into her ear. 'Any man would find this irresistible.' She spun her friend round and dipped her head, nuzzling Carolyn's collarbones and breathing in her scent. 'Your skin's so soft. And you smell so gorgeous.' She drew her tongue along Carolyn's collarbone, and Carolyn shivered. Mandy grinned. Then she stooped, letting her mouth move down over the soft globes of Carolyn's breasts, and took one rosy-tipped nipple into her mouth.

Carolyn gasped as Mandy began to suck. Mandy stopped and looked up, a smile on her face. 'Frigid? I don't think so, sweetheart. I can smell your arousal. All musk and honey and vanilla. Your body's opening, flowering for me. You want to make love. You want someone to touch you and make you come.'

Carolyn flushed. 'I—'

Mandy pressed her fingertip against Carolyn's mouth. 'Don't say another word. Just leave this to me.' She walked Carolyn back to the double bed, then pushed the duvet back, patting the mattress invitingly. Carolyn sat down, and Mandy stripped swiftly. She switched on the small CD on her bedside cabinet. The first few notes of Peggy Lee's *Fever*, syncopated and very sexy, filled the air. 'Appropriate, I think.' Mandy's irrepressible grin was infectious; Carolyn found herself smiling back as her friend joined her on the bed. 'Now, where were we?' Mandy asked. 'Here, I think.'

She dipped her head, nuzzling Carolyn's breasts and taking one nipple into her mouth again, sucking fiercely on the hard peak of flesh. She released her again, blowing softly on her spit-slicked flesh, and Carolyn shivered, closing her eyes. Mandy did the same to Carolyn's other breast, and Carolyn felt a dull ache between her legs. Maybe Mandy was right. She wasn't frigid. She *could* respond – if her lover made love to her in the right way.

Mandy worked her way slowly down Carolyn's body, licking and kissing and nuzzling; when she moved between Carolyn's thighs, spreading her legs, Carolyn made no protests. If anything, she began to encourage her friend, sliding her hands into Mandy's short hair and massaging her scalp with her fingertips. Mandy kissed her inner thighs, and Carolyn gave a gasp of pleasure as she felt Mandy's tongue slide between her labia, licking from the top to the bottom of her musky furrow. Then Mandy stiffened her tongue into a hard point and flicked it rapidly over Carolyn's swelling clitoris.

'See?' Mandy asked softly, putting her fingertip to the entrance of Carolyn's sex and pushing. Her finger slid inside easily. 'You're warm and wet. You feel like velvet or silk; and you're so ready. So ready,' she crooned.

Carolyn had her eyes closed and she was concentrating too much on the way that Mandy's finger was pushing in and out of her to realize that Mandy had shifted, opened her top drawer, and extracted a vibrator. The first thing she knew was when Mandy flicked her clitoris rapidly, then withdrew her finger and pushed the thick tube against Carolyn's sex. It slid in as easily as Mandy's finger had, and Carolyn gasped in shock.

'This is what you need,' Mandy told her softly. 'I don't possess one of those strap-on dildo things or I would have used that instead; but I'm sure that I can make this good for you.' She began to move the vibrator back and forth and, when Carolyn closed her eyes, it was almost as if a man was penetrating her, filling her. Mandy had set up a fast rhythm, plunging in deeply and withdrawing so that the tip of the vibrator was almost out of Carolyn before pushing back in again. Carolyn let herself go, flowing with the sensations that were rippling through her body; almost within seconds, she was moaning and writhing, and then crying out as the inner sparkling of her orgasm filled her entire body, her legs jerking and her internal muscles contracting sharply round the thick tube.

Mandy waited until Carolyn's breathing had slowed before removing the vibrator, then shifted next to her friend, cuddling her. She kissed her gently. 'See? A frigid woman wouldn't have been able to come. I reckon that Rupert must have had a small cock, and didn't know what to do with it, either.'

Carolyn hadn't been able to suppress a laugh. 'That's not fair, Mandy.'

'Maybe, but neither was what he said to you.'

They'd spent the rest of the evening making love, touching and caressing and licking each other; Carolyn had slept better that night, in Mandy's bed, than she had for a long time. She'd felt relaxed and fulfilled and happy, and profoundly grateful to her friend.

The next day, Mandy had acted completely as normal, as if nothing sexual had happened between them. Carolyn had tried to discuss it over breakfast, but Mandy had shaken her head. 'Like I told you, it was a one-off. What else are friends for?' she'd asked lightly.

Carolyn smiled. Yes, what were friends for, indeed? Mandy had given her back her confidence but over the next few days she'd found herself slipping back to the same worries as before. Maybe Rupert was right about her. Maybe most of their problems *had* been her fault.

She put her foot down on the accelerator. Bloody Rupert. He really wasn't worth it. And when she thought about it, she knew that what she had said to Mandy had been the truth. She didn't really want him back. The physical side had been good between them, in the beginning; but that had been when Rupert had been acting a part, the dedicated lover. Once he'd stopped acting that part, their sex life had gone down the pan. Just like the last time they had made love – he'd been the one to come quickly, not bothering to satisfy her. That's why he had wanted her to touch herself. So that he wouldn't feel so bad about the fact that he wasn't able to make her come – or, at least, was too selfish to make the effort.

She thought back to her previous relationships. There hadn't been that many – and they hadn't been that satisfactory on the physical front, either. Which meant either that she was just bad at picking good lovers or that maybe Rupert had a point, and she was frigid. But then again, if that was the case, why had she enjoyed herself so much with the man who had rescued her and sorted out her flat tyre? And why had it worked when she and Mandy had made love?

She sighed. She didn't have the answers. And she didn't want to think about it. Not until she had finished the course and had a day or so to herself, to work out what the hell she was going to do next and where her life was going.

THREE

At last, Carolyn saw the turn-off to Heywood Hall, indicated right, and swung into the narrow gravel drive. She couldn't see the hotel at the end of it because the drive was very long and winding; it was flanked with lime trees that had been trained to meet in the middle above the driveway. Carolyn thought that the dense green canopy would be spooky in the extreme at night or in the middle of winter, and yet cool and inviting in summer. She wondered idly how old the trees were – *at least a couple of hundred years*, she thought. The view from her car was probably pretty much the same as someone would have seen in the eighteenth century from a horse and carriage.

When she reached the end of the drive she slowed down, sucking in a sharp breath as she saw Heywood Hall for the first time. Mandy hadn't shown her the brochure, but Carolyn wasn't surprised that her friend had been impressed by the look of the place. The building itself was gorgeous, a large sprawling place of pale grey and yellow stone, with crenellations, a turret and mullioned windows. Ivy grew around the arched door and trailed around the windows. There was a narrow moat around the hall and the large gravel car park, filled with clear water, and its banks were covered with plants. No doubt there were fish swimming in the moat, too.

Although Carolyn was no expert in architecture, the place looked fifteenth-century to her. No wonder the owner had chosen to turn it into a hotel rather than being forced to sell it or just let it crumble and decay. If she'd lived there, she would have done the same.

If the interior of the hotel was anything like the exterior, her course delegates were going to be thoroughly spoiled for the weekend. She could imagine what it was like inside – all oak panelling, Gothic wrought-iron lights, ancient tapestries and even more ancient wall paintings, almost faded beyond recognition by time. Roaring log fires, paintings of the owner's ancestors in ornate gilded frames, and a long narrow library filled with first-edition leather-bound books . . .

She smiled to herself. She was romanticizing the place already. For all she knew, it had been taken over by developers, the ancient panelling stripped and bleached and the walls painted white, with brass-framed botanical prints hanging on the walls and thick pile carpets lining the floors. It could be a luxury hotel, designed in boring corporate style, rather than the individual and idiosyncratic place she hoped that it would be.

As she pulled into a parking space, her smile faded. In the space next to her was a black BMW, the latest model – and she recognized the personalized number plate. KW 62. It was the car that had pulled up behind hers at Roudham Heath. Somehow, the driver had managed to overtake her, either at some point on the A11, or later on the A14, without her noticing. She flushed. God, don't say that he was one of her delegates . . .

She shook herself. Of course not. The weekend was about writing erotica for women, and the six delegates were all female. So what the hell was her rescuer doing at the hotel? It couldn't be a business trip – not at the weekend, anyway – and he had been alone in the car. Or had he?

Her blood went cold at the thought that someone else had

been in the car, watching what had happened on the bonnet. Male or female, she didn't care: the idea chilled her. Yes, they'd taken a risk, making love outside – but people they didn't know seeing them from a passing car for a couple of seconds was not the same as someone that he knew sitting in the passenger seat and watching everything that was going on, from start to finish. Swallowing, she climbed out of the car, took her briefcase and weekend bag from the boot, then locked the car and strode into the reception area.

To her delight, the place was indeed individual. Although there was a thick pile carpet on the floor in dark blue with a pale yellow fleur-de-lys pattern, similar to one she'd seen in other hotels, the walls of the reception hall had the original oak panelling and the reception desk was free-standing, not built-in to spoil the effect of the hall. There was a roaring log fire in the large inglenook fireplace – a real one, not just a clever gas coal-effect one – with slightly distressed burgundy leather arm-chairs placed on either side of it and a low mahogany coffee table containing a selection of newspapers and magazines. There was a broad sweeping staircase in front of her, again in the rich dark oak with barley-sugar carved banisters and the ubiquitous fleur-de-lys carpet.

She walked over to the receptionist and smiled. 'Good evening. I'm Carolyn Saunders. I'm running the Write Right course on creative writing this weekend. I'm afraid that my colleague Amanda Wedderburn, who was going to run the course, has been taken ill. I believe that my office rang through to tell you about the change, this afternoon?'

The pretty brunette smiled back at her, making no comment on the fact that Carolyn's clothes were soaked and her dark hair was in rat's-tails. 'Of course, Ms Saunders. Your delegates are all here, bar one – Virginia Walker. She telephoned to say that she was running a little late, but she'll be here by half-past seven.' She opened a drawer and extracted a key, together with a standard hotel booking-in form. 'Could you fill this in for me, please? You're in room twelve, which is on the second floor. I'm afraid that we haven't had a lift installed but I can call a porter to help with your luggage, if you like.'

Carolyn smiled back. 'Thanks, but I think that I can manage.' She indicated her briefcase and small bag. 'There isn't that much.'

'Well, the reception your colleague ordered will be ready at eight o'clock in the library. It's sparkling wine and a few nibbles; I hope that's all right. You can go through to the restaurant whenever you're ready; there's no set time for dinner, although we like people to order their meal before ten, if possible.' She smiled. 'Would you like to see the *table d'hôte* menu?'

Carolyn shook her head. 'I'm sure it'll be fine, thanks.' Knowing Mandy, she would already have checked out the food and it would be good. Mandy was fond of all the pleasures of the flesh – good wine and good food, as well as good sex.

'Tomorrow your course will be in the Blue Room, which is next to the library. We've put an overhead projector in there; there's also a whiteboard and a flip chart, and some pens. We've provided paper and pens for the delegates to take notes, and we'll make sure that there's plenty of water available. Your colleague ordered coffee at eleven and tea at three. If there's anything else you need, please let me know.' The receptionist smiled. 'Or Kit, of course.'

Carolyn frowned. 'Kit?'

The receptionist nodded. 'Kit Williams. He's the conference centre manager.'

Kit Williams. KW. Could Kit Williams be the owner of the

BMW? Carolyn didn't like to ask – but there had to be some way of finding out. Her brain clicked into gear. Of course. The hotel brochure. There was bound to be a picture of him in it. She smiled. 'Er – as I stepped in for Amanda at the last minute, I haven't actually seen your conference centre brochure. May I have a copy, please?'

'Of course.' The receptionist indicated a small free-standing display rack. 'Help yourself. Now, if there's anything you need when you get to your room, just dial zero.'

Carolyn smiled her appreciation. 'Thanks. You don't happen to have a garage as well, do you?'

'Not as such. Why?'

Carolyn indicated her wet clothes. 'As you can probably tell by the state of me, I had a puncture on the way here.'

'Oh, dear. In all this rain.' The brunette was sympathetic.

'Mm, it was pretty grim. Anyway, I really ought to have the spare tyre sorted out, in case anything happens on the way home.'

'Well, if you'd like to leave me your car keys, I'll make sure that one of the porters takes your tyre into Cambridge tomorrow.'

'Thanks,' Carolyn said gratefully. 'I don't want to hold up the course – but I don't want to risk travelling without a spare.'

'Neither would I,' the receptionist said, her eyes sparkling with empathy. 'Don't worry, we'll sort it out for you.'

Carolyn filled in the form, then handed it to the receptionist together with her car keys. Then she walked up the two flights of stairs and followed the discreet signs to her room. Room twelve turned out to be large and spacious, again with the blue and yellow fleur-de-lys carpet. Heavy yellow brocade drapes hung at the mullioned window. Her bed was a double; there was a decent amount of pillows piled at the head, and the bedspread was again in heavy yellow brocade, this time with blue fleurs-de-lys patterning it. The bedside cabinets were mahogany and there was a brass reading lamp on each one. There was also a high chest of drawers opposite the bed with a small portable remote-controlled television on it, and a dressing table with a large mirror over it.

She kicked off her shoes and then padded over to the window, drawing the curtains. She put her bags on the floor and headed for the *en suite* bathroom. It was small but plush, with a blue tiled floor, white tiled walls, a big deep bath and an old-fashioned-looking shower fitting, which on closer inspection turned out to be an electric power shower. Carolyn stripped off her wet clothes, leaving them in a squelching heap on the floor, and pulled the shower curtain across, switching on the shower and turning up the temperature setting.

Heywood Hall had thoughtfully provided some shower gel and shampoo – good stuff, too, not the cheap and sickly-smelling toiletries often provided by this kind of establishment. Carolyn stepped into the shower and lathered herself thoroughly, letting the water heat her chilled skin. Again, she thought of Kit Williams. Unless someone had borrowed his car, the BMW was his – which, in turn, meant that he had been her rescuer. *So much for thinking that our paths would never cross again*, she thought wryly. There was a very good chance that she would see him at some point over the weekend. Well, she decided, she would be professional about it. She would pretend that nothing had happened between them, and treat him with the cool politeness that she usually reserved for suppliers.

Even so, she couldn't help thinking about him, and about how it had felt when he'd made love with her. His mouth had been sensitive, slightly vulnerable, and she'd found him incredibly attractive. His blue eyes had been fringed by unfairly long and thick lashes, and his body beneath his suit had been firm and hard and muscular. Just how she liked a man to be.

She continued soaping herself, and was suddenly aware that she was stroking her breasts, toying with her nipples and tweaking them until they were rosy and erect. She flushed, embarrassed; but then again, what the hell? She was doing this for herself, not to please anyone else – and it was the best tension-reliever she knew.

Slowly, she continued to massage her breasts, squeezing the soft globes and tracing the dusky areolae with the tip of her finger. Her thumbs rubbed across the hard tips, sensitizing them even more; she tipped her head back against the tiles, letting the shower jets soak her body and remembering how it had felt in the thunderstorm, when she'd been splayed across the bonnet of Kit's car with the rain beating down on her skin.

It had been good, so very good – as though she'd been at one with the elements. And the way he'd touched her, caressed her . . . She slid one hand down over her abdomen, cupping her mons veneris and parting her labia. Her quim was still wet and slightly sticky from her earlier orgasms – and his. She flushed as a thought struck her: had she smelled of sex when she'd walked into reception? But the brunette at the desk had, of course, been too polite, too well-trained to make a comment about any possible tell-tale odour of sex.

She pushed the thought away, and began to rub her clitoris, letting her finger glide slowly up and down her musky channel. She eased one finger into herself, and added a second, pistoning her hand back and forth. Her rhythm grew quicker as her arousal built; she continued to caress her breasts, pinching the nipples almost cruelly as she worked on herself. She rubbed her clitoris harder and harder, moving her fingers in and out faster and faster; she couldn't hold back the wail of pleasure as she climaxed, her internal muscles clenching hard around her fingers.

When her breathing had steadied down to normal, she finished washing herself, then wrapped her hair in one of the small hand towels, wrapping her body in one of the big fleecy white bath towels and tucking the end between her breasts, sarong-style. She hung her wet clothing on the side of the bath, then headed back out to the bedroom. She unpacked swiftly, hanging her clothes in the wardrobe and tucking her underwear into the chest of drawers. She took her hairdryer from her bag and plugged it in, drying her hair until it was merely damp to the touch; then she went over to the bed again and opened her briefcase.

She glanced through the notes that Mandy had written for her. The course was similar to one she'd taken before, so she felt at ease with the structure; the only difference was that this course was about erotic writing. Mandy had prepared several handouts of examples of good erotic writing, pages photocopied from some of the better erotic novels. Carolyn smiled. Mandy had quite a collection of modern erotica and Carolyn had borrowed a few books from her – in the days before Rupert, that was. She had once made the mistake of letting Rupert catch her reading one of Mandy's books and Rupert had taken it from her, reading passages aloud in a mocking falsetto. She'd been mortified, and hadn't read another one since.

She sprawled on the bed, flicking through the notes; a passage caught her eyes. God, this was so much like the scenario she'd experienced only an hour or so before. Only the location was different: instead of being on a car bonnet next to a main road through an ancient heath, it was set in the middle of a stone circle in deepest Wiltshire.

Philip walked her backwards; she felt the worn edge of the altar stone pressing against the back of her knees. Then he pushed her gently back onto the stone; she could feel the hard cold surface pressing against her skin, and a thrill shot through her. The stone was wet from the pouring rain and, although it was cold, there was also a weird kind of energy which seemed to flow from the stone into her body. A ley-line, perhaps, Cassandra thought with a detached part of her mind. Or maybe it just her imagination – maybe it was just the way that Philip had stripped her in the middle of the stone circle, peeling her wet shirt from her body and dropping it onto the sodden grass, and then unzipping her straight skirt, pushing it down over her hips.

He had left her bra on when he had stripped her earlier, although he had pulled the cups down lewdly to reveal her breasts. He had left her stockings on, too, the lacy welts in sharp contrast to her soft white skin. He had removed her knickers, though, ripping the black silk and letting the ruined garment flutter to the earth. She knew that she looked lewd and wanton, splayed across the altar stone with her breasts and her sex bared, and she loved the thought of it.

It made her feel powerful – she wasn't a victim, lying on the altar stone and afraid of what was going to happen next. She was a goddess, revealing herself to her worshipping follower. This wasn't violation: it was fulfilment. She was the dark-haired goddess, her black hair flowing over her shoulders in a cascade of curls, her green eyes imperious and demanding, and he was her loyal servant, the blond-haired man with dark soulful eyes, a sensitive mouth and a hard firm body. He was going to do exactly what she wanted him to do.

She opened her eyes, looking up at the storm-darkened sky. Lightning flashed across it, splitting the night in two: she smiled again, almost feeling the power of the lightning fizzing through her veins. She felt high, high on sheer pheromones. As she heard the low growl of thunder, she closed her eyes again, lifting her face up to the rain and revelling in the feel of the water spattering her skin. 'I want you to fuck me, Philip,' she said softly, her voice low and resonant like the thunder. 'I want you to touch me. I want you to make me come. Now.'

She widened the gap between her thighs, tipping up her pelvis and exposing her quim to him. Water ran down her thighs, studding the black moss of her black pubic hair like tiny diamonds. She knew that her sex would be puffy and inviting, opening to him like some kind of exotic vermilion flower. She waited, willing Philip to touch her. And then, at last, she felt his finger glide down her musky channel, parting her labia and pushing into her soft wet sex. He touched her clitoris, his thumb feather-light and tormenting against her skin; Cassandra moaned, wanting more, more. She wanted him to fill her, stretch her, make her come.

He teased her, flicking gently at the hard nub of flesh; impatiently, she pushed his hand away, touching herself and rubbing herself harder, harder, as he continued to push his finger into her sex. She wanted to come. She wanted to feel her body flex with the inner sparkling of her climax. She wanted it right now. She couldn't wait. He leaned over and kissed her; her mouth opened beneath the pressure of his, and his tongue slid against hers, a movement calculated to turn her on even more. She writhed beneath him, and his fingers laced with hers, deepening the pressure on her clitoris.

Then she came, her climax rippling through her with the next crack of thunder; her cry of pleasure was lost in his mouth. Her internal muscles clenched sharply round his invading finger; she pushed up towards him, lengthening her climax, and was still. 'Yes,' she moaned as he tore his mouth from hers, and began kissing her throat. 'Yes'.

He continued to kiss his way down her body, nuzzling the pillowy globes of her breasts and then taking one stiff rosy nipple into his mouth, sucking on the hard nub of flesh. She pushed her hands into his hair, urging him on; his hand came up to cup her other breast, squeezing it gently. He rotated his palm on her nipple as he sucked its twin.

Cassandra could feel his erection pressing against her thigh; suddenly, she wanted him inside her. She tugged on his hair, making him lift his face and look at her. She opened her eyes and met his questioning gaze, her irises almost black. 'I want you. I want your cock inside me. I want you to fill me, stretch me. Now,' she said. She was the warrior queen, the goddess, commanding her captain. And he was going to do exactly what she demanded.

'Now,' Philip repeated softly.

She eased one hand between their bodies, curling her fingers round his erect cock. He felt good, long and thick: she smiled with pleasure, and spread her legs wide, inviting him. He smiled back, leaning forward and letting her guide the tip of his cock to the entrance of her sex; then he pushed, filling her to the hilt.

He moved slowly, tantalizingly slowly, pulling almost out of her; she wrapped her legs round his waist, and pushed her heels against his buttocks, easing him back inside her. He smiled then, and began to thrust harder, deeper – withdrawing slowly, and then slamming back hard inside her. She moaned with pleasure, and he cupped her exposed breasts. Her nipples were erect from a mixture of excitement and chill from the storm; he rubbed the dusky tips with his thumbs, sensitizing them still further, and Cassandra cried out, closing her eyes and giving herself up to the ripples of sensation which ran through her.

Philip continued to thrust, taking her to a higher and higher peak; she cried out as her orgasm reached a crescendo, and she heard his answering cry, feeling his cock throbbing deep within her as he, too, came. And all the time the storm raged round them, the lightning streaking through the sky and the thunder echoing through the stone circle.

Carolyn swallowed as she finished reading. God, what was wrong with her? Rupert had accused her of being frigid; if anything, she was beginning to think that she was the complete opposite and had become a nymphomaniac. First there had been that episode with Mandy. Then she had made love with Kit Williams, the tall dark stranger, uncaring who might see them. Then, less than an hour later, she had masturbated herself to a climax in the shower just at the memory of what had happened on the Heath. And now, after reading that passage and remembering how she had felt with Kit's cock deep inside her, she was aroused again, wanting fulfilment. Her sex felt hot and heavy.

She could hardly march down to the conference centre and demand that Kit take her over his desk, there and then – or ring room service and demand that the porter give her a more personal service than he might usually give his clients. Yet, at the same time, she knew that she couldn't face her delegates. Not like this. Not with her sex wet and aching for relief, her breasts heavy and tingling.

There was one thing that she hadn't unpacked. She dropped the sheet of paper she'd been reading on the bedspread and climbed off the bed, padding over to where she'd left her weekend bag. She delved in the bottom and brought out a vibrator. It had been a last-minute decision, one that had shamed her at the time, but now she was glad that she'd

brought it with her. She hadn't used a vibrator for a long time –
since before meeting Rupert, if she didn't count that episode
with Mandy – but she had had a feeling that she would need it
over the weekend. Certainly, the last time that she had
borrowed some of Mandy's erotic novels she'd ended up
masturbating furiously. And spending the weekend teaching
the stuff, reading it . . . Well, it was a fair bet that she would
need her vibrator at some point, to give her release.

She sprawled back on the bed; then, unable to help herself,
she opened the conference centre brochure and flicked through
it. Facing the inside front cover was a photograph of the
manager, Kit Williams. He was dressed in another of the
formal dark suits, white shirt and understated tie – silk, she
guessed – and had been photographed sitting at his desk. His
hair was dry, but she recognized him instantly. Kit Williams
was indeed her nameless rescuer.

She traced the outline of his face with the tip of her finger
and then lay back on the bed, pushing her head back into the
pillows and closing her eyes. She untucked the towel from
between her breasts, letting it fall onto the bedspread; then she
spun the bevel at the base of the vibrator so that the little
machine hummed. Stretching languidly, she brought the
vibrator up, rubbing it against her hardened nipples. A shaft
of pleasure lanced through her, and she gently drew the
vibrator down over her abdomen, anticipating the pleasure
that was to come.

Widening the gap between her thighs, she placed her feet
flat on the bedspread and moved the tip of the vibrator down
the full length of her quim, rubbing it over her perineum and
teasing the openings of her vagina and anus with it. She
repeated the action, moving the machine slowly back and
forth, until her wet sex was flexing with anticipation. Then,

and only then, she allowed the tip of the vibrator to push against the entrance of her sex. She eased it slowly into her warm wet spongy depths, thinking of Kit Williams. The little tube wasn't as long and thick as his cock had been, but it would do her – for now.

The bed was more comfortable than the bonnet of Kit's car had been; she stretched languidly, and began to work the little device harder, plunging the vibrator deeper inside her and then withdrawing it. She teased herself, pushing just the tip back and forth rapidly; then she plunged it in deeply again, right up to the hilt.

Kit Williams. If he were here now, what would he do? Would he just stand there, watching her, his cock swelling and hardening until he could stand it no longer and had to unbutton his trousers, taking out his cock and stroking it? Would he bring himself to a rapid climax, still almost fully dressed and standing over her, letting his seed spurt on to her naked body? Or would he strip, remove the machine from her fingers, and plunge his beautiful cock into her instead, making her buck and writhe beneath him?

Or . . . Her nipples tightened, and she could feel waves of fire flowing through her belly as the idea struck her. It wasn't something she'd actually done, but she had read a scene in one of the books she had borrowed from Mandy and the idea turned her on – big time. If Kit was there next to her, maybe he would turn her over, gently guiding her on to her hands and knees. He would leave the vibrator pushed into her vagina and he would continue to pump the little machine back and forth. But he'd also be kneeling between her thighs, the tip of his cock brushing her perineum. He would moisten his finger and gently press against the puckered rosy hole of her anus, pushing through the tight ring of muscles and massaging her gently. He would gentle her, kissing down her spine and nuzzling her shoulders and telling her how much he adored her; and then he would move his finger in and out, stretching her forbidden passage and turning her on still further.

When she was near to the limit, *then* he would remove his finger, pressing the tip of his cock in its place and pushing in, so very slowly. His glans would be slippery from the clear juices running from the eye of his cock; he would enter her fully, taking her in the most primal way. Though it would be a homage to her body, not a demonstration of his power over her. He would remain still, letting her body grow used to the feel of the way he was invading her – and then he'd begin to move, pushing in deeply but taking it slowly, gently. And all the time he would be working the vibrator inside her vagina, so it would be as if she was being pleasured by two lovers . . .

Carolyn cried out as a powerful orgasm swept through her; she lay on the bed, unable to move, her internal muscles flexing hard round the still-buzzing tube. Eventually, she reached down, switched off the little machine, and removed it. She left it lying on the bed and walked into the bathroom. She needed another wash, she thought; she couldn't go downstairs to her course delegates reeking of sex. Even if it had been solo sex.

Her legs felt slightly shaky, but she took another quick shower and dried herself swiftly. She smoothed body lotion into her skin and stared at herself in the mirror. She still looked slightly flushed and her eyes were sparkling. No wonder, with all the climaxes she'd had that day, she thought wryly.

She returned to the bedroom, and glanced at her watch, giving a stifled yelp as she realized that it was ten to eight. She had about nine minutes to dress, sort out her make-up, and head down to the library for the reception. 'Bloody hell,' she muttered, and sprayed herself with perfume before putting on her underwear. She dressed swiftly, choosing a bright red suit and teaming it with a pair of high-heeled patent leather black shoes, a black shirt, and putting a black velvet Alice band in her hair. She did her make-up quickly, then gave herself one last glance in the mirror. Yes, she looked fine. She looked like a professional tutor, exactly what they would be expecting. Then she opened her door, switched off the light, and headed down the stairs again.

FOUR

The library was clearly marked with italic lettering on a brass plate on the oak door; Carolyn opened the door without knocking. She glanced round before walking into the room: she was the only one there. She heaved a sigh of relief and closed the door behind her.

The room was large, and two of the four walls were filled from floor to ceiling with custom-made bookshelves. One wall contained large French doors which no doubt led onto a terrace or out to the garden; on either side of the doors there were more shelves. The larger books were on the bottom shelves, graduating up so that the smallest books were near the ceiling. There were a couple of library steps in the corners of the rooms for the convenience of the reader. There was also another large open fireplace on the only shelf-free wall, containing a roaring log fire; a large wicker basket of logs rested on the tiled hearth next to the fire, and the smell of burning apple wood drifted through the air.

There were several leather armchairs dotted about the room, including two on either side of the fire, and a square table covered with a white damask cloth. Carolyn walked over towards it and surveyed the spread. Her lips curved in a wry smile. A few nibbles, the receptionist had said. Carolyn had been expecting some crisps and nuts, something small. But there were smoked salmon pinwheels; little redcurrant-and-onion tarts, deep-fried Camembert, tiny cocktail sausages –

which looked as though there were several different flavours, not just the bog-standard pork ones – and tiny bridge rolls filled with tuna, beef and ham. It was virtually a full buffet, she thought.

There were several bottles of chilled sparkling wine on the table, placed in silver ice-buckets next to the champagne flutes, porcelain plates, silver cutlery and starched damask napkins. Carolyn picked up a bottle and smiled in appreciation as she read the label. Sparkling Australian Chardonnay. No doubt another of Mandy's orders. Mandy had a real weakness for creamy Australian fizz and needed little excuse to open a bottle.

A sudden thought struck Carolyn. Supposing that Kit Williams decided to join them? But no. There were seven of everything. Enough for the six delegates and herself, no more. He wouldn't be part of the reception; she wasn't sure whether she was more relieved or disappointed.

There was a hesitant knock at the door. 'Come in,' she called.

The door opened and a woman walked in. She looked as though she were in her mid-thirties, with dark greying hair cut into a neat bob and dark eyes. She smiled shyly. 'Hello.'

Carolyn smiled back warmly. 'Hello. I'm Carolyn. Would you like a glass of wine?'

'Thank you. I'm Peggy.'

Carolyn poured them both a glass of wine and handed one to Peggy. They chatted politely, Carolyn trying hard not to look as though she was assessing the first of the delegates to arrive; within the next ten minutes, the other five had come in. Carolyn poured them all a glass of wine and turned to them with a smile. 'Well, good evening. I'm Carolyn Saunders; welcome to the Write Right course on writing erotica for women. Your tutor should have been Amanda Wedderburn, but I'm afraid that she has the flu. I'm actually the director of new courses, but I've also taught a variety of courses, from copywriting to journalism to fiction, so Amanda asked me to step in for her. Now, I'm not going to start the course tonight with an ice-breaker or anything like that—' there was a ripple of relieved laughter '—but I think that it would be a good idea to introduce ourselves and say what we do and where we come from, before we go to dinner.'

She smiled at them. 'I'll start. I'm Carolyn Saunders, and I used to be a journalist. I discovered that I enjoyed teaching a lot more than writing features, so I became a lecturer at Write Right. I'm thirty, I live in Norwich, and I like reading, music, films and eating out.' And theatre – or she had, before Rupert. But she didn't want to think about him. She turned to the redhead on her left. 'So,' she said quietly, 'tell us about you.'

The redhead smiled. 'My name's Elizabeth Bowes, though everyone calls me Libby. I'm twenty-three, and I'm an actress.' She smiled wryly. 'I don't think I'm bound for Hollywood or being a stalwart of the RSC, but I've been in a few minor West End productions, which is a start. I live in Islington, and I share a flat with two other actresses. I enjoy reading, the theatre – and eating out, when I can afford it.'

Carolyn winced inside. It was just her bad luck that the first of the delegates was an actress. But Libby didn't have the same arrogance as Rupert. She had an inner self-confidence, yes, but she didn't give the impression that she thought she was wonderful and special and everyone should pay homage to her. She was stunning, though. She was taller than Carolyn, around five feet nine, and slender; Carolyn would have bet money that she moved as smoothly as a model. She could have graced any catwalk. She was well-dressed, in a plain black dress with a brightly-patterned shawl thrown over her shoulders, flat black patent court shoes, and silver jewellery. Her hair reminded Carolyn of the Millais painting, *The Bridesmaid*, the way that her red curls tumbled down over her shoulders. Her skin was creamy white, and she had very blue eyes; her make-up was light, yet highlighted her fine cheekbones and sparkling eyes and Cupid's-bow mouth to perfection. 'Thank you, Libby,' Carolyn said.

'I'm Virginia Walker – Gina, to my friends.' The woman sitting next to Libby smiled. 'I live in a bachelor flat in Chichester, with three cats; I was divorced last year, and it was the best decision of my life. I'm forty-three, I don't work, and I enjoy travel. I've spent the past six months travelling round Europe and Australia.'

Carolyn appraised her briefly. She had a feeling that Gina would be one of the livelier members of the group. She had fair curly hair that was brushed back from her face and made her look as if she'd just got out of bed. Her almond-shaped green eyes hinted at mischief, and she had a wide generous mouth. She was about the same height as Carolyn, though thinner. She didn't look as though she was that interested in clothes: her black jersey leggings and loose patterned tunic shirt were chosen for comfort, rather than impact. And yet she still had a sense of style that Carolyn half-envied. *This woman would look good in a bin-bag*, Carolyn thought.

'I'm Suzanne Dryden. Sue,' said the next woman. 'I'm twenty-five, I work as a secretary in an accountancy firm in Birmingham, and I'm married.' She grinned. 'To an erotic writer. So you can guess why I'm here! I like reading, cult science fiction, and aerobics.'

Carolyn couldn't help smiling at Sue. She had a feeling that Sue, like Gina, would be lively and maybe would help to draw out the shyer members of the group. Her cropped red hair was more a strawberry blonde than the rich Titian tones of Libby's hair. She had green eyes and porcelain skin; she was probably the shortest woman in the room, at about five feet two, but she radiated energy. Her clothes were bright, chosen to startle, although the cut of her trousers and casual shirt were flattering.

'Peggy Ridley,' Peggy said softly. 'I'm in my mid-thirties, and I work in an office. I live in Leeds, and I'm married with two children.' She stared at the floor, not wanting to say more. Carolyn's heart went out to her. Even to apply for a course like this must have been a struggle for her. She wondered why Peggy wanted to write erotica. With Gina and Libby and Sue, it was easy to see that they enjoyed the genre and simply wanted to write what they liked reading; but Peggy . . . She seemed more the type to read Austen and the classics, an Aga-saga writer. But Carolyn had a feeling that Peggy had hidden depths. It was just a matter of reaching them during the course.

The next woman was also softly spoken. 'Emma Steward,' she said shyly. 'I'm also in my mid-thirties, and I work in a bank. I'm married, but we don't have any children. I live in Bedford, and I enjoy reading and costume dramas.'

'Thank you, Emma,' Carolyn said. Emma was another of the shy ones, she thought. She had mid-brown curly hair, grey-blue eyes, and was about the same height as Carolyn. She was well-dressed, in a silky pleated skirt and a toning shirt. She was a little on the plump side, which no doubt contributed to her shyness; Carolyn had a feeling that, like Peggy, Emma had hidden depths. There was every possibility that these two would have the most inventive imaginations in the group.

Carolyn turned to the last woman in the group. 'Last, but not least,' she quipped.

The woman smiled. 'I'm Elaine Byford. I'm thirty, and I'm a

freelance journalist. I live in London and I'm single. I enjoy eating with friends, good conversation, and books.' Carolyn immediately felt drawn to her. Elaine had so much in common with her. Though Elaine's confidence was genuine, rather than the sham that Carolyn's had become over the past couple of weeks. Elaine wore her chestnut-brown hair piled on top of her head, managing to give an impression of elegance at the same time as looking as though she'd recently left her lover's bed, and her grey eyes were highlighted with the minimum of make-up.

'Thank you, Elaine. Well, I'm sure that we'll get to know each other very well over the next couple of days. I hope that you're all going to enjoy the course; and if there's anything you think I haven't covered, just tell me,' Carolyn said. 'But tonight I think we'll socialize, rather than work. If we get to know each other a bit better, we'll all be relaxed with each other in the morning and we can go straight into the course then rather than having an ice-breaker. There's plenty of fizzy, so help yourselves; and we can go into the restaurant whenever we're ready.'

'Sounds good to me,' Gina said, refilling her glass and topping up everyone else's within reach.

Carolyn was relieved to note, over the next half-hour, that Peggy and Emma had been drawn into the group by Sue and Gina; the room hummed with a lively buzz of conversation.

'This place is amazing,' Elaine said to her, glancing round. 'It's just the sort of place I'd like to use for the setting of a novel.'

Carolyn grinned. 'I was going to bring that up when I talked about settings tomorrow. But yes, you're right.'

'And this library,' Elaine continued. 'There are so many books here. They can't all be biographies and the complete works of Shakespeare.'

'Mm – anyone who lived here would have to be a sensualist,' Gina agreed, overhearing the conversation and joining in. 'I bet there's some really interesting stuff on the shelves.'

'Let's have a look,' Sue suggested.

Peggy and Emma looked slightly doubtful about rifling through the books; they glanced at Carolyn, who was smiling broadly. Her encounter with Kit, together with the amount of sparkling wine she had consumed on an empty stomach, had made her feel slightly reckless. And the receptionist had more or less told her that she could do what she liked . . . 'Yes, let's have a look,' she said.

Elaine discovered a leather-bound book of John Donne's poems, and insisted on reading one of them aloud: the nineteenth elegy, *On his mistress going to bed.* 'I've always loved that one,' she said. 'The guy who did the lectures on the Metaphysical poets, when I was at university, was gorgeous. He was in his early thirties, and he was a real stunner – a bit like Colin Firth as Mr Darcy. All the girls were sitting there, fantasizing that he was reading this aloud to them and was going to act it out to the letter.'

'There's some fairly raunchy stuff in Keats, too,' Libby added. 'One of my exes was into Keats. There's this poem about two lovers running away, and it's like being in a sweetshop – you can virtually taste everything that happens. I can't remember which one it was.'

'*St Agnes' Eve,*' Elaine told her, smiling. 'Yeah – we did that one, too. And Rochester.' Her lips twitched. 'I bet there's some of his stuff here, too.'

'But,' said Gina, removing a book with a flourish, 'it's not all pre-twentieth century. Look at this. *Erotic Tales, volume seven.*' She flicked through the contents, and her eyes glittered. 'Oh, yes. This is exactly the kind of stuff that

Carolyn's going to teach us to write.'

'Let's have a look.' Libby went over to join her and read over her shoulder. She whistled. 'This is good stuff.'

'Read it aloud,' Sue suggested. 'You're an actress, Libby – you've probably got the best voice of all of us.'

Libby looked at the others. 'What do you think?'

There were several murmurs of agreement; she nodded, and flicked to the next story. 'How about this one – *The Fairground of Desire?*'

'Sounds good to me,' Gina said, sipping her wine. She pulled up one of the leather chairs and sat down, crossing her legs and leaning back to listen to Libby; the others followed suit, including Carolyn.

Libby grinned. 'This is almost like an adult version of *Jackanory!*' she teased.

'Mm, but I think that we're going to enjoy it a lot more,' Elaine said, leaning back in her chair.

Libby began to read aloud. 'Angela woke, her mouth dry and her head reeling. It couldn't possibly be morning already. Apart from the fact that her alarm hadn't gone off, it was still dark outside.

'Or was it? It had certainly been a ringing sound that had woken her; and her room wasn't dark enough for it to be the middle of the night. She stretched out a hand and grabbed her alarm clock, pressing the button to illuminate the time. Three-thirty a.m.

'No wonder she felt so bad. She'd only had about four hour's sleep. Muzzily, she replaced the clock on her bedside cabinet and burrowed back under the duvet. Though her mind refused to let her sleep. It was half-past three in the morning, and she'd been woken by lights and a ringing sound. Which meant that something funny was going on. Maybe one of her neighbours was being burgled and she ought to call the police. Though she slept at the back of the house, not the front, so the chances were that she wouldn't see the lights flashing on any burglar alarm. So what the hell was going on?

'With a scowl, she dragged herself out of bed, went to the window and twitched the curtain aside. Instead of the streaky dawn she'd been half-expecting, it was still dark outside. Though the stars were obscured by twinkling lights, green and red and yellow and blue. She peered out of the window, trying to work out what the lights were: and then blinked in surprise as she realized what it was. A fairground, in the fields behind her house.

'The noise that had woken her hadn't been a ringing sound: it had been the sound of a fairground organ, a carousel. Angela frowned, her grey eyes narrowing. Apart from the fact that she'd heard nothing about a fair coming to town – she had seen none of the flyers that were usually shoved through letter boxes and nailed to trees, or articles in the local newspapers trumpeting the arrival of a fair – it was very late for a fair to be open. Usually, they closed no later than one in the morning.

'She stood watching the lights for a while. Then, on a sudden impulse, she pulled on her underwear, jeans and a sweater. She was past sleep now, so why not go down and join in with the rest of the revellers? It was better than lying there, listening to the music and wishing that she could get to sleep. She slid her boots on, threw her leather jacket over her shoulders, and let herself out of the house.

'As she walked into the field, she glanced back at the houses in her street. There wasn't a single light on; obviously no one else had been woken by the fair. It seemed a bit odd: to her maybe they were all deep sleepers or slept at the front of their houses and hadn't heard the carousel. Shrugging, she turned back to the fair and blinked in amazement when she saw the first stall.

'In the past, she'd seen stalls where men hit a metal rod with a sledgehammer and their prowess was recorded on a meter: *wimp, try harder, average, strong, very strong, Hercules*. This stall had a spongy hole in the middle of the stand, rather than a rod, and the meter read *tadpole, average, large, very large, donkey, bull*. What did it mean? And what was the hole for?

'She soon found out. As she stood there, frowning, the man at the front of the queue dropped his trousers and stood stroking his prick, the familiar motions of his hand soon making his cock purple-tipped and swollen. When he judged himself ready, his penis standing proud and erect, he walked up to the stand and inserted the rigid member into the spongy hole. Lights flashed up: "very large". He grinned, bending his elbow, clenching his fist and drawing it back to his shoulder in the classic gesture of triumph; his friends clapped him on the back. Still laughing exultantly, he withdrew his cock from the machine, zipped up his jeans and walked off.

'The next man in the queue followed suit. Angela watched, fascinated, as he worked himself to hardness. She'd never seen such a large cock, with a girth she would have had trouble curling her hand around. She wasn't surprised when the machine gave him "donkey" status.

'Interested now, she walked through the fair. The popcorn vendor was doing a roaring trade – not least because a beautiful naked man with coffee-coloured skin stood next to the tub of corn, frantically rubbing his cock over it until long strings of milky liquid spewed forth from its end. *Obviously that was meant to be salty popcorn rather than sweet*, Angela thought with a grin.

'The helter-skelter was next. The traditional phallic shape of the ride was made even more so by its purple cap and the red flashing striplights running like veins down its side. The entrance price was "thirty". *Thirty what?* Angela thought. Thirty pence was too cheap. The last time that she had been to a fairground, the cost of the rides had been approaching a pound. Thirty pounds was ludicrously expensive: no one would pay that. So thirty what?

'The answer wasn't long in coming. The woman at the front of the queue knelt before the helter-skelter's attendant. His cock reared in front of him; she cupped his balls in one hand and slicked her red-lipsticked mouth over his glans. Angela watched, fascinated, as the woman's mouth moved over his cock, the red line of her lips sliding up and down the thick tube as she fellated him.

'A second attendant clicked a stopwatch and tapped her on the shoulder. Angela blinked. "Thirty" obviously meant thirty seconds of oral sex. The woman straightened up, smiling, and took the hand of the man who was obviously her boyfriend, leading him towards the stairs.

'The attendant shook his head, tapping the board. The price was thirty seconds per person. The woman gestured to herself – was she to pay her boyfriend's admission price? The attendant shook his head again. Shrugging, the woman's boyfriend sank to his knees, cupped the other man's shaft, and began to tongue it, concentrating on the sensitive groove at the base of the glans before taking it deep into his mouth and sucking hard.

'Angela, not sure whether she was more aroused or un-nerved at the sight, hurried past. *This is one hell of a fair*, she thought. No wonder it hadn't been advertised. It would have been banned by the town puritans. She wasn't sure what would have offended them most: the admission prices, or the rides themselves.

'The ghost train was next. The admission price was six – but not six seconds of oral sex. The attendant there carried a riding crop; each person wanting to ride the ghost train had to bare his or her backside for six strokes of the riding crop. Red marks appeared on the pale flesh of each person's buttocks as they reached the front of the queue and paid the admission price; then, laughing, they vaulted lightly into the carriages of the ghost train, ready for their ride.

'Angela wondered what sort of ghostly surprises awaited them. Would invisible hands reach out to stroke a breast, a thigh? Would a vampire suddenly pop up in a puff of green smoke, opening the traditional black cape to reveal a naked body and an erect cock? Would the cars be stopped and the occupants carried off by "ghosts", to be tied up in a mock dungeon and then brought to a screaming climax by various hands and mouths and cocks? The only way to find out, she knew, was to try it, but she didn't feel ready. Not until she'd seen the rest of the attractions.

'She walked over to the ferris wheel. The attendant there wanted "ten" as her admission price. She was seated on a table, her knees bent and spread wide; her feet were close to her buttocks, exposing her reddened and puffy quim. Each man wanting to ride on the wheel paid ten thrusts of his cock: and the women were given a large black dildo to hold in their mouths and thrust into the attendant, ten times. The attendant's mouth was open with pleasure, and she'd obviously come several times, judging by her glistening intimate flesh

'A juggler walked past, casually tossing penis-shaped batons in the air and catching them. A clown, naked apart from his make-up, fooled around with custard pies, slapping them onto a female clown's quim and then licking the stuff from her with obvious relish. The bulging head of his cock was emphasized with bright red greasepaint. Candyfloss, attached to a stick shaped like a woman's genitals, was being sold from a nearby stall.

'And then Angela came to the merry-go-round.

'This merry-go-round didn't have the traditional smiling white horses with bright red bridles bobbing up and down on golden poles. There were no horses on it: instead, a dozen young men lay on the moving floor, each one of them stark naked. Their cocks rose stiffly towards the ceiling of the ride; a queue of laughing women waited in turn, until the ride's operator allowed them on to the platform. Then each woman lifted her skirt, betraying her lack of underwear, and knelt astride a man, sliding his cock between her thighs so that the head butted against her vaginal lips. The men reached up to open their riders' shirts, exposing their breasts; each woman cupped the fleshy mounds, allowing rosy erect nipples to peep through their fingertips.

'The music started then, the strange music that Angela suddenly recognized had woken her. She watched, fascinated, as the carousel began to turn and the men began to lift their hips, thrusting deep into the women who rode them. This was the one she wanted to try, she thought. This one. She waited impatiently for the ride to stop – noting with interest that the operator didn't slow the carousel down until every one of the female riders had come, very noisily.

'She didn't care that no condoms were provided. The only thing she could think of was the feel of one of those luscious cocks inside her, filling her quim, and the young man's fingers playing with her clitoris, rubbing the hard little nub of flesh until she came.

'When the riders finally climbed off, the men left, too, being replaced by a fresh set. Angela grinned to herself. It was just about every woman's dream – the ride of the decade, and you got to choose the "horse" you wanted. You could have a new horse every time and ride as many times as you liked, reaching climax after climax after climax, until your legs were so shaky that you couldn't stand. She watched as the new "horses" stripped and began stroking their cocks to hardness; the carousel turned round very slowly, so that all the women in the queue could make their choice.

'As the music slowed down again and stopped, the men lay down in position; Angela joined the women thronging onto the carousel, choosing a man with a long and thick cock. He smiled at her as she peeled off her jeans and knickers and straddled him, resting her quim against his sex. "Hello."

' "Hello."

'It's the ultimate zipless fuck, she thought. They wouldn't exchange names – she already knew that, without needing to be told – and she didn't even have to undress him. He was all ready for the taking. She curled her hand round his cock. "Nice," she said approvingly.

' "I'm glad it meets your requirements." He winked at her. "Have a good ride."

'He helped peel off her sweater, tossing it to the side; as she leaned forward slightly, he undid the clasp of her bra, casually laying that aside, too. With a smile, he cupped her breasts, rubbing his thumbs over her erect nipples; the light caress made every nerve ending cry out for more. He raised his upper body and smiled at her then, his eyes a deep and sensual green. She knew what he was going to do and tipped her head back, sliding her hands in his hair as he lowered his lips to one breast. He licked her areola then withdrew slightly, just breathing on her nipple, and her whole skin tingled.

'God, she wanted him to touch her, so much! She almost

groaned in the agony of waiting; and then, at last, he licked her properly, his tongue-tip circling her areola and then flicking rapidly across her nipple. Her clitoris seemed to twitch in sympathy, and she cried out again, digging the pads of her fingertips into his scalp and pushing her breasts against him. She felt him laugh softly against her skin, and then he began to suck.

'Angela had always enjoyed having her breasts kissed and touched, but this was something else. All her nerve endings seemed to ripple, wave after wave of sensation concentrating round her nipple where his mouth touched her skin, then pushing outwards to arouse her whole body.

'He slid one hand between their bodies, stroking her abdomen and then pushing his hand between her thighs; the second that his questing finger touched her clitoris she cried out, the sensation was so good and so sharp. When he began to rub her, she shook, hardly able to bear the intensity; knowing how she felt, he straightened up, letting her sink her teeth into his shoulder to stifle her cries of pleasure.

'When he'd brought her to the edge of orgasm, he lifted her slightly, pausing in his caresses to position the head of his cock at the entrance to her vagina. She lowered herself gently onto the rigid shaft, feeling her internal muscles contract sharply round him. Her blood seemed to be fizzing in her veins, and every nerve end was overloaded with sensation: it was the most incredible thing she had ever felt, and she wanted it to go on and on and on forever.

'He sank back onto the carousel, his hands sliding down to support her; Angela almost laughed with the sheer joy of it, and began to move in time with the fairground music, lifting herself gently upwards and then slamming down hard, grinding her pubis against the root of his cock. She moved her lower body in small circles, flexing her vaginal grip round him; as she bore down on him, he tilted his pelvis, pushing up so that he was enveloped by her soft flesh to the hilt.

'All of a sudden, Angela felt the familiar beginnings of orgasm. The warm rolling pleasure in the soles of her feet made her skin tingle; as it slowly moved through her body, she felt as if her whole being was concentrated on it, her entire body contracting and convulsing in ecstasy. As it coiled up her spine and exploded, her body became a thousand stars imploding, a mass of pulsing energy, and she howled aloud with the sheer joy of it, her voice only just drowned out by the carousel . . .

'The alarm jangled, waking her; with a groan, Angela rolled over and looked at the time. Six forty-five. It was time to get up, have breakfast, and start another day in the office, poring over other people's programs and sorting out their problems.

'*I've had one hell of a dream*, she thought, stretching out luxuriously in the bed. A fairground where all the rides were to do with sex, and you paid in sexual acts. Yes, it had been one hell of a dream, the kind she would quite like to have lived out in real life.

'She got out of bed, a smile on her face. Then she saw the trail of mud across her bedroom carpet to where her ankle boots were lying on the floor. And as she moved, she recognized the sore, slightly sticky feeling between her thighs for what it was . . .' Libby closed the book with a snap. 'And we all know what *that* was, don't we, girls?'

'Mm.' Gina licked her lips. 'I have to admit, I've been to a couple of fairs in the past where I've really wanted to have one of the stall-holders. In the ferris wheel, I think. But I've never seen anything quite like that.'

'No – can you imagine it?' Elaine grinned. 'It would be

banned before they had even finished putting the posters up!'

'Mm, but the idea of it . . . being able to choose the man you want to ride. No strings, no worries. It's the perfect fantasy,' Sue said. 'That, or being one of the attendants. Lots and lots of people willing to pleasure you, for admittance to the rides . . .'

Carolyn glanced at her watch. 'I don't know about you, but I'm starving. Shall we go in to dinner?'

The others agreed and they trooped out of the library, heading for the restaurant.

FIVE

The restaurant turned out to be delightful – an old-fashioned manor house dining room, with panelled walls, faded tapestries, and dark brocade curtains over the long narrow windows. The blue and yellow fleur-de-lys carpet was in evidence again, and the mahogany dining tables were all covered with damask tablecloths set with silver cutlery and fine porcelain, with a tiny blue and white floral arrangement in the centre of each table. The lighting was soft and flattering, and there was another roaring log fire in the hearth.

Their table was at one end of the room; Carolyn glanced round, and was relieved to notice that Kit was nowhere to be seen. She still didn't feel quite up to facing him. Not yet. There were a couple of other groups of people in the restaurant; they were all female, she noticed. No doubt they were delegates for another course; judging by the way that the women were dressed, the courses had something to do with some kind of crafts. Tapestry, perhaps, crewel-work or maybe art.

They went over to their table; after a brief discussion, they ordered four bottles of wine between them, two red and two white, plus a large jug of water. The menu turned out to be as good as Carolyn had hoped: salmon mousse, followed by chicken with asparagus and lemon sauce, and a very interesting-looking sweet trolley.

The conversation soon turned back to the story that Libby

had read to them in the library. 'I wonder how far people put their real lives into a novel,' Gina said.

Sue grinned. 'Put it this way, if my other half did all the things he wrote about, he wouldn't have time to work!'

The others laughed.

'But do you ever read his books,' Elaine asked, 'and see bits of you that you recognize in them?'

Sue thought about it for a moment. 'Come to think of it, yes, he does borrow the occasional thing from real life. And there *have* been times when we've been in bed and I've wondered whether it's me he's with, or whether he's trying out a plot for one of his books on the quiet.'

'Personal fantasies are quite a good place to start from,' Carolyn told them. 'If you're writing about something that you find a turn-on, it's likely that your readers will enjoy it, too.'

Libby eyed her thoughtfully. 'Have *you* ever written an erotic novel, Carolyn?'

Carolyn shook her head. 'I haven't really had the time to write a book.'

'But you were a journalist. They say that every copywriter or journo has a novel in the bottom drawer of their desk, so surely you've had the inclination?' Libby persisted.

Carolyn grinned. 'Not really – though this weekend might change all that!' She was half-tempted to tell them what had happened on the way to Heywood, but decided not to. It would be just her bad luck if Kit came into the dining room, unseen by her, and overheard what she was saying. She didn't want him to think that she would boast about what had happened between them.

'But can you use personal experiences?' Gina asked. 'Quite a few things happened to me on my travels, and I'd like to write about them.'

'You said that you've spent the past six months travelling Europe and Australia, didn't you?' Peggy asked.

Carolyn smiled with pleasure. It looked like Peggy was beginning to come out of her shell. That just left Emma: and then she was in for a very lively course indeed.

Gina grinned. 'Well, I've always wanted to travel. My divorce settlement gave me enough money to do it – and I didn't have a job to complicate things. I packed the bare essentials, and upped and went.' She smiled wryly. 'Mind you, now that I'm back I need to do something for a living. I really don't want to work for someone else, and I enjoy reading erotica – so I thought that I'd try my hand at writing it.'

'Well,' Carolyn said, 'if you've been travelling, you've probably got some good material for backgrounds and settings.'

Libby eyed Gina thoughtfully. 'And you said that you had some experiences, too. Can I ask what kind of experiences?'

Gina shrugged. 'I suppose I lived up to the stereotype – the corporate wife let off the leash at last, who went slightly mad with the heady idea of freedom. I mean, I'm not getting any younger. I could have bought myself a little cottage and mouldered away in the countryside, or even in part of London, but I wanted to do something different. I wanted to do something that I'd never done with David – something that I'd always wanted to do, but it didn't fit in with his idea of how things should be.' She chuckled. 'Luckily, the children saw things my way. My daughter encouraged me to go and enjoy myself.' She took a leisurely sip of wine. 'And that's exactly what I did.'

'So where did you go?' Elaine asked.

'I started off in Paris,' Gina said. She smiled. 'I could have spent a fortune there, but I just about managed to restrain myself. I wanted to travel light – besides, spending my money on clothes I didn't really need would mean that I'd have to stay in less comfortable hotels, or cut my trip short, and I didn't want to do either of those things.' She smiled. 'I don't know if I should really tell you about Paris.'

'Oh, come on, Gina,' Sue said. 'You've whetted our appetite now. You wanted to write about your experiences, so you might as well use us as an audience.'

Gina thought about it for a moment; then her green eyes crinkled with mischief at the corners. 'Well, you asked for it. You've only yourselves to blame if I shock you!'

Elaine grinned. 'I don't know about that. I think that it'd take a lot to shock us. Remember why we're all here.'

Gina nodded. 'Let's just say that I regard myself as a free spirit now. I spent too many years being what other people wanted me to be, being seen only as my ex-husband's corporate wife or the children's mother. So when I decided to travel, I promised myself that I wouldn't fall into the same trap. I wouldn't be one of those middle-aged women who was only interested in pottering around and following her Fodor's guide, or maybe flirted with the equally middle-aged and paunchy guide of a tour. Anyway, Paris. I've always adored Paris.' Her eyes grew dreamy; she sipped her wine. 'They say that it's the city of lovers. I'd spent the day wandering through the streets, just soaking up the atmosphere – the café life, the intimate glances between couples, the culture. It was glorious. There were several street artists painting pastels by the Seine and selling them to the tourists. One or two were drawing portraits and caricatures; there was one in particular who stopped me, saying that he wanted to draw me, but I didn't want to spend my travelling money on a portrait. I still wanted to go to the

South of France, then work my way round the coast – Italy, Greece, Turkey. There was a lot I wanted to see. Ancient ruins, modern cities, vast sandy beaches and private coves.

'Anyway, we started talking and we went for a cup of coffee. His name was Raoul. He was twenty-five and he was an art student. He was rebelling against his parents; they wanted him to settle down into the family financial business, though he wanted to make his living as a painter. He wasn't bad, actually, but making your living as an artist is hardly easy, especially when the competition's as hot as it is in Paris. He was nice-looking, in the way that the young upper-class French are: dark eyes, dark hair, long lashes, fabulous skin. He was just over six feet tall, and he was slightly thinner than the men I was used to – probably because he didn't eat properly, being a student. Anyway, the next thing I knew, I'd agreed to have dinner with him.

'I was staying in a good hotel; he met me there, and we took the Metro to another part of the city – the *Cinquième*, where all the students tended to go. It was an old and almost villagey part of Paris, where you could wander round and just soak up the atmosphere. We went to a bistro; it was cheap and cheerful, not like the top-class restaurants I was used to from my life with David. There were no damask napkins and silver cruet sets and expensive candelabra: it was more rough linen, wood and raffia-covered bottles with candles stuck into them and the melted wax of a few dozen previous candles studding the sides.

'Although the place seemed very basic, it had an amazing atmosphere. And the food was fabulous, French cuisine at its very best. I don't think I've ever had a *cassoulet* to match, before or since. The wine was good, too, soft and rich. As for the place itself: the tables were small, just big enough for two; the chairs were bentwood and slightly rickety; and the walls were painted a rich deep terracotta to echo the flooring, marbled with a paler colour. Paintings hung on the walls – paintings by local artists – and there was a jazz pianist playing old Ella Fitzgerald numbers in the corner.

'Raoul told me his life story, virtually; but he wasn't talking to me as an older woman who could give him advice, a mother figure. He was talking to me as an equal. In return, I told him what I was doing in Europe, and that I wasn't looking for any permanent relationship. When we'd finished our meal, we walked along the bank of the Seine. And then he kissed me. I don't know where he got his expertise – whether someone older had already taught him, or whether he'd just had dozens of lovers – and I didn't ask. I just enjoyed the way his mouth was moving over mine, so sensually. It was obvious that we were going to make love, and I wanted him.

'I suggested that we went back to my hotel. Although part of me would have loved to make love in the middle of Paris, under the stars, I wasn't prepared to take that much of a risk. Maybe you could have done it in the Paris of the Fifties, but it's not a good idea now.' She grinned. 'Not that I was worried about shocking people by our bohemian behaviour, you understand. I was thinking more of muggers stealing my handbag while I was . . . otherwise engaged. Then Raoul said that his rooms were nearby, so we went there instead.

'It was exactly the sort of place that you'd expect an artist's garret to be like. The whitewashed walls were bared, and there were dozens of canvases stacked against them on the floor. There was a small table and one chair, and a narrow bed. The floor was bare polished wood, and his only means of cooking was a tiny gas ring. But the room was at least clean, and so was the tiny bathroom.' Her lips curved wryly. 'I say "bathroom", but he didn't actually have a bath. Just a shower, a sink and a toilet.

'He opened a bottle of red wine, and we sat on his bed. We just sat talking for a long while, sipping wine; but we were both aware of the sexual tension between us. I think I was the one to make the first move. I leaned over and traced his lower lip with my finger. He sucked my finger into his mouth – it was so erotic. He took my wrist then and sucked the tip of each of my fingers in turn before drawing his tongue along my palm, down to the pulse in my wrist. I was wearing a shirt as a light jacket over my sleeveless dress – it was a warm night – and he pushed it up further, kissing along my arm until he reached the crook of my elbow.

'All the time, his eyes were fixed on mine. They were black with desire, and even the way he looked at me was enough to make my nipples harden. I was so turned on. The way he kissed me, caressed my skin – it was though he was a far more experienced man than the twenty-five-year-old student I knew him to be.

'He pulled me to my feet then and pushed my shirt from my shoulders. Neither of us was concerned that the material would crumple. It wasn't important. Then he turned me round and unzipped my dress, pushing that from my shoulders so that it fell, rustling, to the floor. I was wearing my hair up and he bent to kiss the nape of my neck, licking my skin and making me shiver in anticipation. There he kissed his way down my spine.' Gina's eyes were glowing, and her lower lip had grown fuller and redder with the memory.

'He undid my bra and dropped it on top of my other clothes. He was still standing behind me and he slid one hand round my waist, pulling me back against him. I could feel his erection pressing against my buttocks through the thick material of his black chinos; I couldn't help wriggling slightly, and he brought his other hand round to touch my breasts, tracing the areolae and then pulling gently at the hard rosy tips. He buried his head in the curve of my neck, kissing and licking and biting gently; I felt so hot and wet, so ready for him. I remember wishing that there was a mirror in front of us, so I could see what he was doing to me.

'I think he could tell how aroused I was; he spun me round again to face him, and we kissed. All the time, he was stroking my back and squeezing my buttocks and driving me slightly crazy with desire. I tugged his black cotton polo-neck sweater from the waistband of his chinos and he lifted his arms to let me remove it properly. He had a good body, like I said – a little thin for my liking, perhaps, but still very nice indeed. I ran my hands over his pecs; his skin was so soft, so smooth. Whoever termed students the "great unwashed" or said that the French smelled didn't have a clue. Raoul was very clean, and he smelled good.

'Then I undid the buckle of his belt, and the button and zip of his chinos. I pushed them down over his hips and he kicked his shoes off, helping me remove his chinos and taking his socks off at the same time. He was wearing a pair of white cotton underpants and they left nothing to the imagination. I could see the bulge of his cock, long and thick, clearly outlined through the material. We stood there for a moment, just looking at each other. Then he pushed his thumbs into the waistband of my knickers and drew them down, dropping to his knees at the same time.

'I closed my eyes and rested my hands on his shoulders; I knew instinctively what he was going to do, once he'd taken off my knickers. He left my stockings on; I was going to kick off my shoes as he pulled my knickers down to my ankles, but he stopped me, telling me how sexy he found the little I was wearing.' She grinned. 'He said that he still wanted to paint me – but there was something a little more urgent he needed to do first. Slowly, I stepped out of my knickers, leaning on Raoul for balance. He crouched at my feet, running his hands up and down the backs of my legs, massaging my calves and thighs and stroking the sensitive spot at the back of my knees. I kept my eyes firmly closed, giving myself up to pleasure and just enjoying what he was doing to me.

'At last, he ran his hands across my inner thighs, tracing the creamy soft flesh above the lacy welts of my stockings. I widened my stance instinctively, and then I felt his mouth against my thighs, so soft and warm and sensual. Then he used his mouth on me, licking from the top to the bottom of my quim in one movement, and then taking his time to explore the little hollows and furls of my sex. He teased my clitoris from its hood with his tongue, and then flicked his tongue rapidly across its tip, making it even harder and more sensitive, before sucking it hard between his lips.

'He made me come twice, then he turned me round, guiding me so that I bent from the waist, placing my hands on the edge of his bed. He rested his hands on my buttocks and stayed there for a while, just looking at me – for all I know, he could have been memorizing me for a painting – and then I heard the soft rustle of material as he removed his underpants. He came to stand behind me, then reached into the drawer of the little cabinet by his bed. I heard a soft ripping sound, followed by a snapping noise; obviously he was putting on a condom.

'Then I felt the tip of his cock pressing against my sex. He eased in, so very smoothly; it was incredibly good, feeling his body surging within mine. He pushed into me until he was in up to the hilt; then he placed his hands on my hips and began to move, thrusting in hard and pulling out very slowly. He moved his hips in small semicircles, changing the angle of his penetration to give me more pleasure. Just as I was about to come, he pulled almost out of me, then pumped just the very tip of his cock back and forth, very fast and very hard. I nearly passed out when I came, it was so strong – like a tidal wave pulsating through me.' She took another sip of wine. 'And that was Paris, for me.'

There was a slight flush on the faces of the other women at the table; all of them had been able to imagine the handsome young Frenchman and had put themselves in Gina's place as she had described exactly what he had done with her. All of them were beginning to feel distinctly aroused. The married women were thinking of their husbands; the other were remembering past loves. And Carolyn was thinking of Kit, the way that he had made love with her over the bonnet of his car. She knew that the others would appreciate the tale, but she still couldn't quite bring herself to tell it.

'That's quite a story, Gina,' Carolyn said, her voice slightly husky.

Gina grinned. 'The first chapter of my novel, I think. The tale of a woman's journey of self-discovery round Europe.'

'Are you telling us,' Elaine demanded, 'that you had a different man in every country?'

Gina's smile said it all. 'On occasion, more than one.'

'More than one? You mean, at the same time?' Libby asked.

Gina shrugged. 'That'd be telling, wouldn't it?' she teased.

'It's one hell of a beginning,' Sue said. 'Where did you go after Paris?'

'Italy. Not Rome – I know they call it the Eternal City, but I much prefer Florence and Venice. Then I went to Brindisi and took a ferry across to one of the Greek islands. I did some island hopping for a while, then headed up to Turkey. I visited all the monuments – Ephesus, the white cliffs, those kind of places – and I had one hell of a tour in a carpet factory, where the guide and I tried out most of the carpets. Making love on a carpet of pure silk is . . . Well, let's just say that I enjoyed it.' She spread her hands. 'Like I said, I regard myself as a free spirit. I have no ties; I don't have to keep any promises. So there are no barriers to me enjoying myself whenever, wherever and with whomever I choose.

'After Turkey, I caught a plane to Melbourne. I travelled round Australia for a while, visiting the bush, and then ended up at the Barrier Reef. It was amazing, diving in those crystal-clear waters. The colours were incredible. And then I went to the Whitsunday Islands.

'They were incredible. I slept on the beach one night – not because I didn't have any money, but because I wanted to know what it would be like, sleeping on a beach under the stars. The sand was pure white, like talcum powder. I'd always thought that sand was gritty and faintly horrible, but this stuff just caressed your body. It made you want to roll in it. Anyway, I met another man there. His name was Michael. He was about my age, and he was in almost exactly the same circumstances. His wife had left him for another man and, after the divorce, he had lost all interest in his business. He needed some time to himself to work out what he really wanted to do with his life. So he rented out his house, packed a bag, and took the train to France and through to Spain.

'He spent quite a while in Spain, then moved round through the South of France and Italy, then over to Egypt. He had some fairly wild tales to tell about the markets there and the dancing girls he met.' She grinned. 'Though obviously he didn't go into all the details. He ended up in New Zealand, and he'd heard about the white sand on the beaches of the Whitsunday Islands so that was why he was there.

'Like I said, I didn't want to be tied down again; but Michael and I spent a few very enjoyable days together. He was planning to continue travelling after he left the Whitsunday Islands, and he asked me to go with him. I was tempted, but I decided not to. Apart from the fact that I was beginning to run out of money, I'd been travelling for almost six months so I thought that it was about time I returned to England. On our last night, we were talking about fantasies and we wondered how many people would fantasize about being in a place like the Whitsunday Islands and making love on the beach under the stars. We were strolling along the beach as we talked; we watched the sun set and then the moon came out, so big and bright that it almost hurt to look at it.

'The sky was like a sheet of midnight-blue velvet-studded with glittering diamonds; I've never seen the sky so clear or so beautiful. The stars are different in the Southern Hemisphere, bigger and brighter and somehow more mysterious. Michael and I looked at each other. The beach was deserted; and even if it hadn't been, the atmosphere of the place was so relaxed that I don't think anyone would have made any comment about what we were going to do.

'Slowly, we undressed each other. We were both tanned from our travels, but our skin still seemed almost silvery in the light of the moon. He cupped my face in his hands and gently lowered his mouth down to mine. We'd made love a couple of times before, in the short time we'd been together, but we both knew that this would be something special. A kind of parting present, and a new beginning for both of us. For me, the chance to return home and start to pick up my life again; for him, a beautiful memory that would stay with him on the rest of his travels and help to clarify what he really wanted to do.

'He bit gently at my lower lip and I opened my mouth, letting him slide his tongue inside. He was a good kisser – in some ways less sure of himself than my young art student had been but in other ways more sensual. He kissed me deeply, not touching me apart from his fingertips gently holding my face; I felt as though the whole of my body was blooming and flowering for him, my nipples growing hard and rosy and my sex growing wet and puffy and ready to receive him. I arched against him, wanting more, but he was in the mood to take it slowly. He made me wait, still kissing me; and then, at last, he undid my shirt, the backs of his fingers brushing against my swelling breasts.

'He removed my shirt, and then my bra; he cupped my breasts in his hands, pushing them together and up to deepen the cleavage, and circled my areolae with his thumbs. I shivered, arching against him and tipping my head back; he continued to touch me, so very lightly. I wanted him to rub me harder, to take my nipple into his mouth and suck hard, use his teeth – but again, he made me wait, just gently stroking the undersides of my breasts and toying with my areolae.

'Then he drew a trail of kisses along my jawline, down my throat, and licked the hollows of my collarbones. I was so frustrated and impatient; I wanted him right then. But I knew that he was making me wait for a purpose. He nuzzled my breasts, breathing in the scent of my skin; and then, at last, his mouth closed over one nipple. I slid my hands into his hair, urging him on; he was still rolling my other nipple between his thumb and forefinger, and I was almost coming just from the way he was touching me.

'He swapped over, licking my other nipple, his thumb moving over its spit-slicked twin. Although the air was warm, I had goose pimples all over my skin – from excitement, I guess. Slowly, he undid my jeans, pushing them down and stroking my skin as he exposed it. I was itching for him to push the gusset of my knickers to one side and slide a finger into me, to ease the ache, but he didn't. He merely finished removing my jeans, making me lift first one leg and then the other; I held on to him for balance.

'I was expecting him to remove my knickers then, but he didn't. He smiled at me and drew my hands up to the buttons of his shirt. I undressed him, trying to take it slowly – but I didn't have any of his finesse. I wanted him too much. He took my hand, kissing each finger in turn; then he spread his shirt and mine on the white sand, and gently lifted me up. He lowered me gently onto our makeshift bed, then knelt between my thighs.

'He smoothed his hands slowly up my thighs, lifting them and hooking my feet over his shoulders. Then he fitted the tip of his cock to the entrance of my sex. I was already wet and slippery, ready to receive him; slowly, he pushed inside, and then he began to thrust. He took it tantalizingly slowly, setting up a slow and almost dreamy rhythm. I had my eyes open, and I could see the stars sparkling down; it was an amazing feeling, making love under a starry sky like that.

'His eyes were open, too; they were a deep navy blue, almost the colour of the sky. He had fair hair – I'd always thought that I preferred dark-haired men, the proverbial tall, dark and hand-some stranger – but there was something so appealing about him.. Something so English and yet so cosmopolitan at the same time. He continued to push into me until I felt the familiar beginnings of orgasm, starting at the soles of my feet, a rolling warmth that suddenly gathered momentum and swept through me. I think the way my internal muscles spasmed round his cock was enough to take him into his own orgasm; he cried out my name, and I felt him tense against me. Then, gently, he lowered my legs and lay on top of me, not withdrawing; he kept his weight on his hands and knees, though. I think that we both just wanted the skin-to-skin contact.

'We lay there for a while; then he rolled over and got up, drawing me to my feet. He suggested that we had one last swim.' She smiled. 'Swimming in the sea there wasn't like swimming anywhere else. The water was warm, for a start – even though it was night. And there were these fluorescent algae in the water: it was like floating in a sea of molten gold. I looked up at the Southern Cross overhead and thought how bloody lucky I'd been. Everything I'd seen, everywhere I'd been, everything I'd done in those six months. It was more than many people had the chance to do, and I'm glad I did it – I think I'd have always regretted it if I'd played safe and settled down in a nice little cottage with a nice little job.' She spread her hands. 'Okay, so I'm more or less skint now – but those memories are going to sustain me for a hell of a long time. Memories of people and places and feelings . . .' She smiled. 'I think that it's the best thing I've ever done, in my entire life.'

'And there's more than enough material for a book there,' Elaine said. 'I think it has to be every woman's dream, travelling round the world as a free spirit and doing whatever you please, not having to worry about anything.' Her voice was slightly wistful. 'And being able to make love to as many attractive men as you want.'

Mandy would have seconded that, Carolyn thought. All the way.

'That's what I was thinking,' Gina said. 'Though it's a question of where I start. Which is why I'm here.'

SIX

'I know what you mean. Actually,' Sue said, 'I was inspired by something that happened to a friend of mine, Ella. She's a senior in the personal tax department at my firm. Anyway, she was working late one night, trying to finish a set of accounts for a client. She thought that she was virtually alone in the building; the reason that she hadn't taken the file home with her and worked there instead was because she knew it would be too easy to be distracted by a good film or a comedy on the television, and she really wanted to get these particular accounts out of the way. The client was one of the awkward types – you know, the sort who'll ring three or four times a day in the belief that it'll make people work harder and finish the accounts more quickly, whereas all it does is waste the tax consultant's time, time that could have been spent on the actual accounts.

'She'd just about finished them, so she put the file in the typing tray and left the room. She switched off the lights behind her, and it was as she was walking down the corridor to the lifts that she noticed the light underneath the senior tax partner's door. She was a bit surprised, because she hadn't expected anyone to be there. She was about to knock on the door and put her head round it, to see if everything was all right, when she heard a sound. It was the distinct sound of someone crying out – crying out in sexual pleasure.

'Ella froze, with her hand raised ready to knock. There was

89

no way that she could disturb whoever it was – not since they were obviously having sex. But she was curious, all the same. Who was in that room? Was it really Francis Merrick, the tax partner – or was someone else using his room? The doors of the partners' offices were all solid wood, with brass handles and keyplates, so Ella bent down and put her eye to the keyhole. What she saw shocked her. It was indeed Francis Merrick – and he was with his secretary, Sheena.

'Sheena was spreadeagled on Francis's desk, face up, and her wrists were tied so that she couldn't move. Her legs were spread wide and her knees were bent to give him better access to her sex. She was wearing only a black stretch-lace teddy, stockings, and very high-heeled patent leather black shoes – the kind of shoes that Ella knew Sheena never usually wore in the office. Sheena was a very conservative dresser and was more likely to wear flat loafers than something so glamorous. Francis was wearing a black domino mask and was otherwise fully clothed in his dark business suit. He was holding a large black dildo which he was thrusting into Sheena. Sheena had been the one who'd cried out in pleasure, no doubt when Francis had first pushed the gusset of her teddy to one side and inserted the dildo.

'Ella must have made some kind of sound, because she saw Francis pause and stare at the door. He said something to Sheena and walked round the desk, taking off his mask. Ella straightened up and was about to dash down the corridor, but Francis was already at the door. He opened it to find her there and he raised one eyebrow in surprise. "Was there something you wanted, Ella?"

'Ella shook her head. "I thought that I was alone in the office. I was on my way out, and I saw that your light was on. I wondered if anything was wrong."

' "Should there be?"

' "I . . ." Ella flushed. "No. Of course not."

'The look on her face gave her away. Francis knew instantly that she'd seen what was going on, through the keyhole. He smiled. "Ella. You know that people who look at private things are usually calls Peeping Toms. Maybe a Peeping Thomasina, in your case." He smiled again, pleased with his pun. "And people who do that kind of thing are usually punished."

'Ella's face drained of colour. "I . . . er . . ."

' "After all," Francis continued silkily, ignoring her, "you could tell anyone what you saw. And it would be our word against yours."

' "I won't say anything."

' "Quite right – because you're already implicated." He smiled wolfishly at her. "Of course you won't say anything, because you won't want anyone to know what *you*'ve been doing."

'Ella was silent, trying to work out what he meant – then, the next minute, he'd taken her hand and pulled her into the room, closing the door behind him. He produced the key and locked the door, leaving the key firmly in the keyhole and dragging Ella over to his desk.

'Ella really didn't know what to do. She knew that the three of them were alone in the building, so there was no point in screaming. No one would hear her. At the same time, there was this growing feeling of excitement in the pit of her stomach. Francis Merrick was extremely attractive. He was in his midthirties – the youngest of all the partners, and he was a lustobject for most of the single females in the firm.'

Sue grinned. 'And the married ones weren't immune, either. I have to admit, I fancied him, too. Most of us thought that he looked a bit like Charlie Sheen. He had that same dark hair, brushed back from his face, and dark eyes, fringed with very long eyelashes. He had high cheekbones, a beautiful mouth and a nice bum – because Francis was top of the local squash league as well as being extremely bright academically, and he kept himself in good shape. His body was like an athlete's. Anyway, you get the picture. No woman with blood in her veins would turn down a man like Francis Merrick.

'Francis looked at her. "Ella," he said softly. "I wonder what your punishment should be." He traced her jawline with the tip of his finger. Ella had a feeling that whatever her "punishment" would be, it would involve pleasure. Pleasure of the most intensely sexual kind. "What do you think, Sheena?"

'Sheena looked up from the desk, seemingly unfazed at having been caught in such a compromising position. The dildo was still inside her, right up to the hilt, and she had a smile on her face, the kind of smile that you get after several orgasms. "I think, Francis, that you should give her what she needs."

'Francis nodded. "Take off your jacket," he said to Ella.

'Ella looked at him. He couldn't be serious – could he?

' "I said, take off your jacket," he repeated. His voice was still very polite but there was a hint of steel underneath. I'd always thought that Ella was pretty much a feminist and no way would she allow any man to dictate to her – but she did exactly as he said. She couldn't really do anything else, in the circumstances. "Now, sit down."

'Ella sat down on the chair he'd indicated.

' "Good," he said softly. He walked back round to the other side of his desk, and resumed pushing the dildo in and out of Sheena. "You know, Ella, that you're completely at my mercy." His voice was conversational, as though he were discussing some statement of accounting practice, not pleasuring his secretary. "It's going to be a very interesting evening, for all of us. But first, I should reward Sheena for her patience, don't you think?"

'Ella didn't trust herself to reply. She stared at the floor.

'Francis looked at her. "Come here," he said softly. Ella thought about staying put but she decided that it would be better for her to do as he said. She stood up and joined him behind the desk.

' "I think that you'll get a much better view from here," he said. "In fact . . ." He pulled her in front of him and released the dildo, curling Ella's fingers round the end and keeping his hand over hers. "Yes, I think that *you* should be the one to reward Sheena."

'Ella flushed. She'd always seen herself as one hundred per cent straight – and here was Francis, suggesting that she should be pleasuring another woman. The idea shocked her. At the same time there was a tiny beat of excitement in her quim, and that shocked her even more. She'd only ever seen Sheena in a professional context; she'd never thought of her as a potential lover. And now . . . here she was, standing between Sheena's splayed legs, holding a dildo inside her. And not just any dildo – a very large black one.

'Francis slid his free hand round Ella's waist. He tilted her back slightly against him so that she could feel his erection pressing against the cleft of her bottom. Then he began to move his hand back and forth, setting up an easy rhythm. Sheena moaned as the dildo moved within her; Francis smiled then, and spread the fingers of his free hand over Ella's abdomen. Although she was still clothed perfectly demurely in the skirt of her business suit and a plain long-sleeved shirt, she felt suddenly naked. Francis was right. She was completely at his mercy. He could do whatever he liked with her – and she wouldn't stop him. She *couldn't* stop him. She didn't *want* to stop him – and that frightened her even more. Ella wasn't used to being out of control.

'As if Francis sensed her mingled excitement and alarm, he rubbed his cheek against hers and then whispered gently in her ear, his breath fanning her skin and sending a tremor of pleasure through her. "Ella. If I can let your hand go and you continue to give Sheena what she deserves, then I can give you something, too."

'Ella said nothing but, when Francis removed his hand from hers, she continued working the dildo back and forth, twisting it slightly as she moved it and eliciting further groans of pleasure from the bound woman on the desk. At the same time, she felt Francis tip his pelvis against her, sliding his erection against the cleft of her buttocks, and then he was unbuttoning her shirt, tugging it from the waistband of her skirt to give him easier access. He unclasped her bra, then smoothed his hands up and down her midriff. A surge of longing rippled through her. She wanted him to touch her more intimately. Suddenly, she didn't care if he tied her as he had tied Sheena, exposing her completely for his pleasure: all she wanted was for him to touch her, to arouse her and bring her to a shuddering climax – and then more.

'That was when she felt his hands cup her breasts. He rolled her nipples between his thumbs and forefingers, teasing the rosy flesh into hard peaks. She shivered, and he stroked down over her midriff, the pads of his fingertips moving in tiny erotic circles, only just making contact with her skin. He eased his hands round her waist and undid the zip of her skirt. She stepped out of the garment as it fell to the floor.

' "That's a pity," Francis murmured as he saw her tights. "I had you down as a stockings woman."

'A frisson of excitement rippled through her. Francis had been speculating about her favoured choice of underwear? He'd been thinking about her sexually, then.

' "But what are we going to do about these?" Francis continued, tugging at the waistband of her tights. "I think . . ." Slowly, he knelt to the task and began to roll her tights downwards.

'Ella shivered with excitement and continued working the dildo in and out of Sheena, moving faster and faster as her own excitement grew. Francis had rolled her tights down to her ankles; she was about to slip off her shoes to let him remove her tights properly, but his fingers gripped her ankles warningly. She stood still, letting him do as he would. He rubbed his cheeks against the backs of her thighs, and she bit back a murmur of desire. He was teasing her, she thought angrily, and it wasn't fair. She was still wearing her bra and her shirt – albeit in the loosest sense, because neither garment covered her properly – and her knickers, and she wanted to be skin to skin with him.

'As if he knew what she was thinking, he suddenly hooked his thumbs into her knickers and drew them down swiftly. Ella gasped in shock, and she felt rather than heard him laugh against her skin. He urged her to lean forward slightly, exposing her quim to his view; Ella felt slightly ashamed. He'd barely touched her, and yet her quim was already wet and swollen, ready for him to penetrate her. He breathed in the scent of her arousal, making a small noise of approval; then she felt him slide one finger across her labia, exploring her intimate topography.

'She gave a small moan of pleasure as he pushed one finger deep inside her; then she felt a hot sting against her buttocks as he slapped her. "I didn't give you permission to speak," he reminded her softly. Ella, unused to such sophisticated game-playing, froze; then his hands caressed the spot where he had smacked her, and she felt his lips, warm and smooth, against her skin. "Oh, Ella. I can see that I have a lot to teach you," he said. "And you're going to be such a delightful pupil. I've always thought that you were one of the rising stars in the department, so bright and so eager to learn. I'm going to enjoy this, Ella. And so are you. Believe me, so are you."

'She bit her lip as he began to move his finger in and out of her moist channel, adding a second finger and a third. She was still using the dildo on Sheena, who was writhing within her bonds, and pushing her bottom back towards Ella, setting up a rough counterpoint to the way that Ella was teasing her with the dildo.

'Francis wet another finger, and then Ella felt him probing the cleft of her buttocks. She tensed, and he nipped her inner thigh lightly with his teeth. "Ssh, let yourself go. Relax. I know that maybe you haven't done anything like this before, but you're going to like this, Ella," he told her. "It's going to be so good. I promise you, you're going to reach new heights if you let me touch you in the way that I want to touch you." He pushed again at her forbidden portal, and a shaft of dark delight pierced her. She was shocked and excited and scared, all at the same time. She bit back another moan as his finger slowly and mercilessly pushed its way into her; and then Francis began to move rhythmically, working her rapidly.

'Just as Sheena climaxed, moaning loudly, Ella felt her own sex contracting sharply, her sphincter and her quim gripping Francis's fingers. He laughed with pleasure, and kissed her inner thigh as her orgasm ripped through her. When the aftershocks of her climax had died away, he removed his hands, then stood up. Without another word to Ella, he walked round to the front of the desk. He stooped to kiss Sheena lightly on the lips, then held out his hand – the hand that had been delving in Ella's quim and was covered with musky glistening juices. She smiled and stretched forward, licking the nectar from his fingers.

'All the time, Ella was watching, half-fascinated and half-appalled. Then Francis loosened Sheena's bonds. "I think," he said, "that it's time that we gave Ella something to think about, don't you?"

'Sheena smiled, and climbed off the table. "Most definitely."

'Together, Francis and Sheena removed Ella's shirt and bra, and then Francis supported her while Sheena lifted Ella's feet, removing her shoes, tights and knickers. Had Francis not been holding her wrists, Ella would have crossed her arms across her body, protecting herself from their gazes. She felt suddenly shy and embarrassed despite the fact that, only minutes before, she had been almost desperate for Francis to strip her. She knew that it was crazy; after all, she had been the one to bring Sheena to a climax, and Francis had touched her so intimately. Yet still she felt shy.

'Her tension was obvious in the way that she was standing; Francis pulled her back against him, kissing the curve of her neck. "Relax," he said softly. "We're not going to do anything that you won't enjoy, I promise."

'Gently, he turned her round to face him and cupped her face in his hands. He lowered his mouth to hers, nibbling gently at her lower lip until she opened her mouth to let him kiss her properly. She was suddenly shockingly aware that another mouth was also kissing her – Sheena was trailing her lips down Ella's spine, smoothing her skin and massaging the tension out of her body at the same time. Ella felt a frisson of excitement. Was Francis going to tell Sheena to make love to her, in front of him?

'That was exactly what he had in mind. As Sheena dropped to her knees behind Ella, Francis broke the kiss and spun Ella round to face Sheena. He continued to stand behind her, cupping her breasts and toying with her erect nipples; Ella swallowed hard as Sheena pressed the flats of her palms against her inner thighs. Part of her wanted this – she wanted someone to use their mouth on her, bring her to a climax – but she'd never made love with another woman before. The idea terrified her and turned her on in equal measure.

'Sheena was insistent, and Ella was forced to widen her stance. Sheena took it slowly, merely parting her labia and blowing very gently along the moist musky flesh. She stayed there for a while, just looking at Ella's quim; Ella coloured deeply, and her face felt as though it were burning. Francis nibbled her earlobe and whispered in her ear. "Don't you want that, Ella? You're hot, so very hot. Don't you want something to cool you down, something soft and cool against your skin?"

'Ella's shiver said it all. Sheena reached forward and drew her tongue down Ella's musky slit. Ella shivered again and Sheena began to lap in earnest, tracing Ella's intimate folds and hollows with the tip of her tongue, then uncovering the hard pearl of her clitoris and drawing fiercely on it. To Ella's shock, she came almost instantly, her internal muscles flexing hard.

'Sheena stood up again and kissed her very gently, so that Ella could taste her own juices on her mouth.

' "I think that you should repay the compliment now, Ella," Francis directed.

'Ella stood in silence. How could she tell him? She'd never done anything like that before, and she had no idea how to start. To her surprise, Sheena brushed her cheek with the backs of her fingers. "It's OK," she said quietly. "Just improvise. Think of what you like someone to do to you, and do it to me."

'Ella's flush deepened. She felt mortified that these two oh, so sophisticated people had seen so clearly through her inexperience. Yet neither Francis nor Sheena was laughing at her. Instead they were inciting her. Tempting her.

'Sheena pulled the top of the lace teddy downwards, revealing her breasts, then took Ella's hands and brought them up to cup the soft creamy globes. Ella closed her eyes. It was almost as though she were touching herself, feeling that same warm soft heavy flesh against her fingertips. Slowly, she circled Sheena's areolae with her thumbs, feeling the dark rosy flesh pucker beneath her touch and the nipples grow harder.

' "Do it, Ella," Francis said softly. "Touch her. Taste her. Use your mouth on her. Make her come."

'Somehow, Ella wasn't quite sure how, they had moved slightly, and Sheena was sitting on the desk, her legs spread wide and her hands flat on the surface behind her to support her. Francis was still standing behind Ella, playing with her breasts in the same way that Ella was playing with Sheena's breasts, squeezing them gently and sensitizing the nipples, rolling them between finger and thumb and tugging lightly at the hard peaks of flesh.

'At the gentle pressure from Francis, Ella leaned forward and kissed Sheena very lightly. Sheena opened her mouth, deepening the kiss and arching up to Ella as she continued to stroke her breasts. Eventually, Ella broke the kiss and slowly placed a trail of light, moist pocks down the side of Sheena's neck, then across her collarbones; she buried her face in Sheena's cleavage and slowly drew her tongue along the shadowed vee between Sheena's breasts. She took one rosy nipple into her mouth and began to suck; Sheena gasped and lifted her ribcage, pushing against Ella and demanding more.

'Ella's confidence grew at Sheena's reaction and she began to suck harder, transferring her attention to Sheena's other breast. Sheena made a small noise of pleasure in the back of her throat and Francis slid his hands between Ella's legs, stroking her quim and dabbling in her warm wetness. "Do it, Ella," he said softly. "Taste her. She's aroused. Taste the sweetness of her honey. Taste her as I've so often tasted her, her cunt wet and dripping with excitement."

'Slowly, Ella allowed Francis to manoeuvre her so that she was bent from the waist, her hands either side of Sheena's thighs and her own thighs spread to give Francis the access he wanted. As she bent her head and Sheena pulled the gusset of her teddy aside, Ella heard the rasping sound of a belt being undone and a zip being drawn down. Another ripple of excitement flooded through her. While she was making love with Sheena, Francis was going to make love to her.

'Ella had often fantasized about him. She had occasionally lain awake at night, her mind buzzing over some thorny problem with the account she was working on – and then she would start thinking of Francis. Handsome, charming and talented Francis. She would imagine what it would be like to have Francis's mouth between her thighs, his tongue working her into a frenzy before he slid his thick hard cock into her – because she knew that Francis would be endowed with both quality and quantity. He had that kind of air about him.

'And now the fantasy was going to come true – albeit in a slightly different form. Francis's mouth would not be between her legs; her mouth would be between Sheena's legs. But she was going to feel Francis's cock deep inside her. She was going to feel him filling and stretching her.

'She could smell the warm scent of Sheena's arousal, a

mixture of spice and seashore; slowly, she stretched out her tongue to part Sheena's labia. At the same time, she felt the tip of Francis's cock brushing against her own sex. She shuddered as he eased into her; then he rested his hands on her hips and began to thrust, setting up a hard, fast rhythm which Ella matched with her tongue on Sheena's sex.

'Sheena began to writhe as Ella continued to lap her, making her tongue into a hard point as it skated over Sheena's clitoris, then softening its hot wet length again and licking from top to the bottom of her satiny cleft in one long slow sweet movement. At the same time, Ella rotated her hips as Francis continued to thrust into her, plunging in deeply and pulling out until he was almost clear of her before slamming back in, hard.

'When Ella came, her internal muscles clenching the thick rod of Francis's cock, she felt Sheena shudder beneath her and her mouth was filled with a sweet-salt nectar. Almost at the same time, she felt Francis's body tauten against hers and then she felt his cock throbbing inside her, lengthening and deepening her own orgasm. They stayed locked together for a while, unable and unwilling to move; then, finally, Francis withdrew from Ella, and the two women dressed while he restored order to his own clothing.

'Then Francis smiled at her. "I think this will just be our secret – don't you?" '

Sue grinned. 'Except, of course, Ella is a very good friend of mine. We'd been out to see a film – one which had left both of us turned on – and we'd gone back to my place to sink a bottle of wine. Harry – that's my husband – was away for the weekend, or Ella would never have told me the story. Anyway, she did, and I think it would make a hell of a good scene in a book.'

'And how!' Gina said. 'So it actually happened?'

'Sort of.' Sue spread her hands. 'Of course, I've retold it in my words, and embellished it a little bit. I don't think that Sheena was really tied on the desk, and Francis wasn't wearing a domino. He isn't quite as gorgeous as I painted him – though I have to admit, if I wasn't married I'd be very tempted to go and offer him some highly personal services.'

'You need to be careful,' Carolyn said. 'There are the laws of libel. If you use something in a book that happened in real life, you could be sued.'

Sue looked slightly deflated. 'That's a pity.'

'On the other hand,' Carolyn said, 'if you change the names, location, and occupations – and make sure that the characters don't look or sound like the real-life people – there's no reason why you can't use the story as a basis for a scene.'

'Is that what your husband does?' Elaine asked Sue.

Sue chuckled. 'I daren't ask!'

'Excuse me.'

They turned round to see who had spoken. A woman in her early sixties had leaned over from the table next to theirs. 'I couldn't help overhearing what you were saying.'

Sue flushed deeply. 'Look, I'm sorry if I offended you. I think I've probably had too much wine – I forget how loud my voice can be when I've been drinking.'

To their surprise, the woman smiled at them. 'I wasn't offended in the slightest! I was intrigued, actually. What kind of course are you here for?'

'Creative writing,' Carolyn said. 'Writing erotica, to be precise.'

'I thought so.' The woman smiled wryly, her faded blue eyes wistful. 'I almost wish that I could swap courses with you. Except I don't think that any of you would be that interested in cross-stitch.'

'It's meant to be very relaxing,' Peggy ventured.

'Maybe. But what you're all doing is so invigorating. Empowering, almost.' She raised an eyebrow. 'If you're writing from personal experience, I know how you all must feel. I'd love to write about something that happened to me when I was young. But that's another story. Well, enjoy your course.' She turned back to her own group; the others stared at each other, feeling slightly chastened.

'Shall we have our coffee in the library?' Carolyn suggested, breaking the silence.

'Good idea,' Gina said quietly.

Carolyn caught the eye of a waitress and asked if they could have their coffee in the library. The waitress agreed willingly, and Carolyn led the others back into the book-lined room. They remained in near-silence until the loaded tray arrived. Carolyn busied herself filling everyone's cups, and then they drew the leather armchairs round the fire and settled down to their hot drinks.

SEVEN

'I wonder what happened to that woman, that she wanted to write about it,' Elaine mused. 'She must have been in her early to mid-sixties. Supposing it happened when she was twenty – that's, say, forty-five years ago. Some time in the early Fifties.'

'The beginning of rock and roll,' Gina said. 'Actually, she had a marvellous bone structure, did you notice? It wouldn't surprise me if she'd been a model, or maybe an actress.'

'Maybe in films,' Libby suggested. 'The Fifties. James Dean and Marlon Brando. Things were starting to get a hell of a lot more exciting than they'd been in the musicals.'

'Hey, I like musicals,' Elaine protested. 'Especially the Gene Kelly and Frank Sinatra ones. Gene Kelly was gorgeous.'

The others chuckled. 'Let's guess who your first hero will be based upon,' Sue teased.

'You never know,' Elaine said, tapping the side of her nose with her finger and laughing.

'Maybe she met Gene Kelly,' Gina said. 'Maybe that's what happened to her, when she was younger. She went for an audition in Hollywood.'

'Are we talking casting couch here?' Libby asked.

'Possibly,' Gina said.

Carolyn looked at Emma. She was the only one who hadn't spoken since Gina and Sue had told their stories. 'What do you think, Emma?' Carolyn asked gently, wanting to bring her into the conversation and make her feel part of the group.

Emma shrugged. 'I don't know.'

'Make something up,' Libby suggested kindly.

Emma shook her head. 'I don't know anything about acting. You'd be better than I would at describing film sets.'

Libby laughed. 'I doubt that. I've only ever done stage work. I haven't even shot a commercial, let alone a full-length film.'

'None of us know anything about film sets,' Elaine added. 'So make it up. We won't pick holes.'

Emma looked at them. For a moment, Carolyn thought that she was going to refuse; then Emma relaxed, and gave them a shy smile. 'Okay.' She drained her coffee, then sat back in her chair, linking her fingers together and resting them on her stomach, and closed her eyes. 'She has a fairly ordinary name. Mary. But she wants to be an actress. She wants to work in films – and her dream is to star opposite Marlon Brando. She's had a thing about him ever since she heard about his performance as Stanley in *A Streetcar Named Desire*. She didn't get the chance to see it herself, of course – she's never been to the States – but she read every newspaper and magazine clipping about it.

'Anyway, she's got the chance to audition for a small part in a film. Not opposite Marlon Brando or her other hero, Laurence Olivier – but it's a start. One of her other idols is Marilyn Monroe. Mary's heard how she changed her name from Norma Jean Mortenson to something much sexier; Mary decides that she'll do the same. She'll become Angelica Barton. Though she's not going to dye her hair blonde. She's proud of her glossy dark hair, so dark that it's almost black; and it shows off her navy-blue eyes to perfection. Her skin is good, and she doesn't need to wear make-up. Her lips are a perfect Cupid's bow, and she's been blessed with a good figure. She's slimmer than Marilyn Monroe, but just as curvy.

'And, even better, she knows that she can act well. At school, she'd always had the plum parts in Shakespeare plays – Portia, Cordelia, Lady Macbeth – and then she'd spent a couple of years training in London. But her heart isn't in the stage. She likes films. Loves them. They're her whole reason for being, and she knows that eventually that's what she's going to do. She spends almost all her free time at the cinema. She's taken a part-time job as an usherette, so she can see even more films and pick up some tips. And it's paid off. At last, she has the audition she wants.

'The day of the audition itself, she dresses up more than usual. She's borrowed some clothes from a friend, well-cut and expensive clothes that are way beyond her means. She looks good. The dress shows her figure off to perfection, and that particular shade of red highlights the beauty of her hair and eyes. She's taken a lot of care with her make-up, too, and with her hair, pinning it up into a sophisticated style.

'When she meets the casting director, she's surprised. He's younger than she was expecting: not the fat, balding and perspiring fifty-year-old that she'd thought he'd be. He can't be more than thirty-five; and he's gorgeous. He's tall, with dark curly hair that he's greased back in the style of James Dean and beautiful grey eyes. There's something sensual about his mouth that makes her want to reach up and kiss him. She only just holds herself back, but she's aware that her nipples are hardening and that they must be obvious to him through the thin material of the dress. Her quim feels wet and puffy, too, and she only hopes that her perfume is masking the scent of her arousal.

'She does the screen test for him, and she's very pleased with the way it works out. He asks her to wait while he auditions some other actresses; she does so, and she spends her time wandering around the film set, making sure that she doesn't get in anyone's way, but at the same time soaking up the atmosphere and fantasizing about what it would be like to work there.

'Some time later, she's called back to see the casting director; he tells her to close the door behind her and sit down. She does so, crossing one leg over the other, and she's aware that the way that the material falls over her lap does nothing to hide the shape of her legs. She's also aware that he's interested. There's a slight flush across his cheekbones, and his pupils have dilated.

'She looks at his hands. They're well-shaped, and she wonders what it would feel like to have those hands stroking her skin. She shakes herself when she realizes that he been talking to her and she hasn't heard a word. He's waiting for her reply, looking expectant. "I'm sorry," she says. "I . . . I suppose I'm a bit nervous. I didn't quite catch what you said."

'He smiles at her; again, she thinks how attractive he is. She itches to know what that beautiful mouth would feel like against hers, how it would feel against her body. "I said, Miss Barton, you have the job." He spreads his hands. "If you want it, that is."

' "Oh, I want it, all right," she says. She can't stop the slightly husky note from creeping into her voice. And she's sure that he knows she didn't mean just that she wants the job.

'Neither of them moves for a moment; they just stare at each other across his desk. She doesn't take in any of her surroundings – the pile of scripts on his desk, the in-tray full of letters, the photographs on the wall, the cup of dark Italian coffee on his desk, only half-drunk and scenting the room with its bitter aroma. All she's aware of is him.

'Then he stands up and walks round his desk. She stands up,

too, expecting him merely to hold out his hand to shake hers and then dismiss her. She lifts her right hand expectantly; he shakes it, but he doesn't let go. "Miss Barton. Angelica." The way he talks sends a thrill through her. His voice is low, husky, and very, very sexy. He raises her hands to his lips and kisses the backs of her fingers.

'It feels as though she's been burned, where he touches her. A searing, delightful flame; her blood seems to heat from that point and then melt through her body. She wants him. She wants him so badly – even more, perhaps, than she wants to work on his film.

'He turns her hand over again, this time kissing the palm and pressing her fingers over it. Then he starts kissing her wrist, his mouth moving up to the sensitive skin in the crook of her elbow, and then on over her upper arm. He reaches her shoulders and she shivers, feeling how close he is to her. She tips her head back, offering him her throat; his mouth moves softly across her skin, and she can feel her heart beating faster. She wants him to touch her, to ease the ache in her swollen breasts and her hot, moist quim.

'It's as if he can read her mind because he takes her in his arms properly, resting his hands on her buttocks and pulling her close to him so that she can feel his erection. He kisses her mouth, gently at first – and then harder when she opens her lips. He lets one hand drift up her back, slowly unzipping the red dress; then he stands back, pushing the material from her shoulders so that the dress falls to the floor in a rustle.

'He stands there, just looking at her, for a moment; her colour heightens, but she's not going to stop now. Not when she wants him so much. Then he smiles, very slowly, and the look in his eyes makes a pulse beat hard between her legs. He removes her petticoat and then takes her back into his arms. The next thing she knows, he's walked her back over to the door. She suddenly remembers that there isn't a lock on the door; she panics slightly in case they're interrupted, and he strokes her face. "It's all right. No one will come in."

'He rubs his nose against hers, kisses her very lightly on the lips, and takes off his shirt and tie. The look on his face invites her to touch him; she does so, the pads of her fingertips skating so lightly over his skin, his soft pale skin and the dark crisp curling hair on his chest. She finds her hands sliding down over his abdomen. And freezes. This isn't the kind of thing she usually does. She's not experienced, in a sexual sense; although she's indulged in some heavy petting in the past, she hasn't gone that far. But she knows that this is going to be different. She doesn't care about any of the risks – all she knows is that she wants him and he wants her.

'As she snatches her hands away, he smiles at her again. "Beautiful, beautiful Angelica. She walks in beauty like the night . . ."

'She doesn't know how the hell he's guessed it, but that particular poem is one of her favourites and has been ever since school. Byron. She's always wanted a man to think that about her. She smiles back at him, and he kisses her again. She slides her hands round his neck, and he strokes her back and buttocks before unclasping her bra. The white garment falls to the floor, and he brings his hands round to cup her breasts, squeezing them slightly as he lifts them up and together.

'He breaks the kiss and starts nuzzling her shoulders, stooping as his mouth moves lower. She closes her eyes as she feels his lips against her breasts, smoothing over the soft pillowy flesh and then finally taking a hard tip into his mouth. The way he's sucking her feels so good, so good. She slides her hands into his hair, revelling in the clean springy texture beneath her fingertips. He continues sucking for a moment; then he straightens up and kisses her mouth again, sliding his tongue into her mouth and tilting his pelvis so that she can feel his erection pressing against her.

'He eases one hand between their bodies to undo his belt and the zip of his dark trousers. Then he pushes his trousers and underpants down in one movement and lifts her, balancing her weight against the door. He's right when he says that no one will disturb them. With both their weights pressing against the door, there's no way that anyone could just walk in.

'She's still wearing her suspenders, stockings and knickers but that doesn't seem to matter. She wraps her legs round his waist, more by instinct than anything else; then he slides one hand under her buttocks, pushing the gusset of her knickers to one side, and she feels the tip of his cock pressing against her sex. And then he's inside her. It's incredible. She's never experienced anything like this before. The way he'd touched her earlier had made her quim wet and slippery, ready to receive him, and it didn't hurt when he entered her. She isn't quite sure what she'd been expecting – but it certainly wasn't anything like this.

'He kisses her again, his probing tongue echoing the action of his penis inside her. He's moving now, tilting his pelvis and pushing deep inside her. Mary – Angelica – call her whatever you will – is in seventh heaven. She wants this to go on forever. She loves the way he feels inside her, filling and stretching her. It's as if he can feel her relaxing, enjoying herself: because then he changes his rhythm, pushing just the very tip of his cock into her, hard and rapidly. It's enough to push her into her first orgasm, the inner sparkling of her climax fizzing through her veins. She cries out but the sound is muffled by his mouth; and when he feels her quim contract hard round his cock, it's enough to push him into his own orgasm.

'They stay there for a while, locked together, then, gently, he disentangles her legs from his waist and lets her slide down his body to the floor. He pulls up his trousers and underpants, then helps her to dress again. Unbelievably, her sophisticated hairstyle is still in place. The only thing you'd notice about her is that her lipstick needs replacing, and her eyes are sparkling in a different way. He smiles at her again, and kisses the tip of her nose. "The first time, Miss Barton – but I hope that it isn't the last . . ." '

Emma opened her eyes and looked at the others. 'Well, it's just a thought,' she said diffidently.

Libby clapped, and the others joined in. 'Actually, Emma, that was incredibly good. You just made that up, from the top of your head?'

Emma nodded, blushing.

Carolyn smiled at her. With an imagination like that, Emma didn't really need to be taught much. Maybe what she was looking for from the course was confidence – and Carolyn was determined to make sure that she got it. 'Well, I'm not sure whether you really need this course! The only way I think you could improve it is maybe by putting it into the past tense. Novels are fairly heavy going if they're all in the present tense. But I enjoyed your tale very much.'

'Thanks.' Emma smiled back shyly.

'And I don't know about coffee – I think we all need a cold shower after that!' Gina added.

They continued chatting for a while; then Elaine stretched and yawned. 'I know that journalists are supposed to be a hard-living, hard-drinking kind of breed, but I'm absolutely knackered,' she said. 'Must be all the fresh air, after London – or

maybe I'm just getting older,' she added with a wry grin. 'I'll
see you all tomorrow, then,' she said, standing up. 'What time
and where, Carolyn?'

Carolyn smiled at her. 'It's an early start for a Saturday –
nine o'clock in the Blue Room, which is next door. But maybe
we'll see you at breakfast. Unless you'd rather have it delivered
to your room?'

Elaine chuckled. 'That rather depends on what the room
service waiter looks like! Seriously, see you later.'

When Elaine had gone, some of the others started yawning,
too. 'It must be all this travelling,' Carolyn said. 'You've all
come quite a way.'

'Yes, I think I'm going to head for bed now,' Peggy said. She
smiled at the others. 'See you in the morning.' She left the
library and glanced at her watch. Pete would still be awake –
probably watching football on satellite TV, and there would be
an empty pizza box next to him and several bottles of draught
beer. He'd told her that he was going to have a slobby weekend
without her, still, at least he wasn't the type to go clubbing and
pick up some dyed-blonde teenager for a quick no-strings fuck
at the first opportunity.

She smiled to herself. If Pete had been able to hear the
stories that Gina, Sue and Emma had just told . . . Well, he'd
be just as aroused as she was. She unlocked her room and
switched on the light. Then she stripped swiftly, had a quick
shower, and pulled the covers back from the bed. Thank God,
the hotel had put her in a double room. It had been years since
she'd slept in a single bed, and she much preferred the
comfort of a double. It was a shame that Pete wasn't there
beside her, but she did have the next best thing. She picked
up the telephone, dialled nine for the outside line, and then
dialled her home phone number.

The phone rang four times, five; then it was picked up. 'Hello?'

Pete's voice was slightly sleepy and Peggy could hear the sound of televised football in the background. 'Hello, love. It's me.'

'Peggy.' She could almost hear the pleased smile in his voice. 'You got there all right, then?'

'Yes. Sorry I didn't ring you before – I didn't want to be late for the start. We've only just retired for the night.'

'What are the others like, then?'

Peggy paused. 'Carolyn, the tutor, seems nice. Most of them are fairly bubbly. I feel a bit – well, frumpy, beside them.'

'You're not frumpy, Peggy. You're lovely.' Pete's voice was sympathetic. 'They're all a lot younger than you are, then?'

'No – but they're all quite glam.'

'So are you,' he said loyally.

She chuckled, appreciating his attempts to make her feel good. 'Oh, Pete. I wish you were here.'

'Me too. I thought I'd enjoy a weekend of slobbing and scoffing pizza and beer, and watching a bit of footy. But it doesn't seem the same without you here. What's your room like?'

'Okay. At least there's a double bed. This place is amazing, though, Pete. Would you believe, there's actually a moat running round it? It's like an old castle, almost. It's gorgeous.'

'Maybe we should go there for our anniversary, or something,' Pete said. 'A romantic weekend away. So what did you do, this evening?'

Peggy smiled. 'We had a champagne reception. Well, it wasn't champagne,' she amended, 'but it was nice. Aussie Chardonnay. Fizzy. It was in the library and Libby – she's an actress – found this book of erotic stories on the shelves. She read it out to us.'

'Any good?'

'Yes. It was about this fairground, but all the rides were sexual.'

'Oh, yes? Tell me more.'

'Later. Anyway, then we went into dinner. I think you'd like the food here, Pete. And they do Pete-sized portions.'

He chuckled. 'Indeed.'

'Over dinner, we started talking about fantasies. Gina – she's the oldest one, and she's just got divorced and spent a few months travelling round the world – told us that she'd virtually lived out a fantasy. She'd made love with a stranger on the beach on the Whitsunday Islands, where the sand was like white talcum powder, and then they'd gone swimming in the sea afterwards. She said that she wanted to write a book based on her experiences. Then Sue – she's one of the younger ones – told us a story about something that happened to a friend of hers in the office.' She paused. 'She told us a very graphic story – though obviously she'd changed bits of it. And then we realized how loudly we'd all been talking, because a woman from the table next to ours leaned over and said she wished that she was doing our course instead of the one she'd booked.'

Pete chuckled. 'I should say!'

'She said that she'd quite like to write about something that happened to her when she was young. She must have been in her mid-sixties. Anyway, we went back to the library for coffee, and then some of them persuaded Emma – she's another quiet one – to tell us what she thought had happened to this woman.'

'That's something erotic, I take it?'

Peggy nodded, then flushed, aware that of course Pete couldn't see her over the phone. 'Yes.'

'And was it good?'

'Yes.' Peggy paused. 'Even if I'd managed to talk to you before dinner, I think I would have phoned you now.'

'Oh yes?' His voice betrayed his interest. 'Any particular reason why?'

'Because . . .' Peggy chose her words carefully. 'Because,' she said slowly, 'it turned me on, listening to them. Just like when you read a bit from a book to me.'

'Mm.' Pete, too, could remember the instances Peggy was talking about. Whenever he'd read her a scene from an erotic novel, they'd ended up making love. All night.

'If you were here now . . .'

'Yes?'

Peggy's voice grew husky. 'You'd be lying here on the bed. It's old-fashioned, with a large mahogany headboard. There are lots of feather pillows, and the sheets are white and starched. You'd be lying there, on the bed, wearing nothing but four silk scarves.'

'Silk scarves?' he queried.

'Yes. Black ones. You'd be stretched out in the middle of the bed, and your wrists would be tied to the headboard and your feet would be tied to the mahogany rail at the foot of the bed. Not tightly enough to hurt you, of course, but you wouldn't be able to move. And then I'd promise you the best night of your life. I'd undress very slowly in front of you – I'd be wearing that red dress you like, but you wouldn't have a clue what I was wearing underneath until I unzipped it and let it fall to the floor.

'Then you'd see that I was wearing a black lace and silk bustier, and hold-up stockings with lacy welts. And that I hadn't been wearing any knickers, all evening. You could have slipped your foot from your shoe in the restaurant, and slid your foot up between my thighs; and you would have been able to bring me to a rapid orgasm, without anyone else knowing what you were doing. You could kick yourself at the missed opportunity, but it's too late now. Anyway, now you know.'

'Mm. And how,' Pete responded. 'I can just imagine it, Peggy. It'd turn me on so much, knowing that you weren't wearing any knickers when we were out together.'

'I know.' She grinned. She knew his fantasies so well. 'I smile at you, and I push the cups of the bustier down so my breasts are bare but still supported. You can see that I'm already aroused by the thought of what I'm going to do to you – because my nipples are hard, large and dark. Just how you like them to be when you touch them.' She sprawled back against the pillows, closing her eyes. In her mind, she could see exactly the scenario she was describing.

'Oh yes,' Pete said. 'Your breasts are so perfect. Warm and soft and lovely. I don't know which I like most: touching them, looking at them or licking them.'

She chuckled. 'You're supposed to be listening to me, Peter Ridley – not going off into your own daydream!'

'Sorry.' He didn't sound in the slightest bit abashed.

'I walk over to the bed and lean down so that my nipples brush your lips. But before you can open your mouth and taste me, I take one step back again. I'm not ready for you to do that. Not yet. There's something else I want to do first. I smile at you, and slide one hand between my legs.' Peggy began to act out what she was telling him, cupping her mons veneris and sliding one finger between her labia, placing her feet flat on the mattress and spreading her legs wide. 'My cunt is so wet and juicy.' *Both in the fantasy and in reality*, she thought. 'Because I've been fantasizing about this all night. I was watching you in the restaurant, and every time you took a mouthful of food I could imagine your lips against my sex. Licking and lapping and sucking. You know how I love it when you go down on me. I could spend hours just floating, while you work me with your mouth, sucking my clitoris and pushing your tongue deep inside me. I'm in a state of high excitement now, and my finger slides easily into me.' Again, both in fantasy and in real life.

'You can smell my arousal, a honeyed musky scent, and it turns you on. The aroma – and and watching what I'm doing to myself. You love to watch me finger my own cunt and caress my nipples.'

'Oh, yes.' Pete couldn't help the small murmur of pleasure, and Peggy smiled. This was affecting him in the same way that it was affecting her. She hadn't heard the rasping sound of his zip, but she would have bet a large sum of money that her husband had undone his jeans and pushed down his underpants, freeing his erect cock. He was probably stroking it even as she spoke, his fingers moving in a familiar rhythm up and down his shaft.

'I remove my finger and smear the glistening musky nectar over my nipples. Then I lean forward again, this time letting you stretch out your tongue and lick my areolae. You can taste how excited I am, and it makes your cock even harder. You want me so much. You want me to climb on the bed, straddle you, and slide your cock deep inside me. But I'm not going to do that. Not yet.'

'Tease.'

'Mm, but you love it.' She noticed how husky his voice was. *He's definitely rubbing his cock*, she thought. 'I step back again, and slide my hand back between my legs. I start to rub myself, very slowly. Taking it slow and easy, just the way I like it. You're powerless to do anything. You tug against your bonds, in case I've left them loose enough for you to wriggle out of them – but you're out of luck. You can't move. You can't do what you really want to do – lean forward, pull me into your arms, and push your beautiful hard cock into me. Frustrated, but turned on at the same time, you watch me. You watch how my nipples grow even bigger as I pull on them with my free hand, rolling them between my thumb and forefinger. You can imagine how my flesh feels; you're done it yourself, so many times, and you know exactly the texture of my skin. It makes your mouth water to think of it – that, and what my other hand is doing. How my finger is sliding in and out of my warm wet hole; and how I need a second finger, a third, to satisfy me.

'I'm rubbing my clitoris with my thumb, and it's so sensitive, swelling beneath my touch. It feels so good, touching myself, feeling my pussy grow slick and wet. I tantalize you again, withdrawing my hands so that I can smear my juices on your lower lip. You taste my juices, loving the flavour and wanting more. You look pleadingly at me, but I'm not going to give you what you want. Not just yet.

'Then I step back again and continue rubbing myself, bringing myself nearer and nearer to the peak. I'm just at the point where it feels like my whole body is sinking in on itself, melting and growing fluid and then bubbling with a rapid warmth . . . And then I come, my internal muscles flexing sharply round my fingers. I can't help a small cry of pleasure; it feels so good. I love this feeling, this feeling of enormous power surging through me.' *Like a nuclear fusion*, she thought, but didn't say it, not wanting to sound stupid.

'Then I'm ready to start work on you. I climb onto the bed beside you, and lean over so that my nipples rub across your chest. It feels as good for me as it does for you. You make a small noise of pleasure, and I can see that your flat button nipples have grown hard. Your cock's almost twitching with anticipation; you don't know if I'm going to pleasure you with my hand, my mouth, my pussy or all three.'

'All three,' he murmured. 'I want you to lick me, Peggy, lick me and suck me and rub me. And then I want you to ride me, let my cock sink into your beautiful pussy.'

'Mm.' Peggy wanted it too. She began to work herself harder and harder, rubbing her clitoris madly and pistoning her hand in and out of her quim. She knew without having to ask that Pete was rubbing his cock, excited by what she was saying to him and missing her there beside him. 'I kiss you and you open your mouth under mine, letting me explore you with my tongue. Then I break the kiss and reach over to the bedside table, where there's a small bottle of coconut oil. I undo the cap, pour a little of the oil on to my palm and rub my hands together, warming the oil. Then I shift position, kneeling astride you and facing away from you so that you can see my quim, how glistening my intimate flesh is. I lean forward and I trace the tip of your cock with the tip of my nose; you shudder beneath me, wanting deeper intimacy. But you have to wait. First, I cup your balls with one hand, rubbing the oil gently into your skin, and then I curl the fingers of my other hand round your shaft, slicking up and down until your flesh is glistening with the coconut oil.

'I wiggle my buttocks so that you can smell how aroused I still am, and then I push your foreskin back, holding your cock tightly and then rubbing your frenum with the thumb and forefinger of my other hand. You cry out and I push backwards, jamming my pussy over your mouth to stifle your cries. You begin to lick me, tracing my inner furls and hollows with the tip of your tongue, and I begin to masturbate you in earnest. Ten slow strokes, one per second, and ten fast. Ten slow, ten fast. Ten slow, ten fast.'

'Oh, yes.'

She smiled. That was what he was doing, echoing her words. Ten slow, ten fast. Delaying the moment of his orgasm. 'You're writhing within your bonds, but the only thing you're free to do is to lick my quim. And I have no intention of letting you loose – not until I'm ready. I continue masturbating you until I feel that you're near the edge; then I squeeze gently beneath your frenum, delaying your climax. Then, and only then, I dip my head, taking your cock into my mouth.

'I can feel you groaning against my quim, groaning with pleasure as I begin to suck you, taking you as deeply as I can into my mouth. My hand is still oiled and I slide it between your legs, rubbing your perineum. You lift your buttocks, wanting more, and I push my finger against the rosy puckered hole of your anus. You moan again, and lick me harder as my finger slides in, oh, so very, very slowly. I begin to massage you, pushing my finger in and out in the same rhythm that I'm using on your cock. It's too much for you, and you come, your body jerking beneath mine.'

She heard a muffled cry and knew that he'd come, his seed spurting onto his stomach. She wasn't there herself yet – but it was near. So very near. 'But still you keep licking me,' she continued, 'lapping and sucking and using your mouth so professionally, until I reach another climax, flooding your mouth with honeyed nectar.' She paused as her climax surged through her. She clenched her jaw, not betraying herself with a sound. But she knew that he knew that she'd just come, too. 'Then I climb off you and untie you. And then you pull me into your arms and hold me close; we're both sated, and in tune with each other's thoughts.'

'Mm, we certainly are.' His voice was lazy and contented. 'Tell me what you were just doing, Peggy.'

'No.'

'Tell me.'

'You first.'

He chuckled wryly. 'I think you know.'

'Tell me.'

'I was lying on the sofa with my eyes closed, imagining in mental pictures what you were telling me in words.'

'You mean you weren't watching the match?' she teased.

'No. I was thinking about you, Peggy Ridley, and what an enticing witch you can be when you're in that kind of mood. It makes my cock hard just thinking about you – don't you know that?'

'After all this time?' They had been married for fifteen years.

'Definitely after all this time. You're still the most desirable woman I know.'

'I'm glad to hear it. So what were you doing?'

'Like I said, lying on the sofa with my eyes closed.'

'And that's all?'

He laughed. 'No. When you started telling me that little story, my cock grew so hard it hurt. I couldn't stay in that state so I undid my jeans and started stroking myself. Just as you were telling it – fast and slow, fast and slow.'

'Until you came.' It was a statement rather than a question.

'Until I came,' he agreed. 'What about you, Peggy? Were you touching yourself as you spoke to me, rubbing yourself and pretending it was me?'

'Yes,' she admitted.

'And did you come?'

'Yes.'

'Did it feel good, Peggy?' His voice had grown husky again. 'Did it feel good, having your fingers thrust up your pussy as far as you could?'

'Mm – but not as good as your cock.'

'I'm sure we can do something about that – on Sunday night.'

'Sunday night,' she agreed.

'I'll have some fizzy waiting. And then we'll go to bed. You can tell me about the course – and I think you'd better call in sick on Monday morning, because you're not going to get very much sleep.'

She grinned. 'I hope that's a promise.'

'Oh, it is.' He paused. 'Sleep well, darling.'

'You too.'

'And enjoy the rest of your course.'

She smiled. 'Oh, I think I will.'

EIGHT

Carolyn peeled off her clothes and stepped gratefully into the shower. She turned the water to its coldest setting and the needle-sharp jets spattered against her skin, making her feel more awake and taking off the slightly heady feeling produced by the amount of wine she'd drunk. Tomorrow night, she decided, she would drink a hell of a lot less. Not least because the last thing she wanted to do was to drive back to Norwich with a hangover.

It had been quite an evening, she thought. The course delegates had all seemed very nice. Some of them had been livelier than others at first, but she had had a feeling from the start that both Peggy and Emma had hidden depths. As Emma had proved with her fantasy of the elderly woman who had spoken to them in the dining room: the tale had been richly erotic, and Emma had captured the feel of a Fifties office, the Bohemian film set.

Beside Gina, Carolyn had felt slightly gauche and unsophisticated; though she'd felt an instinctive rapport with Elaine, probably because of their shared experience of journalism. Libby and Sue had both been irrepressible live wires, and Carolyn had appreciated the way that they had both tried to bring Emma and Peggy out of their respective shells during the evening. She smiled and turned the water back to a warmer setting, lathering her skin and sluicing the suds away again. She had just switched off the shower, tucked another heated towel round her, sarong-style, and removed her make-up, when the phone rang. Frowning, she padded through into the bedroom and picked up the receiver. 'Hello?'

'Good evening, Miss Saunders. I hope that I'm not calling at an inconvenient time?'

Carolyn froze. She knew that voice. He hadn't said that much to her, but the sound of his voice was indelibly imprinted on her brain. 'I . . . No, no, that's fine.'

'It's Kit Williams, the conference centre manager. I need to discuss a couple of things with you, about your course. Unless you'd rather talk to me first thing in the morning, between breakfast and the course starting, of course.'

'No. No, tonight's fine.' Her mouth was dry. Was he going to offer to come up to her room? Or did he want her to go down to his office?

It was as though he had read her mind. 'Would you like to come down to my office?'

'I . . . Yes, that'd be fine. Five minutes?'

'Five minutes. I'm on the same corridor as the library, but on the opposite side.'

'All right.'

'I'll see you in a few minutes, then. Goodbye.' There was a slightly amused note in his voice, as if he had guessed how much he had flustered her.

Carolyn replaced the receiver, then quickly scrubbed herself dry and slipped into a comfortable pair of leggings and a sweater. She didn't bother putting on any more make-up – as soon as Kit had discussed whatever it was he had to talk about with her, she intended to go straight to bed – and, pulling on a comfortable if somewhat elderly pair of shoes, she headed downstairs to his office.

She wondered what it was that he wanted to discuss with

her. She knew that Mandy had booked the course for what it was, so he couldn't be too fussed about the subject. The receptionist had been fairly clear about the facilities that were needed, and everything seemed to be efficiently organized: so what *did* he want? Or had he recognized her car and found out from the receptionist who she was? Was his talk of needing to speak to her about a couple of details just a front, an excuse to see her?

She took a deep breath. Well, she was here in a professional capacity. Professionally was exactly how she would act. She found his office, and rapped on the door.

'Come in,' he called.

She turned the doorknob and went into the office, closing the door behind her. 'Mr Williams.'

'Miss Saunders. Do sit down.' He indicated the chair in front of his desk.

She noticed with approval that Kit wasn't one of those insecure managers who always had a higher or more comfortable chair than his visitors. The chair he was offering her was similar to his own – black leather, thickly padded, with arms. This was a man who believed in equal partnerships, she thought. She sat down.

He'd changed his clothes, she noticed; he was still wearing a formal dark suit and white shirt, but they were freshly laundered, not the wet clothing he'd had after changing her tyre and making love with her on the bonnet of his car. No doubt those clothes were already in the hotel laundry.

'So what can I do for you?' she asked.

'I just wanted to check if tonight's reception and dinner went as you expected, and to find out if there was anything that we'd missed.'

So why did he want to see her? He could have asked her that

over the phone. 'Dinner was fine. Everyone seemed happy enough.'

'Good. And you need an overhead projector for tomorrow, is that right?'

'Yes.' Relieved that he was talking about such a neutral subject, she switched automatically to professional mode. 'I usually run my presentations through a graphics program on my laptop. Does your projector have an adaptor for a PC?'

He nodded. 'I'll make sure that it's all set up for you. Nine o'clock start, isn't it?'

'Yes, that's right.'

'If you'd like to check the room before breakfast, then you can let me know if there's anything else you need and we'll make sure that everything's ready before the course starts.'

'Thank you.' Was he going to refer to the incident of the tyre, she wondered? Or was he leaving that up to her? She couldn't tell from his voice, although she suspected that if she had the courage to look him in the eyes she'd find that they were sparkling with amusement.

She decided to bite the bullet. 'I was very impressed with your receptionist. She's sorting out my spare tyre for me. And I should add my thanks to you, too, for changing it for me in the first place.'

'My pleasure.'

She risked a glance at him. His eyes were definitely amused: but there was another emotion mixed in with it. Desire. Despite the fact that she was hardly dressed glamorously, he still found her attractive. Perhaps he was remembering the way she had looked, spread over his car bonnet, abandoned to pleasure and the eroticism of the moment.

She swallowed. The worst thing was, she too could remember the way *he* had looked. And the way he had felt against her body, the way he had tasted. The amount of wine she had consumed that evening, together with the provocative tales that some of her delegates had told, had fired her libido rather than suppressed it.

It would be so easy to stand up, walk round to his side of the desk and cup his face in her hands, stooping so that she could kiss him. She wondered how he would react if she did that. Would he be shocked, pull away? Or would he stand up, lift her so that she was sitting on his desk, nudge his thighs between hers and return her kiss?

She flushed as she realized that he was waiting for her to answer something. She hadn't heard a word that he'd said, being lost in a private and very sensual daydream. 'I'm sorry. I didn't catch what you said.'

'I asked you if you'd like to have a drink with me.'

Her eyes widened. Was this Kit in Mr Conference Centre Manager mode, or was this a prelude to something else? 'I . . . Well, the course starts fairly early. I really ought to be heading for bed.'

His eyes flickered with amusement, and her colour deepened. What she had just said could be taken in two ways. And the way the pulse was beating so hard between her legs . . . She knew that her body meant it in the sexual sense, implying that she wanted to head for his bed, even if her mind had meant something totally innocent.

'Surely one glass of wine won't hurt?'

Oh yes, it would, she thought. On top of the wine she had drunk earlier, it would probably be enough to tip her over the edge and she would do something silly, like throw herself at him. 'Make that a mineral water, and you're on.'

He smiled. 'As you wish. But I'm having a glass of wine.' She noticed then that there was a small fridge behind his desk with silver tray containing several glasses on it, together with a coffee filter. She was a little surprised. Surely it would be easier to go into the bar for a drink – or maybe just dial through to reception and have whatever he wanted brought in to him?

It was as though he had read her mind, or maybe she had spoken aloud. She wasn't sure which, and she didn't want to ask. 'I'd rather the staff did what they were paid to do – look after customers, not wait on me. Besides, when I have clients in to discuss conference management, I like to offer them coffee or a drink.'

He opened the fridge door and Carolyn noticed that there were a couple of good bottles of Chardonnay and Chablis in the rack, together with a dozen small bottles of mineral water. 'Would you prefer plain, or Aqua Libra?' he asked.

She smiled. Aqua Libra was a weakness with her. Particularly if she and Mandy had had an evening at the wine bar near their office, sinking more red wine than was good for them. 'Aqua Libra, please,' she said.

He smiled at her. 'It's an acquired taste, but once you have it . . .' He spread his hands disarmingly and took a small bottle from the fridge, uncapping it and pouring half the contents into a glass before handing it to her. He poured himself a glass of Chablis, then returned the bottle to the fridge.

'Well. Cheers.' He lifted his glass in a toast, then sipped his wine. Carolyn echoed the toast, and sipped her mineral water.

An awkward silence fell; Carolyn wondered how soon she could leave her glass and plead tiredness. It was either that, or something was going to happen between them. The air in the room was tense, and she didn't dare to look Kit in the eye.

Instead she concentrated on his surroundings. It had often been her experience, as a journalist, that people's surroundings gave very obvious clues to their personalities. Kit was tidy, the papers on his desk kept neatly in trays; but he wasn't the anally retentive type who insisted on a clear-desk policy. He was efficient, but human with it. Though there were no photograph frames on his desk; so either he wasn't married, or he preferred to keep his personal life very separate from the office.

Her gaze flickered to the painting on the wall. It was a reproduction of a Pre-Raphaelite painting she'd always admired – Burne-Jones's *The Beguiling of Merlin*. It was a good reproduction, too, and had been framed well. It was the kind of painting she would have liked in her own office, or in her house. Rupert had pooh-poohed Victorian art, saying that it lacked the depth of the old masters or the excitement of modern art, but she loved the rich pure colours, the medieval inspiration behind the Pre-Raphaelite movement.

Kit followed her gaze. 'It's a bit fey, perhaps, but I like it,' he said. 'And it somehow seems to suit this place. I'd always imagined Camelot to be a big sprawling place like this, built of honey-coloured stone.' He grinned. 'Though I've never been to Tintagel, or anywhere in Cornwall, so, for all I know, I'm way off beam.' He shrugged.

Carolyn was surprised into looking directly at him. 'So you're a bit of an Arthurian fan, then?'

He nodded. 'My mother read me Malory's tales of Arthur when I was very small. And I suppose that's why I ended up reading English, and specializing in medieval literature.'

Not to mention becoming a knight on a white charger himself – at least, a rescuer in a black BMW. It was on the tip of Carolyn's tongue to say something, but she held herself back. 'So how did you get into conference management, then?'

He spread his hands. 'There weren't that many openings for lecturers in medieval literature, so I decided to go into business instead. I discovered that I liked marketing, and I had a couple of lucky breaks. This job came up, and the owners and I liked each other at the interview. I've been here two years now and the owners have given me a free rein to do whatever I need to build the business. I suppose the conference side of things is my baby.'

'The facilities seem good – at least, what I've seen of them. Otherwise Write Right wouldn't have picked this place as the venue for the course,' Carolyn said.

'So you didn't pick the venue yourself?'

She shook her head. 'I wasn't supposed to be running this course, actually. I'm the director of new courses, so I develop courses rather than lecture nowadays. But Mandy – she's the one who was originally going to run the course – came down with the flu, and asked me to step in.'

'You've taught creative writing before, then?'

She nodded. 'A couple of times. Though it's been romance rather than erotica. I used to run the newsletter and copy-writing courses.'

Kit smiled. 'I'd love to be a fly on the wall tomorrow. It's almost worth asking if I could use CCTV, to catch your lecture!'

Carolyn narrowed her eyes. 'I assume that that was a joke.'

'Of course.' His eyes glittered. 'Though I think, Miss Saunders, that you'd make a very good teacher of erotic writing. You have quite an imagination.'

She felt her skin grow hot again. She knew exactly what he meant; he was referring to that episode at Roudham. She sat upright, lifting her chin. 'Look, Mr Williams, I don't usually behave like that.'

'Neither do I,' Kit said. 'I saw that your car was obviously in trouble. It was pouring with rain, and you looked like you could use some help. That's why I stopped.'

'I could have been a decoy,' she reminded him. 'There could have been some burly male accomplices hiding on the heath, ready to beat you to a pulp and steal your car.'

'True,' he admitted, 'but my gut feeling said that it wasn't a set-up.'

'And, like I said, I appreciate the fact that you helped me.'

'Miss Saunders. Carolyn. I couldn't get you out of my mind, all the way here. I didn't know the first thing about you, not even your name – but you made one hell of an impact on me.' He placed his glass on the desk, and stood up, coming round to her side of the desk. He took the glass from her hand and put it on the table before pulling her to her feet. 'When I walked into the courtyard and saw your car next to mine . . . Well. Call me a romantic – no, make that a Romantic with a capital "R" – but it seemed like fate had brought you back to me.' He took her hand, lifting it to his mouth and placing a kiss into her palms, curling her fingers over the imprint of his lips. 'I asked at reception who owned the car. When they told me, I was tempted to ring your room right then. But I knew that you'd be busy with your course delegates in the library, sorting out ice-breakers and the like, so I decided to wait.'

Carolyn's throat was dry. Her flesh tingled where he had touched her, and she ached for him to touch her more intimately. At the same time she didn't want him to think that she was some kind of cheap tart who made love with anyone, wherever and whenever she pleased. She really *wasn't* like that. What had happened between them at Roudham Heath had been completely out of character for her. Making love in the open, where anyone could have seen them – she wouldn't have done anything so risky, even with Rupert when their relationship was at its strongest. She didn't see herself exactly as a 'sex-only-on-a-Saturday-night-with-the-lights-off' kind of woman. But she wasn't usually the wild and wanton libertine who'd let Kit Williams take her over the bonnet of his car, either. She was somewhere in between.

'I knew that you were having coffee in the library after dinner. The dining staff told me. I was hoping to catch you alone in the library but you left the room before I had a chance to go in and say anything to you. That's why I rang you. I thought that we needed to talk.'

'About the arrangements for the course. So you said.' Carolyn nodded. 'Well, we've done that now.'

Kit's eyes were very bright. 'Not just that. I think that we need to talk about what happened between us.'

She shook her head. 'There's nothing to say.'

'Isn't there, Carolyn?' At her silence, he added, 'I think that there is. Quite a lot, in fact.' He looked shrewdly at her. 'What happened between us – I get the feeling that it was pretty much out of character for you. You're not a natural vamp. One or two of your students – in particular the older one, the one with fair hair – probably are, but you seem much quieter, much more shy. So would you mind telling me why?'

Carolyn flushed. 'You started it.'

'But you responded.'

'Why did you kiss me?' she countered.

He kept her his gaze firmly on her. 'I don't know. Something in your eyes . . . It just made me want to do this.' As he'd done in the rain on Roudham Heath, he took her chin between his thumb and forefinger and lowered his mouth to hers, kissing her lightly. 'Then you responded. And I couldn't stop myself. My brain just shut off and my body took over. I wanted you, and it felt like you wanted me. What happened was a natural conclusion.'

Carolyn hoped that her voice wasn't shaking as much as she

thought it was. 'So you don't make a habit of this kind of thing, Mr Williams?'

'Kit.' He licked his lower lip and Carolyn had a perverse desire to pull his head down to hers and kiss him, pushing her tongue deep into his mouth. 'No.'

'Neither of us has a habit of bonking complete strangers, then.' She tried to keep her tone light.

'I have to admit, I do prefer to know my lover's name before we become too intimate.'

The smile in his eyes was infectious; Carolyn couldn't help responding, smiling back at him. 'Me, too.'

'The only thing is, Carolyn—' he lifted his hand to stroke her face '—I haven't been able to get you out of my mind since it happened. I thought about following you – but then I decided that it wouldn't be fair. The last thing a lone woman driver wants is to have a man following her car; and maybe you had your reasons for leaving without telling me your name. I passed you on the A14 and decided to leave it as a beautiful memory, albeit one I couldn't get out of my head. And then I saw your car outside.' His voice dropped to a whisper. 'And now I know your name.'

She was silent. What now? Was he going to kiss her again? Did he expect her to make love with him in his office? The thing was, she knew that if he touched her, she'd do exactly what he suggested. She was aware that her nipples were hardening, and no doubt he could see the hard points through her loose sweater. Her sex, too, was growing warm and wet, ready to receive him. She wanted him. Part of her was shocked by it. This really wasn't the way she usually behaved. She had never seen herself as a man-eater who would fling herself at any male who passed her way – and yet she couldn't resist Kit Williams. 'We know virtually nothing about each other, Kit.'

He stroked the ring finger on her left hand, running his thumb and forefinger up and down it. 'No ring. So it's a fair bet that you're not married or engaged.'

'My ring might be in the jewellers, being cleaned,' she countered.

'True. But I don't think that it is – is it?' He didn't wait for her to answer. 'Carolyn. We're both free agents. There's nothing to stop us being together now. Even if it's only the very shortest of short-term.'

It was an incredibly heady suggestion. If he meant it. She had to be sure. 'So what are you saying?'

'I'm saying, Carolyn, that I'd like to make love with you again. This time in private – and somewhere a hell of a lot more comfortable. Somewhere where I can worship your body properly. Where I can touch you and taste you and explore you; somewhere where we won't be interrupted by anyone or anything. Where we can be together. Where you can touch me and taste me and explore me, too. Skin to skin, just you and me.' His voice had become husky, sensual; Carolyn didn't need to look down to his crotch for visual proof of his arousal. She could tell from the slight flush on his face and the expanded pupils of his eyes.

'So what's it to be? You're perfectly at liberty to slap my face and tell me to go to hell.' He drew her hand back up to his mouth, kissing her fingertips one by one. 'Alternatively, you could say yes.'

'And if I *do* say yes?'

He dipped his head to rub his nose against hers. 'Then I'll take you to my suite. And I'll spend most of the night making love with you.' He smiled. 'Though I promise that you'll get *some* sleep. I wouldn't want to ruin your course by making you a complete zombie.'

'What were we saying about not bonking complete strangers?' she quipped.

He chuckled. 'But you're *not* a stranger, Carolyn. We know each other, in the Biblical sense. And I know your name. I know what you do for a living, I know where you're from, and I know that you're one of the most desirable women I've ever met.'

She shook her head. 'I'm ordinary, Kit.' It was an echo of what she'd said to Mandy a couple of weeks before, when Mandy had proved to her that Rupert's taunt about her supposed frigidity had been a lie.

'*You* might think so,' he told her softly, 'but I don't. There's something about you. I can't define it, but I can't resist you either.' Again, he brushed his lips very lightly against hers and she had to fight the urge to kiss him back. 'It's your choice, Carolyn. No strings, no pressure.' He punctuated his words with tiny butterfly kisses.

No pressure. And yet he was teasing her with kisses, inciting her to say yes. She knew that she ought to refuse – that she ought to leave then and there and return to her own room, alone. Temptation beckoned, though, and she found herself returning his kisses, nibbling at his lower lip. His mouth opened beneath hers, and she slid her hands into his hair, holding him closer. She slid her tongue into his mouth, exploring him; and she pushed her pelvis hard against him, so that she could feel his erection pressing against her.

When she broke the kiss, he stroked her face with the backs of his fingers. 'Do I take it that that was your answer?'

It was ridiculous, she knew, but she felt suddenly shy. She lowered her gaze and nodded.

He held her close, stroking her back and rubbing his cheek against hers. 'You won't regret it. I promise you,' he whispered in her ear. 'We'll be good for each other.'

In silence, he led her from the room, switching off the light and closing the door behind them. He led her to the far end of the corridor, away from the main reception, and on up some narrow spiral stairs. She realized with delight that Kit's suite was in a tower. Bearing in mind what he'd told her about his love of medieval literature, this place must be paradise for him.

Kit's room was furnished in a similar fashion to her own, with the blue and yellow fleur-de-lys carpet, heavy brocade curtains and mahogany furniture. The main difference was the bed. Kit had a king-size old-fashioned wrought-iron bedstead, hcapcd with pillows and a thick duvet, all of which were obviously goose-feather.

She wondered how many women he had brought back here – then stopped herself crossly. It was none of her business. He'd been honest with her, anyway, telling her that there were no strings and it was a short-term relationship. What did she expect? Undying declarations of love?

As if Kit had sensed her doubts, he spun her round, placing his hands on her waist and looking deep into her eyes. 'Second thoughts?' he asked softly.

Carolyn paused, then shook her head.

He smiled. 'I'm glad,' he told her. 'Because I want you, Carolyn Saunders. I want you very badly. Almost as much as I did when I saw you standing in the rain, your clothes plastered to your body and your hair soaked.' He bent his head to kiss her; Carolyn responded, twining her hands round his neck and arching her body against his.

He tugged at the hem of her sweater and she lifted her arms, helping him to remove the garment. He gave a sharp intake of breath as he saw her breasts, and he ran his fingertip along the edge of her bra. 'Did I tell you that your skin feels like silk?'

She chuckled. 'Obviously none of your studies rubbed off on you!'

'Meaning?'

She grinned. 'Well, if that's your idea of seductive or poetic language . . .'

He laughed. 'I'd better shut up and let my body do the talking for me, then.' He unclasped her bra and cupped her breasts in his hands, pushing them together and up slightly. He stroked the soft undersides, tracing her areolae with his thumbs at the same time.

She closed her eyes and tipped her head back, offering him her throat. He lowered his mouth, licking her skin and finding the sensitive parts before nibbling very gently at them. Carolyn gasped, and she felt rather than saw him shrug off his jacket. Then he dropped to his knees in front of her, hooking his thumbs into her leggings and pulling them down over her hips, drawing down her knickers at the same time. She kicked off her shoes, then lifted each foot so that he could finish undressing her.

'Beautiful,' he murmured huskily, stroking her legs and squeezing her buttocks. He nuzzled her midriff, and Carolyn felt desire jolt through her. She knew what he was going to do next, and she wanted it, so very badly. She rested her hands on his shoulders as his mouth tracked lower; gently, he slid his hands between her thighs, pressing the flat of his palms against her skin and urging her to widen her stance.

Then she felt his breath, warm against her quim. He stayed there for a moment, just breathing in the musky scent of her arousal. Then she felt his tongue part her labia, and he was licking her, lapping at her musky juices and making his tongue into a hard point as he teased her clitoris from its hood. She gave a soft moan of pleasure as he took the hard coral bud into his mouth and began to suck. While he worked on her clitoris, he slid one finger against her sex, then pushed into her warm wet depths.

Carolyn moaned as he added a second finger and began to move his hand back and forth. She dug her nails into his skin as his rhythm grew faster, stronger; and she cried out as her orgasm flared through her, making her whole body seem on fire. He waited until her climax had ebbed away before removing his hands and standing up again. Carolyn's legs still felt shaky and she clung to him, scared of losing her balance. He kissed her deeply, sliding one hand beneath her hair to caress the nape of her neck and cupping her buttocks with his other hand.

When he broke the kiss, Carolyn helped him to undress. Naked, he looked even better than she had hoped, or than she remembered: his body was firm and muscular, and no doubt he used the gym and the pool which Heywood Hall had thoughtfully provided for its guests.

He smiled at her and led her over to the bed. He pushed the duvet back, then sat on the bed and patted the mattress. Carolyn felt slightly disappointed that he hadn't taken the macho route of lifting her up and carrying her to his bed; on the other hand, she appreciated the fact that he was treating her as an equal. She sat down next to him and he pulled her into his arms, kissing her again. His tongue probed her mouth and he stroked her body, lingering over her midriff and her breasts. She could still feel his erection brushing against her, thick and long; the memory of how he'd felt inside her made her want him again.

She rolled onto her back, spreading her legs invitingly; he kissed her lightly, and smiled. 'I had something else in mind. Last time, I took you; this time, I think it's your turn to take me.' He licked his lower lip, then rolled onto his back, giving her a sensual look. 'I'm all yours, Carolyn. Do what you want with me.'

It was an invitation that she couldn't resist. She shifted to a kneeling position beside him, then slowly drew her hands over his body, tracing the outline of his ribcage and waist. She teased him, bringing her hands within millimetres of his erect cock, then moving lower, caressing his thighs. He felt just as good as he looked; making love with him, she thought, would be more than a pleasure.

She followed the path of her hands with her mouth, nuzzling the crisp hair on his chest and teasing his flat button nipples with her lips and tongue. She nuzzled his abdomen and he tensed, clenching his fists; she could tell that he was only just stopping himself begging her to take him into her mouth. She smiled, and traced the end of his cock with the tip of her nose; he groaned, arching up towards her, and she breathed on his shaft, tormenting him. Then she moved lower, nuzzling his thighs and drawing a trail of kisses down to his knees.

He groaned, and Carolyn moved again, parting his legs and kneeling between them. Then she cupped his balls with one hand, ringing his cock with the thumb and forefinger of her other hand, and slowly bent her head. This was going to please him, she knew: but it was going to please her just as much. She wanted to taste him, to feel his cock throbbing under her lips and tongue.

There was a clear bead of moisture in the eye of his cock; she licked it, savouring its musky tang, then opened her mouth to ease the tip of his shaft between her lips. Kit gave a gasp of pleasure and closed his eyes, pushing his head back into the deep feather pillows; Carolyn began to work him, setting up a counterpoint between her mouth and the fingers ringing his erection. All the time she caressed his balls gently, massaging his skin and stroking his perineum, her fingertips moving along the satiny cleft between his sac and his anus.

She began to work him harder, harder; as she sucked him, she felt his body tense beneath hers and he came, filling her mouth with salty fluid. She swallowed every drop, then crawled up the bed again, straddling him and kissing him deeply so that he could taste himself on her mouth. He held her close, stroking her buttocks and returning her kisses. Eventually she felt his cock growing erect again, and she rocked back and forwards so he could feel the warmth and wetness of her quim against his flesh.

Kit gripped her buttocks and lifted her slightly; she curled her fingers round his cock, then fitted its tip to the entrance of her sex. Slowly, Kit lowered her onto his cock, giving a low groan of pleasure as he felt her warm wet depths engulf him. He sat up then, kissing her hard; with one hand he caressed her breasts, teasing her already erect nipples and tugging gently on them. With the other, he sought her clitoris and began to rub the little nub of flesh in a figure-of-eight pattern as she lifted and lowered herself on him. She rested her forearms on his shoulders for balance and continued moving over him, rocking her hips in tiny circles as she pulled herself up and then slammed back down again, grinding her pubis against his.

She could feel her orgasm beginning again, a warm rolling sensation in the soles of her feet that rapidly gathered momentum and pressure as it moved up through her calves, through her thighs, and snaked into her gut. Kit was still kissing her, and her yelp of pleasure at her climax was lost in his mouth. Her internal muscles gripped his cock, squeezing hard. But Kit didn't stop there. Somehow, he managed to manoeuvre their positions so that she was lying on her back and he was kneeling between her thighs; all the time, his cock had stayed buried deep within her.

He continued to move, thrusting hard; Carolyn wrapped her legs round his waist, lifting herself up so that he could penetrate her more deeply. Although their lovemaking in the thunderstorm had felt good, filling her with a kind of raw power, this was equally satisfying, she thought. She had the comfort of the mattress beneath her, in such sharp contrast to Kit's hard body driving into hers.

He took her to a higher peak, and then a higher one; she felt her climax ripple through the whole of her body, making her tremble and quiver. It was as though her body fused with his, the tremors in her innermost depths pushing him to his own climax; he gasped and then lay still, resting his cheek against hers and keeping his weight supported on his hands and knees.

Eventually he slipped from her and rolled over onto his back, tucking her into his side. He kissed the tip of her nose. 'Thank you,' he said softly.

Carolyn swallowed, unable to speak; she tipped her head back for a kiss instead, hoping that he'd understand. From his smile, she knew that he did; he stroked her face, and pulled her closer. 'Lovely, lovely Carolyn. Can I persuade you to stay with me for a bit longer, I wonder? I'd just like to sleep with you in my arms.'

Which was exactly what she wanted, too. To sleep with her lover, share a deeper and more vulnerable intimacy with him. Short-term or not, it was what she needed. To feel wanted and cherished by such an attractive and physical man as Kit Williams – to wipe out Rupert's harsh comments, his cruel betrayal. 'Yes,' she said softly.

'Good,' he said, and switched off the light.

NINE

The next morning, Carolyn woke to find herself alone in Kit's bed. There was a note beside her on the pillow; she picked it up and read it. *Had to be up early, but didn't want to wake you – though there's an alarm call for 8.15, so you don't miss your course.*

It was signed only with his initial, and she was half-amused to notice the flamboyance of the letter K, compared with the rest of his very neat and formal script. She stretched, then glanced across at the clock on the bedside table. It was quarter to eight. There was more than enough time for her to return to her own room, shower, change and head down for breakfast. She stretched luxuriously. She felt slightly tired, yet exhilarated at the same time. Kit had made love to her twice more during the night, his touch sure and sensual. It had been good for both of them, and it had proved to her beyond doubt that Rupert had been lying. A frigid woman wouldn't have been able to respond to Kit in the way that she had, giving herself up completely to climax after climax.

No, a frigid woman wouldn't have straddled Kit, touching her own breasts as she rode him. A frigid woman wouldn't have welcomed Kit's mouth exploring every inch of her skin, from the hollows of her ankles to the furls of her quim. And a frigid woman wouldn't have delighted in kneeling beside him, taking his cock as deeply into her mouth as she could. If she'd been less than perfectly responsive to Rupert – well, it hadn't been all her fault.

She yawned, and turned her face to the pillow. She could smell Kit's masculine scent, mixed with the tell-tale aroma of sex, on the cotton of the pillowslip. Half of her was tempted to remain where she was and wait for him to come back to bed; but then again, she couldn't let her students down. Besides, Kit was busy. That was why he'd left without waking her.

She reread what he'd written, and her eyes narrowed. He hadn't mentioned anything about seeing her again. *When he'd said short-term, the previous night, he'd meant* very *short-term*, she thought wryly. *Like just one night*. Still, she was an adult. She'd had the choice – and she'd agreed to go to bed with him. There was no point in getting upset about the fact that it was over now. It had been an incredibly pleasant interlude, but now she had to get on with her life.

She crumpled the note into a ball, then climbed out of bed, dressed swiftly, and left the room. To her relief, she wasn't spotted padding round the corridors. She reached her own room, showered, dressed swiftly, and headed downstairs. She glanced into the Blue Room, and noticed with pleasure that everything was set up exactly how she wanted it. The desks were even arranged in a horseshoe shape, rather than a classroom layout – in exact accordance with Mandy's instructions. Luckily, she and Mandy taught the same way. She smiled, and headed for the dining room.

Elaine, Peggy and Emma were sitting at the one of the tables, drinking coffee and chatting. Carolyn went over to join them. She didn't have time for a large breakfast, but she wasn't really much of a breakfast person anyway. She had never been able to face a fry-up, even on a weekend morning. A cup of coffee and a croissant would do her nicely.

'Good morning,' she said cheerily. 'Did you sleep well?'

'Definitely,' Peggy said. 'This place is wonderful. How did you find it?'

'I can't take the credit for that, I'm afraid,' Carolyn said, pouring herself a cup of coffee. 'That's all down to my colleague Mandy.' She grinned. 'And believe me, Mandy wouldn't stay anywhere that wasn't comfortable, didn't have good food, or sold barely-drinkable wine.' She paused. 'Have I missed the others?'

Emma shook her head. 'I think they decided to have breakfast in their rooms.'

'I nearly did, too,' Carolyn lied. 'But as I wanted to check the room first, I thought that I might as well have breakfast down here.' She glanced at her watch. 'A quick breakfast, that is!' She buttered a croissant, adding jam to it; when she'd finished it and drained her coffee, she wiped her fingers on the napkin and glanced at her watch. 'Well, if you're all ready, shall we go?'

The others nodded, and they left the dining room. Gina, Libby, and Sue were already waiting for them in the Blue Room; Carolyn noticed with pleasure that several jugs of iced water had been brought into the room since she'd inspected it. Kit's team really were professional. 'Good morning,' she said. 'I hope you all slept well.'

'You bet.' Gina was as enthusiastic as Peggy had been. 'And we're all raring to go.'

'Good.' Carolyn smiled at them. 'As this is a residential course, and we all met each other last night, I don't think that we really need to bother with name plates or any ice-breakers. Unless you'd all prefer to do that?'

Elaine pulled a face. 'No, I don't think I could handle either having to find out something unusual about the person sitting next to me, or coming out with three statements about myself, one of which is an outrageous lie!'

Carolyn chuckled. 'Oh dear. The next course that I design, I'll make sure that I come up with a different ice-breaker!' The others laughed. 'But what I would like to know,' Carolyn continued, 'is why you all want to write erotica.'

'Mine's easy,' Sue said. 'Like I said last night, my husband writes erotic novels. I want to write one that's as good as – no, better than – one of Harry's.'

'Does he know that you're here?' Gina asked.

Sue nodded. 'But he thinks that I'm brushing up on my shorthand.' She gave them all a wicked smile. 'Potentially, in six months' time, he's going to have one hell of a surprise.'

'Good on you,' Elaine said. 'Well, I always wanted to write a novel. I must have written half a dozen romances. You know how it is – they always say that a journo has a novel in her bottom drawer. Though I've had an awful lot of rejection slips, mainly because the publishers said that I needed to tone down the sex scenes. But I felt the books would be too watered-down if I took out the sex scenes; that's why I decided to turn to erotica.'

'I've always enjoyed reading,' Peggy said. 'A friend bought me one of those erotic novels for women – and I really loved it. And the more I thought about it, the more I wanted to write one myself.'

'Me, too,' Emma said. Carolyn paused, hoping that Emma was going to amplify her comment, but Emma merely flushed and stared at her desk. Carolyn sighed inwardly. It looked as though Emma had gone back into her shell. It was a shame, after her performance, the previous night; or maybe Emma needed a few glasses of wine before she could break through her inhibitions.

'Well,' Gina said, 'I'm broke. I need to earn some money, and I'd like to do something I enjoy to earn money. Like I said, I've travelled a lot recently, and I think that I could write a book about my experiences. Fictionalized, of course.'

'Libby?' Carolyn asked.

'Pretty much the same as Peggy,' Libby said. 'Though I didn't enjoy the first book I read. It was dire, and I thought that I could do better – and also that it'd be a nice way to earn a living while I'm "resting".'

'Fair enough,' Carolyn said. 'Well, I can't promise that what I'm going to teach you will guarantee publication – or that you'll all be as rich as Croesus if you do get something published – but at least the course will start you off on the right lines.' She poured herself a glass of water. 'Throughout the course, feel free to interrupt me at any time – it's probably easier to ask questions as you go along rather than wait until the end of a session and then forget what you wanted to ask.'

There was a murmur of assent.

'Now, can anyone give me a definition of erotic writing?'

'Something that turns you on,' Gina said.

Carolyn nodded. 'Anything else?'

'Something that involves all the senses,' Elaine said. 'Something that involves touch and taste and smell and sight and sound.'

'Yes. Anything else?'

'It needs a plot,' Emma added shyly.

'Definitely,' Carolyn agreed. 'Actually, I have a definition here. An erotic novel has a plot, characters and motivations, just like any other novel. The one element that distinguishes it from the mainstream story is that it contains explicitly described sexual encounters that are integral to the plot: without the encounters and explicit descriptions, the story would seem flat and meaningless.'

'It's not just one bonk after another, either,' Libby said. 'Not like the one I read.'

'Exactly.' Carolyn smiled at her. 'Mandy's given me a story that she says is a really good example of the definition: without the sex, the story is pointless – but there's a definite plot there, too.' She paused. 'Apart from the fact that I'm sure that you don't all want to listen to me droning on all day, I murder stories when I read them out. Would anyone like to volunteer?'

'It just has to be Libby,' Sue said, smiling.

Carolyn nodded. 'Libby, would you mind?'

'Of course not.' Libby spread her hands. 'It makes a change from reading lines, anyway!'

Carolyn handed her the paper, and Libby began to read.

'The Game, by Eleanor Richmond.' She cleared her throat. 'Alison looked closely at the package, wondering who had sent it. The neat type on the label gave nothing away – it was Times Roman, the same font that almost everyone she knew used – and the postmark was too blurred to read. She didn't think that it was anything to do with work, because the office would never give out her address without checking with her first; besides, she always picked up her review software from the office and she'd called in the previous day to collect the batch that was currently sitting on her desk in her study. She couldn't remember sending away for anything, and she'd never even heard of the company whose logo sat neatly in the top left-hand corner: Wonderland Inc.

'There was only one way to find out what it was.

'She opened the package and laughed as she saw the contents. It was just an ordinary black high-density computer disk, with a white label bearing the Wonderland Inc logo and demanding "Play me". "What's going to happen next?" she said, with a grin. "Alison in Wonderland shrinks to the size of a dormouse, or suddenly becomes eight foot tall?"

'It was obviously a promotional stunt from a software house that wanted her to review their latest "Pick-'em-up" or "Shoot-the-aliens" game, and she gave them a few extra marks for originality. Well, it wasn't a bad try – they had probably had to put in quite a bit of effort to find out her address in the first place – but it would have to wait its turn. She had half a dozen others to review first.

'She walked into her study and slid the topmost disk from the pile on her desk into her computer, heaving a sigh and wishing that she could summon up some enthusiasm for the task. How many overworked executives would love the idea of being a computer games reviewer, working mainly from home and spending most of their time playing games and reviewing them for a magazine? How many people would love to swap jobs with her? She really should be grateful that she wasn't tied in to a normal nine-to-five routine – or, as it seemed to be with most of her friends, an eight-till-seven office job.

'It had been fun at first. But, after a while, it grew boring: playing the same tired old game day after day, though in a slightly different package with different graphics and a different title. She might be picking up different icons from different places, but the principle was the same. Alison hadn't reviewed one really original game in the entire previous year, and the one she had just started was no different from the rest. The second was the same, and so was the third. Boring, boring, oh, so bloody boring. The graphics on the third game were the best of the bunch, but not one of them would get more than five out of ten in her column. There just wasn't that spark of excitement about any of them.

'She was about to put the fourth disk from the pile in the disk drive, and stopped. The way the Wonderland Inc disk had

been packaged had amused and intrigued her. Maybe the game
might be as original as its promotional pack. It certainly
couldn't be any worse than the previous three she'd played
– at least, she hoped that it wouldn't be. She picked up the disk,
slid it into the drive, switched to DOS, and typed "Play me".

'The screen went blank. She sighed, her blue eyes narrowing, and raked a hand through her short dark hair. It looked
like this was going to be a complete waste of time. Knowing
her luck, they'd sent her a duff copy or duff instructions.
Maybe "Play me" hadn't been the right command. Maybe it
wasn't a DOS game in the first place. Maybe it needed
unzipping and installing properly into her PC, and would
turn out to be one of the new games with 3-D graphics:
though it was unusual for there to be only one disk for that
kind of game. It was always either a CD-ROM or half a dozen
floppies. She was about to switch into the file manager and
scan the contents of the disk when the cursor flickered for a
moment, and words came up on the screen.

' "Hello, Alison."

'She frowned. She hadn't even typed in a user name. How
could the program know who she was? Unless someone had
pre-programmed it especially for her. There was always a
chance that whoever had sent her the disk had personalized it,
hoping to score extra points. Well, she might as well play it.
That's what she was paid to do, after all. "Hello," she typed
back.

' "You're bored, aren't you?"

'She was surprised. When the words had first come up, she'd
been expecting some kind of adventure game where you'd be
given a situation and had to decide what to do next – one of the
incredibly old-fashioned kind that had gone out with the ark
and was only worth playing again for the retro novelty value.

But this seemed a bit different. She frowned at the screen; then her face cleared. It was probably just a joke from one of her friends in the office. *Well let's see what you make of this, guys,* she thought. "So?" she typed.

' "Want to do something about it?"

'She grinned. She'd been right. It was either a joke or a chat-up line from one of the lads who worked on the business software reviews. Probably the new guy, Mark – judging by the way he'd been trying to look up her skirt the last time she'd been in the office. He was attractive enough. Average height and build, dark curly hair, soulful dark eyes, and a pouty smile that reminded her of Antonio Banderas. Nice bum, too, as their secretary had pointed out. Whatever Mark Roper did in his spare time, he certainly took care of himself. If it was him, then Alison would certainly be interested. "What do you suggest?" she teased.

' "Oh, I'm full of ideas."

'I bet you are, you lecher, she thought, still smiling. "Such as?" she asked.

' "Go over to your CD player."

'Oh, so you know the layout of my study, do you? she thought. Obviously whoever had sent her the disk had been at her flat-warming party the previous month, and had checked out her flat thoroughly at some point during the evening. So it could have been Mark. She'd invited everyone in the office as well as her circle of friends outside the magazine, and her flat had been packed to bursting. She was fairly sure that Mark had been there that night. "Why?"

' "Because I want you to play some music," the answer came back patiently. "Something with a slow and heavy beat. Soft rock, or whatever makes you open to ideas."

'Whoever he was, he had a very different approach, she

thought. "Okay," she typed. She quickly turned on the CD, choosing an old Paul Rodgers compilation, and walked back over to her computer. The cursor was flashing expectantly. "What now?" she typed.

' "Put your headphones on – and, as they say, lie back and enjoy it."

'Alison chuckled, her face relaxing into prettiness. This was one hell of an interactive program. It wasn't one of the situation games, after all: it was more like the kind where the computer genius would answer your questions and help you improve your life. The ones she'd used before, where you could type in something and the computer would "answer" your questions, had all been very low-tech, and it had been easy to see how the program had been structured to recognize certain words and phrases and put them into a new order to "answer" the player's comments. This was a lot more inventive. Whoever had developed this certainly had more imagination than the game developers she'd met in the past. Or maybe it was her own boredom sending her imagination into overdrive. Maybe she was imagining that the computer was chatting her up, trying to cajole her into a sexy mood. "Enjoy what?" she fenced.

' "Your trip through Wonderland, Alison."

' "That's a bit corny, isn't it?"

'The computer screen went blank for a moment, as if the machine was thinking about her answer. "Well, you don't have to. No one's making you do anything. It's your choice."

'Alison grinned again. "Huffy-puffy," she typed back.

'The screen didn't change.

'Are you still there?' she typed.

'The screen still didn't change.

'*Damn*, she thought. *This could have been fun, and I've blown it by being a smart-arse.* "Hello?" she tried. "Talk to me."

' "I'm thinking about it."

'She hadn't expected that. This looked like a truly interactive game. How the hell could the programmer have known what her responses would be? However he had done it, she was impressed. "I'm sorry," she typed. "Can we start again?"

'If computers could smile, Alison thought that hers would have been sporting a broad cheesy grin. She was half-surprised that a smiley-face graphic didn't flash up on the screen.

' "It's a deal. Is the music on?"

'She put on her headphones. "Yes."

' "Then follow the instructions on the screen."

'She waited expectantly.

' "Sit back in your chair and listen to the music," the program told her. "Feel the beat."

'She did as she was told, letting the slow bluesy music relax her. Her body began to sway automatically in time to the beat. The computer screen seemed to be waiting for her to make the next move. Smiling and relaxed now, she typed in, "What next?"

' "Let yourself go. Let your shoulders lead you."

' "My shoulders?" Alison typed, surprised.

' "Oh, yes. You have beautiful shoulders. Undo your shirt and bare them for me. Let me see you."

'Part of her balked at the command; part of her was intrigued. Besides, the music was beginning to have an effect on her. She'd chosen the kind of music she liked to play while making love and it was beginning to arouse her, put her in just the kind of mood to be receptive to suggestions like that. Slowly, she pulled her loose white cotton shirt from the waistband of her jeans, unbuttoned it, and shrugged it down to bare her shoulders.

' "Take it right off," the computer demanded.

'She let the shirt fall to the floor.

' "Now move with the music."

'Alison couldn't help herself. "You mean, pretend I'm a tree, like kids do at infant school?"

'The reply was instant. "Well, if you're not going to take me seriously, forget it. I'll just GOTO END."

'*It was one hell of a moody program – or programmer,* Alison thought. "OK, I'm sorry. I won't tease you again."

' "Good. Now move for me."

'Slowly, Alison swayed in her seat, her arms raised away from the keyboard and her hands moving in time to the music. As the program had demanded, she led with her shoulders, her upper body snaking in front of the screen.

' "That's nice. *Very* nice," the screen told her. "Now, take off your bra."

' "My bra?" Alison typed, surprised.

' "Stop parroting."

' "I'm not."

' "Then take off your bra. White lace is very sexy, I know, but I want to see a bit more of you. I want to see your breasts. I want to see your nipples grow hard and rosy as you touch them. I want to see your breasts swell as you grow more aroused."

'Alison was a little nervous about how much the program seemed to know about her – how the hell could it know that she was wearing a white lace bra? It wasn't as though she always wore the same colour underwear; she had a drawerful of jewel-coloured bras and knickers. Maybe it was a lucky guess. But she did as she was told, unclipping the white lace garment and letting it fall on top of the shirt.

' "Beautiful," the program said. "Your skin's so smooth, so pale. I can imagine how it feels, how it tastes. Soft and warm

and creamy. I'd like to taste you, Alison. I'd like to touch you –
but I can't, right now."

'*You can say that again.* Alison thought.

' "So I need you to do it for me. Cup your breasts, and keep
moving."

'Feeling suddenly shy, Alison brought her hands up to cover
her breasts.

' "I said cup them, not cover them."

'*How the hell did it know what she'd just done?* she thought
with shock, sliding her hands down to cup her breasts, as
instructed, and lifting them up slightly. Her nipples began to
harden: instinctively, she brushed her thumbs across her
areolae, feeling her flesh begin to pucker under her touch.
She stroked her nipples with a circular motion, closing her eyes
for a moment as desire lanced through her. Then she shook
herself and stared back at the screen.

' "That's good," the program said approvingly. "Now touch
yourself a little harder. Touch your nipples the way you'd like
a man to touch them. And keep moving for me. Let me see you
enjoy yourself, enjoy the way your body feels."

'She massaged her nipples between her thumbs and forefingers, still swaying in front of the screen. It felt good, she had
to admit; she could imagine a man standing before her, touching
her breasts in that way, stroking the soft undersides and
tugging gently on the hard peaks of her nipples. A man like
Mark Roper. Touching her, just before he bent his head and took
one nipple into his mouth, flicking his tongue across the rosy
nub of flesh and then sucking hotly on it. She drew one hand up
to her mouth, wetting her finger and thumb before touching her
breasts again, pretending that her spit-slicked fingers were his
mouth. She could almost smell his clean male scent, mingling
with the sweet musky smell of her own arousal.

' "That's perfect. Just perfect," the program told her. "Now slide your right hand down to your jeans. Feel the softness of your skin as you caress your midriff. It's soft and warm and waiting – and you know exactly where you want to be touched next. You know where your body's aching for contact."

'Alison did as she was told. And yes, the screen was right. It felt good. She was soft and warm, and the touch of her fingers against her midriff made her shiver with longing. She wanted to touch herself much more intimately now.

' "Unzip your jeans, but do it slowly. And keep your left hand where it is. Keep touching your breasts, arousing yourself more and more and more."

'She could hardly believe that she was doing this – being seduced by a computer program. *But it certainly beat the hell out of picking up keys and hearts from clouds and rocks, or pretending she was in some kind of dungeons-and-dragons world,* she thought, unzipping her jeans.

' "Take off your jeans."

'Her eyelids were beginning to feel heavy, and she licked her lower lip. The program had virtually tuned in to her thoughts, knowing exactly what she wanted to do. She stood up.

' "No, not like that! Sit down and do it slowly. Weave your way out of them. Use your hips."

'It was easier said than done, and Alison was sweating slightly by the time she'd removed her jeans. "Very nice," the computer said approvingly. "Now run your hands down your sides, put your hands to your waist, and move to the music."

'It only took a couple of seconds for her to carry out the commands.

' "Mm, you're ready now," it told her. "Warm and wet and ready for me. I can almost smell your arousal. And I can imagine how you'd taste, your sweet nectar on my tongue.

Slide your right hand down to your thigh."

'Alison did, and obeyed the next command, to draw her fingers across the crotch of her knickers and press in against her quim. She felt a melting rush of excitement as she did so.

' "Mm, that feels good, doesn't it? You can feel your clitoris swelling, and it's tormenting, having your knickers between it and your fingers. You need to be skin to skin. It's too much, having that cotton barrier there. So do what you want to do, what your body's screaming out for you to do. Open your knees and cross your ankles. Lean back in your chair, and slip your right hand inside your knickers. Rest the heel of your palm on your mons veneris, then slide your middle finger between your labia."

'She felt as though there was a furnace building inside her quim; she followed the instructions to the letter.

' "Feel how hot you are; the lightest touch is going to send you up in flames. It's going to be so good, Alison, so very good. You're going to enjoy this. You're going to pleasure yourself for me now – and for you."

' "Oh, yes," she murmured, cupping her sex.

' "Now rub your middle finger, very slowly, across your clitoris. Up and down, very lightly, then round and round."

'Whoever had written the program was a real expert, someone who knew exactly how to turn on a woman – and particularly this woman. She did as she was told, feeling the swelling hardness of her clitoris as she played with the little bud of flesh, very gently and very lightly.

' "Now explore a bit deeper. Feel how soft and wet and hot you are, how your sex is opening like a flower beneath your touch. Warm wet hot petals, like a tropical orchid in a rain forest."

'She wasn't so sure that orchids grew in rain forests, but she was in no state to argue. And it was true: her flesh *was* warm and slippery under her fingertips. She groaned as her finger slid inside her sex, sucked in by her warmth and wetness.

' "Now move back a bit," she was instructed. "Rub your clitoris a little harder this time. Do it like you'd want a man to do it for you."

'She played her part to the letter, dipping her finger into the wetness of her quim and then trailing it over her clitoris, lightly at first, then harder, harder, until she was gasping and writhing on her chair.

' "Now taste yourself," the program demanded.

'Trembling, Alison brought her hand up to her mouth, tasting the dampness on her fingers.

' "The sweetness of sea and salt and honey," the program informed her. "Touch yourself, Alison. Feel how good it is. Let yourself go. Make yourself come for me. Pretend I'm right there, doing it to you. Pretend it's my hands, my mouth, on your sex. Pretend I'm going down on you – that it's my lips, my tongue, playing with your clitoris."

'All her inhibitions vanished, and she let her right hand slip down again, rubbing the soft swollen flesh and closing her eyes. She brought her left hand down and gave herself up to her fantasy. Yes, there was a man in front of her, crouching by her chair; he was rubbing her clitoris, his dark eyes watching her intently. Watching the way she bared her teeth in pleasure and gripped the arms of her chair as he continued to work her, the way her bottom moved against the chair, rocking so that she was spread wide open for him. Then he was dipping his head, drawing his tongue along her sex and then sucking her clitoris, nipping it gently with his lips, while he pushed a finger deep into her quim, pushing his hand in and out, in and out, as though he were fucking her with a tiny and inexhaustible cock.

'Then the sharp contractions of her climax started, moving out through her body in waves; she felt as though there was some kind of connecting cord between her throbbing nipples and her pulsing clitoris. Her internal muscles spasmed round her fingers, clutching her tightly. Drained and panting, she withdrew her hands and slumped in front of the screen.

' "Good?" the program asked hopefully.

' "Yes," she typed languidly. "But who *are* you?"

' "Wonderland," the screen informed her smugly.

' "So how come you know so much about me?" she asked. "How come you knew how I'd react, that I would do exactly what you told me to do, and when?"

'If computers could blush, Alison's would have been glowing a rich red as it answered, a little shyly, "Look at your modem."

'Alison did as she was told, and her eyes widened in surprise. So much for the "interactive" disk. It had merely triggered her modem and set up a link between her computer and another, with the person on the other end of the line waiting for her answers. No wonder the program had been so fast with its reactions to her replies. And whoever it was must have known that she'd modified her modem to make it almost silent, so there hadn't been the tell-tale sound of the modem dialling up and the hissing noise as it connected. "OK, I see how it works. But how did you know that I was following your instructions?"

'It was definitely bashful now. "I just do."

' "Come on. I've played your game. Now you play mine," she demanded.

' "Now?"

' "Now." She was adamant.

'There was a pause. "OK. Turn your screen round ninety degrees, and look out of the window."

'Frowning now, Alison did. And saw the new reviewer, Mark, at the window in the flat opposite hers – holding a pair of binoculars.'

Libby placed the paper on her desk. 'Well,' she said. 'Tell me, Elaine – is it really like that in an office? Do people really seduce each other like that?'

Elaine chuckled. 'Not on the magazine where I work at the moment! Men are pretty rare in our office – and most of the ones I meet through work turn out to be gay. I'd be bloody surprised if one of *them* sent me an erotic e-mail. They're all too busy criticizing my fashion sense, or lack of it.'

'So what did you all think?' Carolyn said. 'Did the story fit our definition?'

Gina nodded. 'I think so. The whole point of the story was a seduction by computer; without that, there wouldn't have been any story. The sex scene was described explicitly; but I would have preferred a little more description of the main character. We didn't really know a thing about her – other than that she had short dark hair, blue eyes, and liked rock music.'

'Yes, we didn't know her age, if she lived alone, or what she liked doing with her spare time,' Sue added.

Emma shook her head. 'But how can you really get any deep characterization in a short story? There isn't enough time.'

'Even so, I think it has room for improvement,' Gina said. 'Though I did enjoy it. I have to admit, I quite like the idea of someone telling me what to do – and knowing that I have the choice whether I obey or not.'

'Would you have done it, in her place?' Peggy asked.

'I think so,' Gina said. 'If I was in the right kind of mood – fed up with what I was doing, feeling a little horny, listening to the kind of music that always makes me want a man inside me . . . then yes, I think I would have done it.'

'So you thought it was believable?' Carolyn prompted.

'Ah, but don't forget about the willing suspension of disbelief,' Elaine said with a grin. 'I mean, some of the novels I've read are far from believable. People just wouldn't act like that in real life. But you can let yourself go with it, if the characters are strong enough.'

Carolyn nodded. 'That's what I'm going to cover next. Characters and setting. But first, I think we all deserve a coffee break.'

TEN

During the coffee break, Carolyn checked that her presentation would work properly through the overhead projector. She was relieved, but not particularly surprised, to find that everything worked perfectly. She couldn't imagine Kit allowing anything to run less than efficiently.

Gina and Sue had gone outside for a cigarette break; when they returned, and the others had finished their coffee, Carolyn launched into her presentation, explaining how important it was that the characters were believable, and that their readers could identify with them and sympathize with them. 'And if you don't find your characters' lovers sexy, you can't expect your readers to find them sexy, either.'

'But how do you know that other people fancy the same kind of people that you do?' Libby asked. 'I suppose it's like music, or films – everyone has different tastes. I might fancy someone whom you think is completely repulsive.'

'True,' Carolyn said, 'but the trick is to carry your reader along with you. If you don't fancy your lead character, no one else will. If you do, then maybe your reader will put her own fantasy man in place of yours – what she'll identify with are the emotions and the way you deal with them.' She paused. 'And you don't have to have a tall, dark, handsome stranger in every single book.'

'I dunno,' Libby said. 'Give me Colin Firth, any day!'

Peggy chuckled. 'Yeah, I think that picture of him as Mr

Darcy must have gone up on every office pin-board. I know that my office was really buzzing the day after the scene where he was in wet breeches!'

'And there's a starting point for you. If your lead male character reminds you of Colin Firth, it'll be easy for you to describe him, and to describe how your lead female character reacts to him. That way, your readers will be able to "see" the characters that are in your mind. You also need to make sure that your characters are consistent – I know that Charlotte Brontë got away with changing the colour of her heroine's eyes halfway through *Shirley*, but I bet that all her readers picked up on it.' She shrugged. 'It's the same with all other physical details – like if your male lead is circumcised, don't have someone rubbing his foreskin back and forth in a later chapter.'

'Is there a way of making sure that you keep things consistent?' Emma asked.

'Apart from reading it through at the end and checking for yourself, you mean? Yes, you might find it useful to write yourself a little thumbnail sketch of each of your characters. Their height, their body shape, their hair – cut and colour – their eyes, any distinguishing physical features, whether they smoke or are vegetarian, what they usually drink – that kind of thing. You could do it on an index card, or even scribble it on a piece of paper: whatever you find easiest to keep by you.'

'Right.' Emma made some scribbled notes.

'What about names? Should they be exotic?' Gina asked.

'Not necessarily. If you have an Angelica and a Gabrielle and a Margaretta . . . It's all a bit over the top. By all means use one or two exotic names, but don't overdo it. There's no reason why you can't have a Jane as a heroine, or a John as a hero.'

'There's a John in our office,' Sue said. 'He's repulsive.'

'So there's your anti-hero, if you use one,' Carolyn said. She smiled. 'It's more or less the same principle for settings. If there's a particular place that you find really erotic, use it in a book. It could be anything from the park of your local country house through to Gina's deserted beach in the Whitsunday Islands or the *Cinquième Arrondissement* in Paris. Your setting is important – what happens to your characters doesn't happen in a vacuum. And the settings will help to define your characters, and maybe even the conflict between them. For example, if you have a high-flying finance executive stranded in the middle of the Scottish moorlands or the Yorkshire Dales in the pouring rain, she'll react very differently from the way that a farmer or a hiking guide would react.'

'What if you haven't actually been to the place in your book, like Paris or this deserted beach?' Elaine asked.

'Research it. Talk to someone who has, and get them to describe the atmosphere. Read magazines and reference books and brochures about the place. There might even be a video you can borrow from your local travel agent,' Carolyn said. 'Of course, you could always use it as an excuse for a holiday . . .'

The others laughed.

Carolyn continued explaining about how to develop settings, and how to draw thumbnail portraits to help; then she paused. 'Now, I've done enough talking for the moment, so I'm going to set you a task, to put what we've just been talking about into practice. I want you all to think of a character you find really attractive, and a setting, and be ready to describe that character and setting to the others. I'll give you ten or fifteen minutes to sketch a rough thumbnail, and then we'll start.' She smiled at them. 'And, in the meantime, I'll go and find us some more coffee.'

While they began to scribble on the conference paper that the hotel had provided, Carolyn left the room, intending go to reception to order more coffee. As she closed the door of the Blue Room behind her, she realized that Kit had just left his office and was standing in the corridor in front of her.

He smiled at her. 'Hello, Carolyn.'

She smiled back, deciding to take her lead from him. If he wanted to be chirpy and friendly, that was fine by her. She wouldn't expect anything more. 'Good morning.'

'How's the course going?'

'Fine, thanks.' She looked at him. 'I thought I'd order some more coffee while they're working on an exercise.'

He nodded. 'I can do that for you, if you like.'

'That's OK. I could do with the break, to be honest – I usually lecture standing up, but it's not the same as walking around.'

He brushed a stray tendril of hair from her face. 'There are so many things I want to say to you, Carolyn. But you're in the middle of a course, and I have a meeting in Cambridge.' He paused. 'Maybe we could talk, later this evening?'

'Maybe.' *Definitely*, she thought; but she didn't want to appear too eager.

He smiled at her. 'I'll come to you, then. I'll ring you first.' For one moment, she thought that he was going to kiss her; instead, he gave her a very camped-up wink, and strode off down the corridor.

Carolyn watched his long easy stride as he walked away. He looked almost as good from the rear as he did from the front. And she knew every inch of his body, beneath that formal suit. The knowledge thrilled her – but it worried her at the same time. She really didn't need any complications in her life at the moment, or another relationship. She'd just split up with Rupert, and she needed time to get over it. Plus she knew that a long-distant relationship between two workaholics simply couldn't happen. But then again, there was no reason why she couldn't enjoy the rest of the weekend at Heywood . . .

She smiled wryly, and went to reception to order more coffee and biscuits. On her return to the Blue Room, she found everyone still working diligently. She glanced at her watch. Five more minutes. She wondered what kind of characters and settings everyone would choose. Gina would probably go for something exotic, as would Sue. A gipsy in Turkey, or maybe something set in Egypt. Peggy and Elaine would choose something from the world of business. Libby might draw on her background as an actress; and Emma was a complete enigma. She could turn out to have the raunchiest imagination of all of them: certainly, her story about the actress had been uninhibited. Or maybe that had just been the wine.

Eventually, she coughed. 'OK. Time's up. Who'd like to start?'

There was a silence. Then Peggy spoke up. 'I'll do it, if you like.'

'Thanks. So, tell us about your character and your setting.'

'I've gone for the exotic name. He's called Jordan Davies. He's about thirty-five, and he's about six feet tall, with dark straight hair, which he wears brushed back from his face. He has hazel eyes, which look almost grey in some lights; he has one of those wounded puppy-dog mouths that make you want to pull him into your arms and kiss him, and he's a computer programmer.'

'A computer programmer? But aren't they all spotty nerds?' Libby asked, surprised.

Peggy grinned. 'Not all of them. There's one in our office who's completely gorgeous – though Jordan Davies isn't quite based on him. Anyway, he usually wears a black polo-neck cotton sweater and chinos and desert boots, adding one of those big black coats in winter. In summer, he wears well-cut, almost knee-length shorts and polo shirts. Because what he does is such a specialized job and he doesn't have any contact with the general public, he can get away with dressing less formally than everyone else in the office.'

'Are the chinos tight?' Elaine asked.

Peggy nodded. 'Definitely. And the way he moves – I suppose you'd describe it as loose-limbed. It's sort of fluid and graceful. He moves more like a dancer than anything else.'

Carolyn thought of Kit. Different colour eyes, different clothing – but very similar in looks and the way he moved. The idea made her stomach clench with longing. And Kit was going to come and see her, later that night. She glanced surreptitiously at her watch. In less than twelve hours. God, how could she wait that long, to feel his body against hers again?

'He plays a lot of sport in his spare time,' Peggy continued, 'rather than sitting hooked up to the Internet for hours. So his shoulders are broad and his hips are narrow. He's lean without being skinny, and developed without being a gorilla. He has the kind of body that makes you want to see exactly what he looks like without his clothes. Say after a rugby match, in the shower, when you could soap away all the dirt and sweat and grime, and then do exactly what you wanted with him.'

'Mm, sounds good to me. What's his voice like?' Gina asked.

'Quite well-spoken. Not posh, exactly; just ordinary Home Counties. Fairly soft, too.' Peggy smiled. 'Imagine an English Fox Mulder.'

'Now you're talking,' Sue said. 'He's gorgeous. I could eat that man alive.'

The others laughed, agreeing.

'What about your setting, Peggy?' Emma asked.

'The office, I think. It's a modern building, a late 1980s design, in red brick with large windows. Inside, the walls are magnolia.'

'Aren't they always?' Sue groaned.

Peggy grinned. 'Yeah. And there are the usual Venetian blinds at the window, little narrow black ones. Then there are up-lighters around the room, which is open-plan – there are sound boards between the clusters of desks. There are four to six desks per cluster, the kind that look as if a large semi-circle has been cut from them to give you more working space. The sound boards and carpets are all in a very soft blue, because the design consultants have said that that particular shade of blue is a relaxing colour. There are tubs of plants, big leafy ferns and ivies. And there are a couple of tasteful framed prints on the walls – because this is the kind of office that frowns on silly postcards and badly-photocopied notices about people having to be mad to work there. The sound boards are more or less bare, apart from the odd schedule or list of names and phone extensions, because the manager is a bit sniffy about the area looking scruffy.'

'I hope you don't think I'm being hypercritical,' Gina said, 'but can an office really be erotic?'

'I think so, yes,' said Elaine. 'The thing is, what might seem ordinary on the surface could be completely different underneath. There could be all sorts of undercurrents.'

'Exactly,' Carolyn said. 'That's where your characters come in. It's the way they interact with your setting that makes it work. That, and their motives.'

'So what happens with this Jordan Davies guy?' Emma asked.

Peggy chuckled. 'I haven't got that far yet. But that story about seduction by e-mail . . . Well, that's certainly given me an idea for a scene. Can you imagine that you're working hard, concentrating on something entirely mundane – and you get an e-mail from the most attractive man in the office, making suggestions to you about what he'd like to do with you?'

'Mm, particularly if you're having the day from hell, your boss is suffering from the male equivalent of PMT and is taking it out on you, and all your deadlines have suddenly moved forward by a couple of days, so there's no way you'll get everything done on time,' Sue said feelingly.

'All part of the setting,' Carolyn told them. 'Now, when it comes to plot you need some kind of conflict between the characters to make things interesting. They might be on opposing sides in their jobs – for example, the female head of a development company and a man who's trying to keep that particular field as a nature reserve. I don't know if any of you know the Kipling rhyme, about six honest serving men?'

Elaine nodded. 'I remember it, just about, from my journalism course. "I have six honest serving men; They taught me all I know. Their names are what and why and when, And who and where and how." '

'That's the one,' Carolyn said. 'Your readers want to know what is happening, where and when it's happening, who it is happening to, and why it's happening. That's basically the book's action, setting, characters, and plot. The "how" is how you tell it, of course.'

'Right.' Sue nodded.

'So if we take our story of Jordan Davies in the office forward a bit – we have a character and a setting. What we need now is a plot.'

'What about the female character?' Elaine asked.

'Over to the floor,' Carolyn said. 'Tell me about her.'

'He's got a gorgeous name, something unusual, so hers needs

to be a bit more ordinary to balance it out,' Emma said. 'Let's call her Jane.'

'Jane Burroughs,' Gina added. 'She's about five foot six, with dark hair worn in a bob. She wears smart office suits – usually navy or black – with demure shirts and she uses flowery chiffon scarves to accessorize them. Oh, and flat leather court shoes, and minimal jewellery.'

'She wears contact lenses,' Emma said. 'Coloured ones. Bright blue, because her eyes are quite a pale blue and she wants to be a bit more glamorous.'

'She doesn't wear heavy make-up, though,' Peggy said. 'Subtle. She's not in sales; she's fairly quiet, really. Hard-working and ordinary.'

'She's a secretary,' Sue said. 'I can identify with that. And she'd be using e-mail a lot, to cope with messages for her boss. That's when she gets the erotic e-mail.'

'Is the e-mail she receives for her – or her boss?' Libby asked.

'That depends on whether or not her boss is male. I mean, the occasional homoerotic scene really turns me on. There are a couple of scenes in *Interview with a Vampire,* between Tom Cruise and Brad Pitt, where it really . . . Gina gave an exaggerated shiver of lust. 'Well. No, let's make her boss female. Lynda.'

'Lynda Meadows,' Libby agreed. 'She and Jane are complete opposites. And they don't really get on that well. Lynda's quite loud. She has big hair, with lots of blonde highlights. She's in sales, and she wears power suits, big earrings and very bright colours, usually pillar-box red or jade green. She's a high heels and stockings woman, and she wears chiffon shirts that you can always just see through, so if she's in a meeting with a man, he's so transfixed by what he can see of her breasts that he'll agree to anything. She wears lots of make-up, and very strong perfume.'

Carolyn chuckled. 'I take it that you don't like saleswomen?'

'It's not that, so much,' Libby said wryly. 'But when I've been resting, I've occasionally done some tele-marketing so I can pay my share of the rent. I've come across one or two real stereotype women sales managers – loud, bossy and not very sensitive. I think that kind would be a real contrast to our quiet and nice Jane Burroughs.'

Carolyn grinned. 'I don't think you need me to tell you much about plot, from the sound of things. You've already got the idea – it's what happens to the characters, and how they interact. There needs to be some kind of conflict. Jane picking up an e-mail that was really meant for Lynda, but thinking that it's meant for her – yes, that's a good one. Mistaken identity. Or maybe she misinterprets it deliberately, because she doesn't like Lynda and fancies Jordan herself. So think what kind of conflict you're going to have, and how you're going to resolve it.' She paused. 'I think, as you're working so well together as a group, I'd like to just take you through a few slides about the do's and don'ts of plotting, then ask you to work on the plot of the story together, rather than all have separate stories.'

'That's fine by me,' Gina said.

'Me, too,' Sue added.

There was a general murmur of assent, and Carolyn ran through the next set of slides. Then she glanced at her watch. 'I make it lunchtime. How about we break now, and you have a chance to think about the Lynda, Jane and Jordan scenario over lunch? Then I'll give you an hour to put it together, and we'll go through it and see where you've done well and where you could do things differently and make it even better.'

'Do you have a portable printer with your laptop?' Peggy asked.

Carolyn nodded. 'I usually bring one with me, in case I need to print extra copies of handouts.'

Peggy smiled. 'Could we use your laptop to write our group story rather than do it in longhand, please?'

'Of course. Though I think that you should take turns in typing – otherwise it'll be too easy for one of you to be the group's typist and not get a chance to add in your own ideas,' Carolyn warned.

'We'll do a couple of paragraphs each,' Gina promised.

'Great. Well – time for lunch.' Carolyn smiled at them, and led them from the room.

Lunch turned out to be a self-service salad-bar affair, and Libby's eyes widened at the choice. 'Wow. I really could get used to living like this,' she said, heaping her plate with green salad, melon, tuna niçoise and scalloped potatoes. 'It makes a nice change from beans on toast or a cheese sandwich – that's if someone hasn't scoffed all the cheese.'

Elaine laughed. 'That sounds very much like how things were when I was a student. Either there was no food in the house or someone had left something shoved to the back of the fridge and no one noticed it until it virtually walked out of its own accord!'

They sat down and all of them chose freshly-squeezed orange juice rather than wine. 'I need a clear head to write,' Emma said wryly.

'And I think that I sank more than enough last night,' Gina added. 'I want to pace myself.'

Over their meal, they discussed what was going to happen between their characters – their motivations, the conflicts between them, and ways they could be resolved. After coffee, Carolyn smiled at them. 'Would you prefer me to leave you all on your own for an hour or so, or would you like me to stay in the room so you can bounce ideas off me?'

'Stay. You're part of us,' Sue said warmly.

Carolyn nodded, and they returned to the Blue Room.

'This is the worst bit,' Peggy said. 'Where do we start?'

'With Jane at her desk,' Sue said. 'She's just had a clash with Lynda, and she's trying to get through the extra pile of work Lynda's just given her. A lot of amendments to an urgent report, and Lynda's writing is almost illegible.'

'Though she's been Lynda's secretary for more than six months now – since her previous boss, who was male, retired. So she's used to Lynda's scrawl,' Emma added. 'It just annoys her that Lynda can't be bothered to make an effort.'

'Tell you what – you start talking, and I'll do the first bit of typing,' Peggy said.

Carolyn unhooked the connection between her laptop and the overhead projector and handed the little machine to Peggy. 'The word processor I use is a pretty standard package,' she said. 'While you're beginning your story, I'll fetch the printer from my room.'

'Thanks.' Peggy smiled at her and switched into the program while the others moved their chairs so that they were all sitting in a circle round the laptop. 'Okay. Sue, you had the idea for the beginning. Start talking . . .'

When Carolyn returned, carrying the small printer, Peggy and Sue had changed places and Libby was talking them through the next few paragraphs. Sue's quick fingers were easily able to keep up with Libby; then Sue changed places with Elaine. All six of them were animated and seemed to be enjoying the challenge of writing a story between them.

'How's it going?' Carolyn asked when they reached a natural pause.

'OK. It's almost like playing a very long and very interesting game of consequences,' Emma said. 'Especially when you can make the whole story change direction so quickly.'

Carolyn nodded. 'Well, keep at it. You've got another three quarters of an hour.'

'Right.' Gina grinned. 'I think we ought to ban you, actually. So the whole thing's a surprise when you hear it.'

'Fair enough. I'll go and have a stroll,' Carolyn said. 'If you need any more water or anything, just dial zero for reception; and if you need me, I'll be somewhere in the gardens.' She smiled at them and left the room again. It was working well, she thought. They'd all settled in nicely, and Peggy and Emma were taking just as much a part as the livelier members of the group.

She wandered along the stone-flagged terrace outside the hotel and leaned over the balustrade at the end, looking down at the moat. Heywood really was the most gorgeous place, she thought. And every part of it was different. It was mainly fifteenth century, but there were also some later additions, from the sixteenth and seventeenth centuries. Most of the windows were stone and mullioned but, on one aspect, there was a room in which the diamond panes were set at different angles, making it look as though the windows were rippling in the sunlight.

Carolyn stared at the building for a while, looking at the tower that spiralled up one corner. Kit's tower. The tower of the White Knight. She grinned. Now, that really *was* fantasy. Medieval knights – at least in the courtly conventional sense – didn't seduce women. They were gallant, like Lancelot and Gawain. Though she knew that in real life most of the knights had been soldiers for hire, behaving in exactly the same fashion as modern-day mercenaries. Fighting for money, not glory, and doing what the hell they liked in between. Kit wasn't like that, either.

She headed down the stone steps to one of the lower reaches of the garden and sat down on the grass. She was relieved to find that the ground wasn't damp, and the moss within the grass made the turf cushioned and inviting. Smiling to herself, Carolyn reclined fully, putting her hands behind her head as a makeshift cushion. She closed her eyes, letting the sunlight beat down on her face. She had no intention of lying there sunbathing for a long period — she'd read too many articles about the damaging effects of sunlight – but five minutes wouldn't hurt, she thought.

Unbidden, Kit's face came into her mind. Supposing he were to walk into the gardens and discover her there ... What would he do? Would he assume that she was sleeping and lie down beside her, kissing her awake? Or would he pick one of the longer stems of grass, and tickle the end of her nose with it until she opened her eyes in outrage, ready to push him away? And then he'd bend his head, kissing her deeply and turning her anger into passion of the best kind, arousing her until she didn't care who could see them, ending up by making love with him on the lawn ...

Carolyn opened her eyes again and sat up. It was ridiculous, having romantic dreams about Kit Williams. Whatever had happened between them the previous day – and whatever was going to happen between them later that evening – she knew that it wasn't long-term. She really didn't want anything long-term, either; so it was pointless, fantasizing about him like this.

She smiled wryly. She had read somewhere that the sun was an aphrodisiac. Or maybe it was sun after champagne: whatever, lying here and thinking erotic thoughts about Kit Williams wasn't going to help. She had to concentrate on her course. She owed it to her students. She glanced at her watch and realized with surprise that she'd been outside for longer than she'd thought. Time to go in and find out how they were getting on. She always felt slightly guilty, setting a writing exercise as part of the course: but then again, it was a chance for her students to put the theory into practice, and it gave them a break from her voice.

Yawning, she stood up and went back to the Blue Room. As she opened the door, they all looked up at her.

'Five minutes?' Emma asked.

She nodded. 'Five minutes. I'll check that our coffee's ready, and then perhaps one of you can read the story to me.'

'It has to be Libby,' Gina said.

Libby groaned. 'I wish I'd told you all that I worked in an office now!'

'We would have picked you anyway,' Sue said. 'You have such a good voice.'

'Flattery will get you anywhere,' Libby teased.

When Carolyn returned to the room again, they were all ready. While Peggy poured the coffees, she hooked up the printer and printed out the story, putting it on Libby's desk, before connecting her laptop to the overhead projector again.

ELEVEN

As soon as they'd finished their coffee, Libby picked up the papers. 'Switchback, by Madeleine Harper,' she said. 'That's our composite author's name.'

'OK,' Carolyn said, settling back in her chair and listening.

Libby began to read aloud. 'Jane looked at the report and grimaced. Lynda wanted it back by lunchtime, she'd said – six copies, with all the graphs in colour. Fat chance. Printing it would take nearly that long, let alone making the umpteen minor alterations that Lynda had marked in her near-illegible script on nearly every page. Alterations which Lynda really should have made in the previous draft.

'Jane pulled a face at her boss's door. She'd been working for Lynda for six months now, since John Green had retired. She'd liked the old sales manager. He'd been a bit crusty, but at least he'd been approachable. The glamorous and glitzy Lynda was anything but. She fitted every stereotype going. The sassy confident sales person, wearing short skirts and high heels, jewel-bright colours and heavy perfume. The woman manager who tried to be more of a man than the men against whom she competed, a pushy autocrat who believed in power-dressing. The boss from hell, who changed her mind every five minutes and expected instant results, not caring whether her staff had to work late to meet her demands.

'Sighing, Jane switched into the report and began making the alterations. Work had become more and more intolerable lately. Sometimes she thought that the only reason she stayed there – apart from her monthly salary cheque, of course – was for the chance of seeing Jordan Davies. Jordan was the computer whizz-kid who'd joined the firm about nine months before Lynda had and had set up the new telesales program from scratch.

'He wasn't like the rest of the guys in the computer department. Apart from the fact that Jordan didn't look like he spent his weekends in an anorak, tapping away on the Internet, he actually spoke to people. Most of the computer buffs lived in a world of their own, speaking their own jargon and not communicating with anyone outside their team except in terms of COBOL or PASCAL. Jordan, on the other hand, always made a point of stopping by Jane's desk on his way back from a meeting with Lynda, to say hello and ask her how her day was going. It didn't seem like he was just being polite, either; it was as if he really meant it, as if he really was interested in whether or not she was having a good day.

'And he was gorgeous. Everyone in the telesales department had noticed that. He was about six foot tall, with straight dark hair brushed back from his hazel eyes, and a vulnerable mouth that made you just want to kiss him. He dressed more casually than many people in the office – most of the computer buffs did, scruffing around in jeans and trainers and T-shirts with obscure sci-fi slogans – but, at the same time, Jordan always managed to look smart. Most of the women in the office fantasized about peeling off his stone-coloured chinos and his polo-neck sweater.

'Jane wondered what Lynda thought of him. If Lynda had been a more approachable woman, the sort to go out with the team for a drink after work on a Friday night, then Jane might have asked Lynda if she, too, thought that Jordan was sex on legs. As it was, Jane could only speculate. She had a feeling that Lynda was the kind of woman who enjoyed sex. Lynda always wore chiffon shirts, sheer enough and light enough to make her bra clearly visible through the material, saying that if men were going to gawp at her breasts instead of concentrating on her proposals, then she'd take advantage of it to push her ideas through.

'That wasn't the attitude of a woman who was afraid of her body; but Jane had no idea what kind of men Lynda liked. Did Lynda prefer older men, the more sophisticated type who would wine and dine her? Did she like them young, so she could train them to her standards? Or did she like the odd "bit of rough", the kind who would take her out on a long ride on a Harley Davidson until her quim was throbbing and aching for cock and would then drape her over the back of the motorbike, taking her to a series of short sharp orgasms?

'Still, it wasn't any of her business. And knowing Lynda's erotic tastes wouldn't change anything. It wouldn't make her any more approachable – or Jordan, for that matter. Although he was always friendly towards her, that was all. There was nothing more to it than that; and Jane had no intention of making herself the focal point of the office gossips by propositioning him and being turned down.

'She concentrated on the report, her fingers rattling swiftly over the keyboard. She'd almost finished the first section when her machine bleeped. An e-mail had just arrived. She thought about ignoring it. After all, the report had to be her first priority. On the other hand, the e-mail might be about Lynda's lunch meeting, and that would affect the report. Besides, she'd already done most of the work. She deserved a quick break, to let her brain concentrate on something else, so that she'd be refreshed when she checked through the printed copy for any final errors. She checked her printer, set the report to print, then flicked into the e-mail program.

'There were a couple of private messages from friends, confirming what they were doing that night: going out for a few glasses of wine and a pizza, then to the pictures to see the latest Brad Pitt film. There was a message about Lynda's diary, someone wanting to book a morning out with her on the following Wednesday; and then there was one with no title. She frowned, and selected it.

'Her eyes widened as she'd read the first line. *I've been thinking about you all morning.* Who had been thinking about her? And why? She read on. *Fantasizing, to be precise. I'd like to be alone with you. So you're standing in front of me, looking up at me with those beautiful blue eyes. I wouldn't be able to help lowering my face to yours, and kissing you. I've been dreaming about kissing you for weeks. Kissing you. Touching you. Unbuttoning your shirt and caressing every inch of skin as I reveal it. Tracing the creamy skin of your breasts with my fingertips. Then sliding my fingers under the edge of your bra and touching your nipples; you'd be so responsive, hardening almost instantly.*

'Jane's face flamed. Who the hell had sent this to her? She flicked down to the bottom of the message; it was simply signed with a "J". Then she flicked back up to the top again, and her colour deepened even further as she read the identity of the sender. Jordan Davies.

'Half of her wondered whether it was some kind of wind-up. Maybe he had gone to a meeting and left his mailbox open, and one of his colleagues had thought that it would be a good joke to send her an erotic e-mail from Jordan. On the other hand, it could be genuine. But he'd never given her the impression that he fancied her. Her eyes narrowed. What the hell was going on?

' "Is that report ready yet, Jane?" Lynda's strident tones cut into Jane's thoughts; guiltily, Jane switched out of the e-mail program.

' "I'm just checking it through for errors. Then I'll sort out the number of copies you want."

'Lynda rolled her eyes. "I wish you'd stop daydreaming and get on with what I pay you for."

'Jane bit back a sharp retort and took the document from her printer. She checked through it, corrected the couple of mistakes that remained, then printed off the half a dozen colour copies that Lynda had requested. When they'd finished printing, she clipped them together and walked into Lynda's office. "The report's done."

'Lynda didn't look up from her work. "Good."

'*Not even a "thank you",* Jane thought crossly. *Bloody woman. Why couldn't she observe even the least bit of office politeness?* She kept her temper in check – just – and resisted the temptation to slam the copies of the report down on Lynda's hands, placing them in her boss's in-tray instead. She returned to her desk, and reread the e-mail that Jordan had sent her. The more she thought about it, the more she was convinced that it *was* a wind-up. Well, she could take a joke as well as anyone else. She created a new message, and typed in: *Come and get it, big boy. Lynda's office, twelve o'clock.* If Jordan's mailbox was still open . . . well, his friends would spend the next half an hour wondering whether she had really fallen for it.

'At five to twelve, Lynda would be leaving for her meeting, and Jane would be going to grab a sandwich. She would leave him a copy of the e-mail, with a post-it note telling him to make sure he didn't leave his mailbox unattended in future – or at least when his friends were about to send other people messages on his behalf.

'Then she continued with her work. At five to twelve, she was deep in the middle of sorting out Lynda's monthly expenses and made no comment when her boss left for her meeting. She'd completely forgotten about the e-mail she'd sent Jordan, until she felt a hand on her shoulder. She jumped, startled, and looked up – straight into his eyes.

' "I thought that I'd come and have a word with you. Twelve o'clock, like you said." He nodded towards Lynda's office. "Gone to a meeting, has she?"

'Jane flushed. "I can explain . . ."

' "I think we'd better go in there."

'She swallowed, closed the file on her desk and slid it back into her in-tray, then walked into Lynda's office. Jordan closed the door behind them, and turned her to face him. "That message you sent me."

'She closed her eyes. "I forgot the time. I intended to leave you a copy of the e-mail your pals sent me – in your name – with a note reminding you to log out of your mailbox when you leave your desk."

' "What e-mail?"

'So she'd been right. It had been a joke. Although she'd been fairly sure that it was a wind-up, she was still slightly disappointed. The idea of Jordan Davies fantasizing about her was a very pleasant one. Quickly, she tapped into Lynda's computer, logging on to the e-mail program. She flicked through her mailbox, and selected the one she'd received earlier. "Here."

'Jordan leaned over Lynda's desk to read it, then whistled. "I'm surprised you didn't come right over to me and slap my face after you'd read that!"

' "Well, I thought it was probably a wind-up."

'He looked at her, and she noticed that his pupils had

expanded slightly. "I didn't send it, Jane – but what if I were to tell you that it's true?"

'Jane didn't quite believe her ears. The office sex-god was telling her that he fancied her? Hardly. She wasn't glamorous: although she always looked smart and professional, wearing a suit to work and keeping her dark hair cut in a neat glossy bob, which she usually pushed back from her face with an Alice band, she wasn't the type to attract a second glance. Not like Lynda.

'Jane?'

' "I . . ." She really didn't know what to say.

'Jordan took the initiative, stroking her face with the backs of his fingers, then tracing her lower lip. She could so easily imagine him carrying out what that e-mail had suggested, kissing her and sliding his tongue into her mouth, then unbuttoning her shirt and touching her breasts. A pulse began to beat hard between her legs.

'He walked over to the window of Lynda's office and pulled the blinds closed. Then he returned to Lynda's desk, switching on her up-lighter before standing in front of Jane again. "Jane," he said softly. "I didn't have anything to do with that e-mail."

'So he wasn't going to kiss her. Jane's throat was dry with disappointment.

' "But I wish that I had." He glanced at the piece of paper, then at Jane's face. Slowly, he bent his head, touching his lips lightly to hers. Jane froze in shock; then she found herself responding, opening her mouth under his so that his tongue could slide between her lips and explore the sweetness of her mouth. Her hands came up to twine round his neck and she kissed him back, pushing her tongue against his.

'The next thing she knew, he had unbuttoned her shirt and was tracing the edge of her bra with one fingertip. Her nipples

hardened in response, their sharp points clearly visible through
the lace of her bra; he finished unbuttoning her shirt, tugging it
free from the waistband of her skirt, and slid his fingers under
the edge of one cup, pushing it down to reveal her breast. He
did the same with the other cup, then stood back with his
hands on her shoulders so that he could see her properly.
"Beautiful," he breathed.

'His voice was husky, and Jane knew that he wasn't faking
it. She risked a glance upwards to meet his eyes, which were
almost black, his pupils had expanded so much. Yes, he fancied
her as much as she fancied him. "Jordan," she breathed.
"Touch me. Taste me. Make love with me."

'He needed no second bidding. His hands came up to touch
the soft creamy globes of her breasts, his thumbs tracing her
areolae and teasing the hard rosy peaks of her nipples until
Jane tipped her head back, thrusting her ribcage upwards. He
bent his head, taking one rosy nipple into his mouth and
sucking fiercely, and Jane nearly cried out, it felt so good.

'While he continued caressing and kissing her breasts, his
other hand was busy hitching up her skirt, bunching up the
hem and pushing the material upwards until it was round her
waist. Jane wished that she'd been wearing something more
sexy than the opaque black tights she usually wore to work,
but Jordan didn't seem in the least bit disappointed. He merely
searched for the waistband of her tights, then pulled them
down over her thighs.

'He pushed the papers on Lynda's desk to one side and
hoisted Jane onto the bleached ash surface. Then, gently, he
continued to roll her tights downwards, removing them and
her shoes at the same time. He kissed the hollow of one ankle
and moved upwards, his mouth sure and sensual against her
skin. Jane's breath grew ragged as he moved upwards, licking

the sensitive spot behind her knee and then moving higher, kissing the creamy soft skin of her inner thighs. Her quim felt on fire, and she wanted him to use his mouth on her.

'As if he could read her mind, he pushed the gusset of her knickers to one side and urged her back against the table. Jane closed her eyes, widening the gap between her thighs, and clenched her fists as she felt Jordan's warm breath against her heated sex. And then his tongue was parting her labia, seeking the stiff coral bud of her clitoris and sucking hard on it before exploring the folds and hollows of her sex, tasting her nectar. She came within moments, and she felt him smile against her skin. "Oh, Jane. You're so sweet, so responsive. I want to do more than just touch and taste you."

' "Yes." The word was ripped from her. She wanted more, too. She wanted to feel him inside her, his cock filling her and stretching her.

'She heard the rasp of his zip, and then she felt him bend over her. He'd obviously removed his sweater, because she felt the crisp hair on his chest brushing against her nipples, the friction driving her wild. He kissed her again, his tongue probing her mouth; and then she felt the tip of his penis pressing against her sex, easing into her slowly until he was inside her up to the hilt.

'She could hardly believe that it was happening. Jordan Davies, the office sex-god, was screwing her on her boss's desk. Anyone could come into that office and see them together . . . Though she knew that no one was likely to interrupt them. Lynda's meeting wasn't due to finish for a good hour; and no one was likely to drop in on the off-chance that she would be back early. Lynda had made it very clear that if anyone wanted to see her, they should book time in her diary. Jane clenched her teeth together, holding back a cry of pleasure as Jordan began to move, his hips rocking in small semicircles as he thrust into her. He'd lifted her knees, holding her legs on either side of his waist so that he could penetrate her more deeply, and it was so good, so very good . . .

'She felt the beginnings of her orgasm ripple through her, a soft coiling sensation that tightened and tightened until the pressure was almost unbearable before exploding in her solar plexus. As if he knew that she was going to cry out as she climaxed, he jammed his mouth over hers again, kissing her deeply. The way her quim was rippling round the thick shaft of his cock was enough to tip him into his own orgasm; she felt his cock throbbing deep inside her, and then he was holding her close, shuddering as his body poured into hers.

'He broke the kiss. "Jane. Thank you."

'Before she could say another word, she heard the door open, and there was a shocked gasp . . .'

Libby smiled. 'And that's as far as we got. To be honest, I feel that it's more like part of a chapter in a novel than a short story.'

'Yes, I think you're probably right,' Carolyn said. 'Did you have any ideas sketched out about what happened next? And who was in the doorway?'

'Lynda,' Gina said promptly. 'Her meeting had finished early. And when she saw what was happening on her desk . . . Well, either she would have sacked Jane on the spot for indecency, or she would have joined in.'

'I think she would have joined in,' Sue said. 'At least, in one of my husband's books she would have joined in.'

'I'm not sure how I feel about the idea of a threesome,' Peggy said. 'I mean, I've never made love with another woman, or with two men at the same time. I don't know how I'd begin to describe it. How can you put in things that you haven't experienced?'

'Read a lot – and cheat,' Emma said, surprising everyone. 'If you imagine what your husband feels when he touches you, that's how another woman would feel if you touched her.'

Carolyn chuckled. 'I feel a complete fraud here. It doesn't sound to me as though any of you really need to be on this course at all!'

The others laughed, shaking their heads. 'I dunno,' Libby said. 'Without you to crystallize our ideas, we'd all be floundering along.'

'Well, it's nice of you to say so.' Carolyn looked at her watch. 'I'd like to set you a final writing exercise. It's up to you whether you do it here, in your rooms, or even outside in the garden. I'd like you all to write a short story for me, based on the characters and settings you thought up earlier. If you need a theme to get you going, choose some kind of special occasion.'

'What do you mean by "special"?' Gina asked.

'Anything you like. It could be an anniversary, a prizegiving ceremony . . . anything you like.' She smiled at Peggy. 'Peggy, if you want to do something different with Jordan Davies and the office, that's fine; I'm not expecting you to come up with more characters, unless you want to. I'd like you all to give me your stories tonight at dinner – we'll meet at half past eight, in the restaurant, to give you a little more time – and I'll mark them this evening. Then we'll go through some of the best ones, tomorrow, and you can all have a chance to comment.' She paused. 'Any questions? I'm in room twelve if any of you need me, or if you have any questions.' She gave everyone a thick folder. 'In here there are examples of good and bad erotic writing, plus a hard copy of my presentation, to remind you of a few points and give you some ideas about the various different types of character, which settings work and which don't, and how to structure a plot. If you don't manage to finish your stories, that's not a problem – just do a few bullet points so I know how it ends.'

'See you at half eight, then,' Elaine said.

Carolyn smiled at them all, unplugged her laptop, and left the room.

She returned to her bedroom. Rather than killing time before dinner by watching television, she decided to take advantage of the leisure facilities that Heywood Hall offered. She hadn't brought the right clothes for the gym, but she'd packed her swimming costume in the hope that there might be a pool. She rummaged in the drawer, then took her swimsuit down to the Leisure Centre on the ground floor.

The pool was kidney-shaped and it was deserted, to Carolyn's surprise and pleasure. She collected a towel and a robe from the attendant and went into the small changing room. She hung her clothes neatly on a peg, together with the towel, then shrugged the robe on top of her swimming costume. On the way back to the pool, she noticed the sauna; she decided to take a quick sauna before her swim. Again, the place was deserted; obviously the other guests at Heywood were either busy in their course rooms or had gone shopping in Cambridge. So much the better, Carolyn thought, removing her robe and spreading it across the pine slats of the sauna bench.

She sloshed more water on top of the coals, then stretched out on top of her robe, putting her hands behind her head as a makeshift pillow and closing her eyes. Part of her would have liked to strip off properly, but she didn't quite have the courage – in case someone else came in. Unless it were Kit, of course . . . Yes, she could imagine making love with Kit here. She could imagine him stripping the belt from her robe and tying her wrists to the top bench, guiding her to lean forward so that her quim was exposed to him. And then he'd rub the tip of his penis along her vaginal lips, tantalizing her, letting his cockhead press ever so slightly against her vulva and then skimming it forward again to brush against her clitoris, teasing the hard nub of flesh and making her wriggle against him.

Then he'd enter her, thrusting deeper and resting his hands on her hips, guiding her back and forth in direct counterpoint to his thrusts, increasing the friction to their mutual satisfaction. He'd pump harder and harder, making her groan and writhe; and then she'd come, her internal muscles clenching sharply round the thick hard rod of his cock. Or maybe he wouldn't tie her. Maybe he'd sit on the lower bench and she'd kneel astride him, facing him; and *she*'d be the one to dictate the pace, raising and lowering herself on his erect cock, her movements becoming faster as her excitement grew.

Carolyn shivered as she realized that she had automatically splayed her legs and that her fingers were stretched along her quim, pressing through the gusset of her swimming costume. God, she had to stop this. Anyone could have come in and caught her on the point of masturbation. This had to end, right now. She hauled herself up to a sitting position and picked up her robe as she stood. Then she headed for the pool. The water would be warm, but it would be cooler than the sauna – and she needed something to cool her down.

The pool was indeed warm, and it wasn't really long enough for Carolyn to get rid of her excess energy by doing furious lengths; she contented herself instead with doing circuits. Somehow swimming had a calming effect on her, and she began to relax. She'd just completed her twentieth circuit when she became aware that she wasn't the only person in the pool. She stopped and clung to the side for a moment to catch her breath. Her stomach lurched as she half-recognized the body powering through the water towards her.

He stopped as he reached her, resting his arms against the edge of the pool and letting his legs float upwards. 'Skiving off?' he teased.

Carolyn flushed. 'No. I set them a writing exercise, and I thought I'd have a swim before dinner.'

Kit's eyes sparkled. 'I thought that it was you, when I walked past.'

'So that's why you're here?'

He shook his head. 'Actually, I've been in the gym. I usually finish a workout with a swim and a sauna.' He gave her a sidelong look. 'Care to join me?'

She shook her head. Having a sauna with Kit would be far too dangerous. It had been bad enough having a sauna alone. Her thoughts then had been erotic and about him – and if he were sitting next to her she knew that she wouldn't be able to control herself. She'd end up making love with him, regardless of who might come in and catch them together. 'I had a sauna earlier.'

'How about the steam room, then?' he suggested.

Again, she shook her head. 'I don't think so.'

'Coward,' he teased, his voice low and husky. 'Seeing you with your hair wet, Carolyn, does things to me.'

She said nothing. She knew exactly what it did to him. Exactly the same as seeing *him* with wet hair did to *her* – it stirred up memories of Roudham Heath and what they'd done together in the thunderstorm.

'This isn't peak time, Carolyn. We're not going to be disturbed. Come into the steam room with me.'

She shivered. 'Kit . . .'

'I promise you, I won't do anything that you don't want me

to do. We can just sit and talk, if you like.'

As if, she thought. She knew damn' well that as soon as she and Kit were in that steam room they wouldn't be able to keep their hands off each other. He wasn't even standing particularly close to her at that moment, and yet her breasts had grown heavy and swollen with desire, and her nipples ached for his touch.

'Just for five minutes,' he coaxed.

Although he wasn't even touching her, Carolyn could almost feel his mouth against her skin. She shivered. 'All right.'

Without another word, he hauled himself from the pool. Carolyn did likewise and followed him over to the steam room.

'Be careful as you go in,' he directed, holding the door open for her. 'There's a vent just inside the door.'

She stepped carefully into the narrow room and sat down. Kit closed the door behind him and seated himself opposite her. Their knees touched, but that was all. Carolyn swallowed hard. The nearer he was to her, the more she wanted to make love with him. What the hell was wrong with her? Why couldn't she just act normally with him, be professional, like she would have done with just about any other male?

'It's the same for me,' Kit said, surprising her.

Carolyn realized that she must have spoken her thoughts aloud. 'Kit – I'm not normally like this.'

'Neither am I. My secretary says that I'm driven, and all the staff here think the same. They've even taken to calling me "Jack" – as in "all work and no play makes Jack a dull boy",' he said.

She smiled ruefully. 'Dull isn't exactly the word I'd use to describe you.'

'Thank you. Though I wasn't fishing.'

The steam had given their skin a fine sheen. Carolyn

couldn't help reaching out to brush some of the moisture from his face; he caught her hand and kissed the palm, curling his fingers over the place where his lips had touched her skin. 'Carolyn, when you touch me, I lose control,' he warned.

'I know.' She regarded him keenly. 'It's the same for me.'

'Oh God,' he muttered, and pulled her towards him; she found herself sitting sideways on his lap, her hands round his neck and her mouth opening under his. He stroked the bare skin on her back, making her arch towards him; he broke the kiss just long enough to untangle her arms from round his neck and slide the straps of her swimming costume over her shoulders. 'I don't care if anyone comes in,' he said hoarsely. 'I need you too much. I need to see you, Carolyn. I need to touch you, to taste you.' He pushed the costume down to bare her breasts, then bent his head to bury his face in the creamy globes.

Carolyn's nipples hardened instantly, and Kit shifted his head slightly so that he could take one hard rosy tip into his mouth. She slid her hands back into his hair, urging him on, and he transferred his attentions to her other breast, licking and sucking and using his teeth very gently to graze her flesh. She arched against him once more and he pushed her costume down still further. She lifted her buttocks to let him pull the garment down over her thighs; he gave a sigh of pleasure and eased his hands between her legs, cupping her mons veneris and squeezing it gently.

'Oh, yes,' she murmured huskily. 'Touch me, Kit. Do it,.'

He needed no second bidding and stretched out his fingers, pressing them against her quim. She sighed with pleasure as he parted her labia, his fingers gliding up and down her already moist flesh. He kissed her again as he pushed one finger deep into her sex; Carolyn returned his kiss hungrily, wanting more. He began to piston his hand back and forth and she rocked against him, tilting her pelvis and widening the gap between her thighs.

He brought her to a shimmering climax within moments; then he removed his fingers and licked every scrap of the creamy nectar from his skin. 'You taste divine,' he told her, his eyes a very deep blue. 'I want to taste you – but even more than that, I want to fuck you, Carolyn. I want to feel your glorious cunt wrapped round me, like hot wet silk.'

She thought of the scene she'd envisaged in the sauna, and a shudder of pleasure ran through her. 'Then do it,' she said. 'Fuck me. Now.' She stood up, resting her hands on the bench and leaning over to give him a perfect view of her quim.

She wasn't sure whether it was her words or her action that finally snapped his control, but he groaned and got to his feet, pulling off his swimming trunks. He curled his fingers round his cock, letting the tip glide up and down her quim, teasing her perineum; she wasn't quite sure what he was going to do, and tensed slightly. The fantasy she'd had about him on her first night at Heywood was one thing; doing it was something else. It was something she'd never done, and the idea both thrilled and scared her.

Then she felt his cock push against her sex; he gripped her hips and began to thrust, pushing in deeply. Carolyn's breath came from her in short sharp grunts as he continued to pump his hips back and forth; her groan was muffled by the steam in the room as she felt him lift one hand and smooth his thumb along the cleft between her buttocks. He pushed against the puckered rosy hole of her anus, and she moaned as she felt the digit invade her flesh.

Kit began to massage her, setting up a fast rhythm that had her baring her teeth and trying to contain her cries of pleasure.

Just as she thought that she couldn't take any more, her internal muscles contracted sharply, her quim rippling round his sex and her sphincter clutching at his thumb. It was enough to tip him into his own orgasm, and she felt his seed flood into her, the power of his climax lengthening her own.

When the aftershocks of her climax had died away, Kit withdrew gently and turned her round to face him, pulling her into his arms and kissing her deeply. 'God, Carolyn, you're so lovely. So responsive. You drive me insane, do you know that?'

'You have the same effect on me,' she told him shakily.

'What I want to do now is to take you back up to my suite, have a shower with you, and then spend the rest of the night drinking champagne with you and eating grapes and strawberries from your body,' he said.

She stroked his face. 'Nice idea, but I have work to do. My students are expecting me to have dinner with them. I can't let them down.'

He rubbed his nose tenderly against her. 'I know. You sound like me,' he told her with a wry smile. 'But later tonight, I'll call you. Once isn't enough for me, Carolyn. I need to make love with you again. I need to feel your beautiful body wrapped round mine.' He kissed her deeply. 'And right now, I'm going to let you put on your swimming costume and walk out of here. Because if I touch you again, I won't be able to let you go.'

She nodded. 'Later,' she said huskily. She bent down to pick up her discarded swimsuit, pulled it back on, and left the steam room.

TWELVE

Carolyn gave her towel and wrap back to the attendant, then collected her clothes and returned to her room to shower and wash her hair. Her legs still felt shaky from the series of climaxes that Kit had given her in the steam room. If anyone – Mandy included – had suggested to her that something like this might happen during the weekend, she would have laughed in disbelief. But it *was* happening.

She sat at the dressing table to dry her hair. Her skin was glowing and her eyes were sparkling: *the tell-tale signs of good sex*, she thought. Her lips curved. She was tempted to join in with the others in telling erotic tales, focusing on Kit – although, at the same time, this was something that she wanted to keep to herself. She didn't want to share it with anyone.

When she'd finished drying her hair, she glanced at her watch. There was still some time to go before dinner; her exertions in the pool and what she had done with Kit had made her feel slightly sleepy. She programmed the phone to ring at half past seven, waking her in enough time to dress for dinner, then curled up on the bed and went to sleep. The nap refreshed her, and when the phone rang to wake her Carolyn stretched luxuriously, yawning and picking up the receiver to cancel the alarm. She hadn't felt this good in months.

She dressed for dinner, choosing a dark chiffon patterned shirt, a pair of tailored black trousers, and soft kid loafers. She pushed her hair back in an Alice band, added make-up and perfume, then headed for the dining room. The only one sitting at the table was Emma, who smiled shyly at her. 'Hi.'

Carolyn smiled back and slid into the seat next to her. 'Hi. How did your story go?'

'OK. It's a bit offbeat, maybe; but I chose Christmas as my special occasion.' Emma shrugged, and handed Carolyn some folded sheets of paper. 'I just hope that you can read my writing.'

Carolyn unfolded the paper and glanced at the first page. 'I only wish that mine were half as neat,' she said. Emma's writing was very clear, the kind that was a joy to mark. 'How are you finding the course?'

'I'm enjoying it,' Emma said. 'I know I'm not as outgoing as Gina and Sue, but that's just me. It doesn't mean that I'm not happy in the group, or anything.'

'We're not here to work on assertiveness,' Carolyn said gently. 'We're here because you want to write erotica. And if your story is anything like the one you told us in the library, I'm going to enjoy reading it. Very much.'

Emma flushed. 'Thank you.'

Elaine came to join them, followed by the others; all of them handed Carolyn some sheets of paper. 'Mine isn't finished, I'm afraid,' Gina said apologetically. 'But I've done some bullet points so you know how it's going to end.'

'That's fine.' Carolyn stacked the papers together and put them in the folder she'd brought down for the purpose. 'I'll go through these later this evening, and make a few suggestions if I think that you need to make some changes. I'll give you all some one-to-one feedback tomorrow morning – say in sessions of twenty minutes each – while the rest of you get a chance to try out the leisure centre. Then I'll ask a couple of you to read your stories out tomorrow afternoon, and we'll have some group feedback.' She glanced at their faces. 'If you're all comfortable with that, of course; if you'd rather just have one-to-one feedback and then make the afternoon a question-and-answer session, that's fine by me.'

'I'm happy to have group feedback – on the basis that seven heads are better than one, and I could do with all the constructive criticism I can get,' Sue said.

'Great.' Carolyn smiled. 'Does everyone else feel the same?'

'Yes, Sue's right. And the group writing exercise we did really helped,' Gina said, 'although we all use different words.'

'That's understandable,' Carolyn said. 'It's like people's tastes in men differ: I might really dislike some words whereas those same words really turn you on, and vice versa.'

The waiter came up to take their order; when he'd gone, Elaine turned the conversation back to the subject of words. 'I really hate the word "cunt",' she said. 'But I suppose it's because I've heard it used as a term of abuse so often.'

'Maybe we should reclaim it,' Gina suggested.

'In the right place, though, it's OK,' Libby said. 'In D.H. Lawrence. You know, *Lady Chatterley*.'

'Oh God,' Elaine groaned. 'I can remember doing lectures about him, in my second year. He had this idea that the pillar of blood – i.e. his erect cock – could save the world.' She pulled a face. 'I think I would have hated going to bed with him. He'd have been too busy talking about his wonderful ideas to do anything about pleasuring me.'

'Not to mention using a word you really hate,' Gina said.

'I think I prefer the word "quim",' Sue said. 'Harry made himself a dirty thesaurus. He got me to add a few words.' She wrinkled her nose. 'I took a few phrases out, too. I really hate the terms "prick" and "prick-end".'

'Mm, "the tip of his cock" sounds better,' Peggy agreed. 'Or "penis".'

'The worst one I ever heard was in the office,' Elaine said. ' "Purple-headed womb warrior".'

The others collapsed into giggles. "Oh, honestly!' Peggy said. 'That sounds more like something from *Viz* than anything else.'

'It probably was,' Elaine said.

'Mind you, it's better than "his male hardness",' Gina said. 'I can't bear those coy romances – the ones where you know they really want to say cock and clit, but they end up with stuff like "his masculinity" or "the centre of her womanhood".'

'So that's where I went wrong,' Elaine said, laughing. 'They didn't like the word clitoris!'

'Mind you, all the squelchy ones are foul,' Emma said. ' "Sopping love-crack", and that kind of thing.'

'Ugh,' Libby said. 'Or when they talk about a woman's "hole".'

'Yes, that's coarse rather than erotic,' Gina agreed. 'I think I prefer "moist sex-flesh".'

'Mind you, a touch of vulgarity can sometimes be quite fun,' Peggy said.

'Yeah, but only if it's a touch,' Libby said. 'I prefer a bit of variety. I hate reading a book where a woman keeps asking a man to fuck her – it's boring if she's only got the one phrase. Especially when she could have so much more fun going into detail about exactly what she wants him to do to her.'

'So would your heroine be a dominatrix?' Sue teased.

'No. But she'd know what she wants and wouldn't be afraid to ask for it in fairly explicit terms,' Libby said seriously. 'I don't think I'm one of the whips-and-chains brigade.'

'There are nicer ways of being tied up,' Emma agreed,

surprising everyone. 'Like with a silk scarf. Something soft and sensuous that feels good against your skin.'

'That's the difference between men and women, basically,' Gina added. 'Men think with their cock, and women think with their whole body, using all their senses.'

'Does Harry ever use a female pseudonym?' Peggy asked.

Sue nodded. 'Occasionally. And he does write differently if he uses a woman's name. He writes more from a woman's point of view, and his vocabulary's different.'

'More "musky cleft" than "sopping crack", then?' Elaine asked.

'Mm. I wonder why men are so obsessed with bodily fluids?' Gina mused.

'They always have been. Look at John Donne – or Keats,' Elaine said. 'Right through literature, men have been fascinated by fluids.'

'Honeyed nectar,' Sue said.

'But definitely not "jism",' Emma said with a shudder.

'Or "spunk",' Libby said.

'I think that's what your heroine would have – in the other sense of the word,' Elaine said. 'Actually, I know what you mean – I think I'd rather read about a feisty woman who was sexually honest and told a man exactly what she wanted. I imagine that most men would like it, too, having a woman explain in very graphic detail exactly what she was going to do to him, or what she wanted him to do to her.'

Elaine suddenly realized that the wine waiter was standing next to them. He'd brought the three bottles of Chardonnay that they'd ordered; she flushed. He'd obviously overheard what she'd just said, judging by the knowing and slightly amused look in his brown eyes. She moistened her lower lip, embarrassed, and his smile broadened.

'Would you like to taste the wine first, madam?' he asked Carolyn.

She shook her head. 'It's the same wine that we ordered last night. I'm sure that it will be fine, thanks.'

He nodded. 'Well, if there's anything I can do for you, just call me.' His eyes met Elaine's again, this time telegraphing a completely different message.

Elaine swallowed. She didn't know his name, or anything about him – other than his job, of course – but he was the type she usually went for. Tall, with dark hair, dark eyes and slightly darker skin, as though there was Mediterranean or Indian blood somewhere in his family. He had a generous mouth, with slight grooves at either side as though he laughed a lot; there were no betraying wrinkles around his eyes, and she guessed that he was a couple of years younger than she was.

She glanced at his hands. His fingers were long and sensitive, and the nails were scrupulously clean; there was no trace of a wedding ring, or even a tell-tale white band where a ring had once been. She could imagine those hands working on her body, and the thought made a shiver of pleasure run down her back. Again, she moistened her lower lip, keeping her eyes fixed on his. She knew that what she was doing was obvious – tarty, even – but she didn't care.

He smiled again, and gave her just the hint of a nod; a frisson of excitement rippled through her. The attraction was mutual – and not just because of what he'd overheard her saying. She knew with sudden clarity that they would make love at some point that evening. She wasn't sure where or when, but it would happen.

They continued discussing the merits of various words throughout dinner, laughing and teasing each other; between the main course and pudding, Elaine excused herself to go to the toilet. As she walked across the dining room, she was aware of someone watching her. She knew exactly who it was. The wine waiter.

'Allow me,' a voice breathed in her ear, opening the door for her. She didn't turn to say anything to the man behind her – she knew who it was – but continued out of the room. She knew that he was following her, even though she couldn't hear his footsteps on the thick carpet.

Without speaking, he held the door of the Ladies' open for her; then he followed her through it and closed the door behind them, locking it. Elaine was relieved to see that the toilets at Heywood weren't the usual cubicle type; there was only one, so no one would come in and guess what was happening. They'd just wait outside, thinking that whoever was in there was taking a long time because she had a stomach upset, or something like that.

She turned to face him; he smiled at her and took her hand, drawing it up to his lips and kissing the tips of her fingers. 'I couldn't help overhearing what you were saying, about women telling men exactly what they wanted. I know that your course is about creative writing, and you were discussing novels – but it looked to me as though you meant it on a personal basis, too.'

His voice was low and well-spoken; Elaine had the impression that he wasn't just a wine waiter. Either he was a student supplementing his grant with a weekend job, or he was a management trainee who was going through an old-fashioned programme, spending a few weeks in each job to help him understand the way the hotel ran, the problems that the staff faced and where their service could be improved. Not that it was important. The only thing that mattered was the sheer chemistry between them.

He really was very attractive, she thought. Seen at close quarters, he was even more good-looking than she'd first thought. His skin was smooth and soft, his hair was clean, and the curve of his mouth made her itch to kiss him. Without another word, she slid her hands round his neck and pulled his face down to hers, kissing him hard and sliding her tongue between his lips as he opened his mouth. His hands curved round her buttocks, squeezing the soft globes, and then he eased one hand under the hem of her sweater, stroking her back and making her shiver.

'Tell me what you want,' he said as she broke the kiss.

'I want you to make love with me.'

He shook his head. 'If you want that, then you'll have to ask me slightly differently.' He grinned. 'You were right when you said that it turns a man on when a woman tells him exactly what she wants him to do to her, in graphic detail. And using coarse words, too – I love to hear a well-spoken woman talk dirty.'

Elaine's eyes widened. Was this something he'd done with other guests at Heywood, too? No doubt most of the female clientele at the hotel were well-off, nicely spoken; did this young man make a habit of seducing the likeliest-looking women, inciting them to talk dirty to him?

He tilted his pelvis, pressing against her so that she could feel the bulge of his erection pressing against her pubis, and she stopped thinking. Her body's needs overruled her mind. 'I want you to take off my sweater,' Elaine said, her voice low and husky. 'I want you to take off my bra, and touch my breasts. I want you to stroke them, caress them, and roll the nipples between your thumb and forefinger until my breasts are swollen and my nipples are hard. Then I want you to kiss my neck, letting your mouth trail southwards over my skin until you reach my nipples. Then I want you to take one nipple into your mouth and suck it. I want—'

He dropped a kiss on the end of her nose, pressing his forefinger against her lips to silence her. 'That'll do for now,' he said. 'We'll take it step by step.' Gently, he tugged at the hem of her sweater; Elaine lifted her arms, letting him pull the garment over her head. He undid her bra, taking that off too and dropping it on top of her discarded sweater. Then he spun her round so that she was facing the full-length mirror. 'I thought that you might like to see what I'm doing to you, as well as feeling it,' he said softly in her ear.

Elaine shivered as he stroked her ribcage, and arched against him. 'Mm,' she said, closing her eyes.

He nipped her earlobe. 'Open your eyes,' he said. 'Watch what I do to you, how your body reacts to my touch. I think you'll like it.'

Elaine gasped and opened her eyes again, watching him in the mirror. He kissed the curve of her neck, and licked her skin like a cat. She shivered as his fingertips moved in tiny erotic circles over her ribcage; she longed for him to touch her breasts, squeeze her nipples and stop the ache in her sex – but he was taking his time, making her wait. His skin seemed in such sharp contrast to her own, olive on cream. What she was seeing looked as good as it felt, and he was right – it turned her on even more, watching him touch her.

She wriggled impatiently against him, pressing her bottom back against his erect cock; he laughed softly and at last he cupped her breasts, splaying his fingers over them so that her nipples peeked through his fingers. Then he closed his fingers together again, squeezing those same nipples. The pressure felt delicious, and Elaine made a small noise of pleasure in the back of her throat, low and husky.

He smiled, nipping her skin very gently as he kissed the curve of her neck. Then he pulled away from her, drawing her back slightly before moving in front of her. 'Like I said, I want you to see exactly what I'm doing to you,' he said softly. Then he dropped to his knees in front of her, and a shiver of delight ran down Elaine's spine as he cupped her breasts again and took one nipple into his mouth. Again, she was struck by the contrast between his dark curly hair and her creamy white skin; she could see his head moving back and forth very slightly as he sucked one nipple. He continued squeezing the other between his finger and thumb; Elaine could see her breasts growing heavy and swollen with arousal, and the sight sent a thrill through her.

He switched his mouth to her other breast, licking the areola and blowing gently on it; sensations coursed wildly through her skin. She wanted more, more. 'Suck me,' she demanded. 'I want you to suck my nipple. Use your teeth – not hard, just enough for pleasure.'

'As you wish, madam,' he said, his voice amused rather than subservient; Elaine moaned as he carried out her wishes to the letter. It felt so good, almost as if a cord was connecting her breasts with her sex; with each suck, she felt a pulse beat between her legs, harder and harder.

'Go down on me,' she said. 'I want you to take off my trousers. I want you to touch me between my legs.' She felt him grin against her skin, and looked down. 'What's so funny?' she demanded.

'I was expecting something a little more . . . shall we say, explicit?'

She lifted her chin. If that was what he wanted, that's exactly what he would get. And how. 'I want you to take off my trousers,' she repeated.

He nodded and undid the button and zip of her black chinos, pulling the material over her hips and easing the garment downwards. She rested her forearms on his shoulders for balance, slipping her feet from her shoes and then lifting each leg in turn so that he could remove the chinos properly. He sat back on his heels and looked at her. 'Beautiful. What a woman,' he said, his voice husky and admiring. 'I wonder if you taste as good as you look and smell?'

'There's only one way to find out, isn't there?'

His eyes crinkled at the corners, and he raked a hand through his hair. 'You're the one who's calling the shots. Tell me what you want.'

'I want you to take off my knickers – with your teeth. I want you to open my legs, and I want you to kiss my inner thighs. I want you to part my labia and draw your tongue along my quim. I want you to suck my clitoris until I come. I want you to fuck me. And I want you to tell me exactly what you're going to do to me, just before you do it.'

'Then that,' he said softly, 'is exactly what you're going to get. Keep watching the mirror.' He bent his head, nuzzling her midriff, and desire kicked through her loins. Unable to help herself, she cupped her breasts and began stimulating her nipples while the young waiter continued to rub his cheeks against her abdomen. Then he bent his head still further, taking the waistband of her knickers between his teeth and tugging downwards. Elaine parted her legs slightly, making it easier for him, and he pulled her knickers downwards, using only his teeth, until they were halfway down her thighs. Then he hooked his thumbs into the lacy material and removed them properly. He placed the flat of his palms on her inner thighs and pressed; Elaine widened her stance obligingly and he smiled, rubbing his face against her legs.

'I can smell your arousal,' he said. 'It's rich, like honey. I can tell how your cunt is dripping for me. I know that you want me to use my mouth on you, and that's exactly what I'm going to do. I'm going to lick you and suck you, probing deep inside you with my tongue. I'm going to explore every little hollow and furl of your sex with my mouth. I'm going to suck your clitoris. And I'm going to keep licking you and licking you and licking you until you come.' He looked up at her. 'Though I take it that if you're as liberated a woman as you seem, you'll return the compliment.'

Elaine met his gaze. *Yes*, she thought. She liked the idea of changing places with him afterwards, stripping him and then kneeling before him on the tiled floor, taking his cock into her mouth and letting him watch her in the mirror as she sucked him. 'You'll have to wait and see,' she said teasingly.

'It'll have to be mutual, or it's no deal,' he whispered huskily, drawing one finger along her quim and dabbling in her warm wetness. 'So what's it to be?' He removed his finger and rocked back on his heels, watching her.

The threat was too much for her. She couldn't let him stop now – not now. She wanted him. She wanted to come. Using her own right hand wouldn't be enough. 'It'll be mutual,' she told him hoarsely.

'I was hoping that you'd say that. And now, I'm going to lick you. I'm going to use my mouth on your delectable cunt until your legs are shaking.' He smiled and bent his head, breathing in the musky aroma of her sex, and then made his tongue into a hard point, exploring the folds and hollows of her quim. Excitement ripped through her as she watched what he was doing to her, seeing the way his arms clasped her thighs and his head moved as he licked her. It was like watching her own very private movie – with the added bonus of being able to feel everything that was happening as well as see it.

Elaine continued to massage her breasts as he licked her; her movements grew fiercer, more frenzied, as he found her clitoris and teased it from its hood with the tip of his tongue, then drew the hard bud of flesh into his mouth and sucked deeply on it. As he continued to work her with his mouth, she felt her orgasm begin to bubble through her body, fizzing through her veins. She wanted to watch what he was doing into her, but the excitement was too much for her; she closed her eyes and cried out softly as her climax reached its height.

When her pulse had slowed down, he stood up, taking her into his arms and holding her close. Elaine leaned against him, feeling slightly shaky; when she recovered her composure, she tipped her head back for a kiss. He tasted of her, the sweet musky nectar of her arousal, and it turned her on even more. She wanted to taste him, too. She wanted to feel him come in her mouth, and wanted him to watch exactly what she was doing to him.

Slowly, she undid his waistcoat, then removed his bow tie. His pristine white shirt followed, and then she copied his earlier action, turning him so that he faced the mirror and then dropping to her knees in front of him. She undid the buckle of his belt, and then the button and zip of his trousers. Then she eased the material down over his hips, leaving his trousers just below his knees. She peeled his underpants from him, too, and her eyes widened as she saw his cock. It was long and thick, uncircumcised; *this*, she thought, *is going to be good*.

He rested his hands on her shoulders, and she bent her head, nuzzling his midriff. He smelled good, clean and very masculine; there was a slight arrowing of dark hair down to his groin, and it tickled her nose, making her laugh. She made a trail of tiny kisses round his navel, then dipped lower so that she could trace the outline of his cock with the tip of her nose.

He groaned with pleasure, and she stretched out her tongue, making it into a hard point and drawing it along his frenum. His grip on her shoulders tightened and she curled her fingers round his cock, moving her hand up and down until his erection was blown up to full proportion. Then she took the tip of his cock into her mouth, swirling her tongue over his glans. He moaned and she took him deeper, so that his cockhead was touching her soft palate.

Then she began to move her head back and forth, massaging his balls at the same time. He shivered, and she took his cock from her mouth, squeezing just below the frenum to delay his climax. Then she ran her tongue along his shaft, teasing him, before taking his balls into her mouth and sucking him. He groaned again, and she made her thumb and forefinger into a tight ring round his shaft, taking the length of his penis into her mouth again and rubbing it as she sucked.

'Oh God,' he groaned. 'That's so good, so good. Do it harder, baby, harder. Take me deeper. Take my cock as deeply as you can.'

She could tell that he was nearly losing control and slid her other hand between his thighs, massaging his perineum. He jerked his hips, and she continued to suck him, concentrating first on just the tip of his cock and then taking him deeply into her mouth again. She felt his balls lift and tighten, and then her mouth was filled with warm salty liquid, his cock twitching between her lips. He bit back a cry as he came, shuddering.

When he'd finished, she sat back on her haunches and licked her lips. 'Mm. Nice,' she said softly.

He drew her to her feet, pulling her into his arms and holding her fiercely. He pulled the pins from her hair and kissed her hard, not caring that he could taste his semen on her mouth; Elaine was amazed to discover that his cock was growing hard again. *He's definitely younger than me, with a recovery rate like that*, she thought.

He tore his mouth from hers. 'Thank you,' he said softly. 'I don't think anyone has ever done that so well to me before.'

She inclined her head in acknowledgement. 'I've had a little practice.'

'Whoever he is, he's a lucky man.'

Her smile broadened. 'That's corny. And I'm single, for your information.'

'I'm married,' he told her; at her widened eyes, he added, 'to my job. I've had offers since I've been here, but I haven't wanted to take up any of them.' He caressed her back and her buttocks. 'Guests or staff. Until I saw you tonight. I couldn't believe it when I heard what you were saying. You looked like an angel, and you spoke like . . .'

'A slut?' she finished.

He shook his head. 'No. Like an honest and sensual woman. A real woman, one who knows what she wants and isn't afraid to do something about it. I knew that something was going to happen between us. If you hadn't left the table, I would have found out who you were, and delivered some champagne to your room, courtesy of room service.'

She grinned. 'Perhaps I should have waited, then . . .'

He grinned back, recognizing that she was teasing him. 'Maybe. Though it could still be arranged.' He brushed her cheek with the backs of his fingers. 'In the meantime, we have a little unfinished business.'

'Indeed?'

'Indeed.' He took her hand, curling it round his erect cock. 'And I think I can guess what you'd like me to do with this. The same as I'd like to do with it. I want to be inside you, sweetheart. I want to feel your beautiful sexy quim enfolding my cock.' He backed her over to the mirror, and lifted her up. Elaine wrapped her legs round his waist, and he tilted his pelvis so that the tip of his cock rested against the entrance of her sex. Then he pushed, sliding into her warm moist depths. 'God, you feel so good,' he said.

'Mm. And just supposing that I'd really wanted to go to the toilet,' she teased.

He chuckled. 'Golden rain. I don't have a problem with it.'

She wasn't expecting that answer; to cover her discomposure, she jammed her mouth over his. He kissed her deeply, his tongue echoing the action of his penis inside her; he pushed deeply into her, taking it slow and easy and letting her climax build up to a crescendo before changing his rhythm to short sharp thrusts.

Elaine's orgasmic wail was lost in his mouth; her quim rippled round him, but he didn't stop. He kept going, taking her to a further peak; by the time that she felt his cock throb inside her, she was shuddering, her breasts mottled with the rosy flush of her climax and her eyes glittering. His shoulders were covered with the crescent-shaped marks of her fingernails where she'd dug them into his skin.

Gently, he withdrew, and let her slide down his body until her feet were on the floor again. He held her close for a moment, then rubbed his nose against hers. 'I think your friends might have noticed that you've been gone a while.'

Elaine shrugged. 'I'll tell them that I had to make a phone call, or something like that.' Her eyes narrowed. 'Won't they have missed you, too, in the restaurant?'

He grinned. 'I'll just tell them that I had to do a little room service.'

She chuckled. 'Service' was a crude way of describing what he had just done with her; yet the *double entendre* appealed to her. 'We'd better get dressed, then,' she said.

'Indeed.' He smiled at her. 'And I'm afraid I've made rather a mess of your hair.'

'That's okay.' She smiled back at him. 'I think that your trousers might be a bit crumpled, too.'

'No matter.' His eyes glittered, and he dressed her in silence, caressing every inch of skin before he pulled her clothing over it to cover her again. While Elaine restored order to her hair, he dressed quickly; by the time he'd finished, he looked almost as immaculate as when he'd first brought the wine to her table.

'We're lucky that no one else wanted to use the toilet,' she said softly.

'You make your own luck,' was his lugubrious reply.

Elaine didn't understand until they left the room and she saw the notice on the outside: *Cleaning in progress. We apologize for any inconvenience.* She chuckled. 'My God, you really do believe in taking risks.'

'Only when they're worth it.' He lifted her hand and kissed the tips of her fingers again. '*À bientôt*, then.'

'*À bientôt*,' Elaine echoed softly; then she walked back towards the dining room while he walked in the other direction. They still hadn't told each other their names, she remembered suddenly; but then again, it wasn't important. She had a feeling that she'd need something from room service later that evening – and she knew exactly who would arrive with whatever she'd ordered.

THIRTEEN

When Elaine rejoined the others at the table, no one made any comment about her flushed face and sparkling eyes. Only Peggy, who was sitting next to her, nudged her. 'Okay?' she asked, her voice low and concerned.

Elaine nodded. 'I just had to make a quick phone call to someone.'

Peggy accepted the lie easily. 'You missed Gina telling us her favourite fantasy,' she said, refilling Elaine's glass. 'As you can probably guess, it involved water. A waterfall, to be precise.'

'Mm.' Elaine shivered. She could imagine making love with the young wine waiter under a waterfall, the sparkling clear water sliding over their bodies in the sunlight as he thrust into her, uncaring who saw them.

'The sweet trolley's good tonight,' Emma said. 'We waited for you.'

Elaine flushed. 'Sorry. You should have started without me.'

'Don't be silly. I needed a break, anyway.' Gina patted her stomach. 'I'm going to have to spend the next month working out, to make up for what I've eaten this weekend.'

'But you're still going to have the Death By Chocolate with cream,' Sue teased.

'Too right. Chocolate has to be one of the world's best pleasures,' Gina said. 'Sometimes even better than sex.'

'If we're talking unsatisfactory sex and Belgian chocolate,' Peggy said, 'then you have a point.'

They ordered pudding – Gina and Elaine choosing the Death by Chocolate, and Emma plumping for early English strawberries. Peggy and Carolyn opted for cheese, Sue chose the pavlova, and Libby picked the lemon syllabub.

'I think that my favourite fantasy has to involve chocolate,' Sue said, when they'd finished their puddings and were sipping their remaining wine.

'I'm surprised you didn't go for the Death by Chocolate, then,' Gina said.

Sue shook her head. 'Not when there's raspberry pavlova. Anyway, I mean a different kind of chocolate – like Belgian chocolate, in the bath.'

'In the bath? That's a bit decadent,' Elaine remarked.

'It's the best pick-me-up I know,' Sue said.

'I thought that that was supposed to be sex,' Gina said mischievously.

'Both together,' Sue added with a grin.

'Oh, no. We're not going to hear a Mars Bar story, I hope,' Libby groaned.

'Nope. A Belgian chocolate story.' Sue took a sip of wine. 'You know what it's like when you've had one of those really hectic days – the kind where everything that could go wrong goes horrendously wrong, and you miss your lunch trying to sort things out. You feel like death warmed up by the time you get home. The only thing that can make you feel better is a long, deep, hot bath. Preferably with lots of aromatherapy bubbles, a glass of good wine, and a box of chocolates. Belgian chocolates – truffles, I think. The kind with little flakes of chocolate on the outside, rich and dark.' Her face grew animated as she warned to her theme. 'I'd have a couple of candles on the windowsill – a soft romantic glow, rather than a harsh overhead light; and I'd have an aromatherapy burner in between the candles, using the same oil as I'd put in the bath. A relaxing mixture of lavender and neroli.' She smiled. 'And some music to help me unwind. Something sensuous. Bach, I think. A Bach cello concerto.'

'Sounds good to me,' Carolyn said feelingly. 'The perfect pick-me-up, after a difficult day.' It was the kind of thing that she had liked doing – until Rupert had moved in and hogged all the hot water before a performance, forgetting to switch the immersion on again for her.

'But it gets better,' Sue said. 'Say you have ten minutes or so to let the tension soak away. Then the man in your life comes into the room. All he's wearing is a pair of faded denim shorts – cut-off jeans from several summers ago, so the material's all soft and it's tight against his body, so you can see the perfect curve of his buttocks. We're talking about Mr Gorgeous here.'

'So Harry has little cut-off jeans, does he?' Gina teased.

Sue grinned. 'He does indeed. Remind me to show you a picture of my other half, after coffee. He looks like Bruce Willis at his cutest.'

'Oh, wow, if we're talking about *Moonlighting* . . .' Peggy licked her lips. 'I used to love that programme.'

'Me, too. And then I met Harry.' Sue's lips twitched. 'Which reminds me of another film . . . Anyway, he kneels down beside you and takes the soap from the edge of the bath. Then he lathers his hands and urges you to lean forward so that he can wash your back. He starts at your shoulders and works down, soaping your skin. He uses long, sweeping strokes, smoothing upwards with his fingers and then pressing downwards with his thumbs, one on either side of your spine. Up and down, up and down, stroking your skin and kneading you, until all the hard knots of tension in your muscles have dissolved and you're feeling lazy and relaxed.'

'Mm,' Peggy said, leaning back against her chair. 'Sounds wonderful. Can we have this now, please?'

Sue chuckled. 'I don't think you'd like the next bit to be in public. Because by now, the foam has started to dissolve – as it always does as soon as soap comes anywhere near it – and your breasts are revealed to him. He's relaxed you so much that you've forgotten what a bitch of a day it's been, and you're beginning to feel aroused. Your breasts have grown heavier with desire, swelling at the thought that he'll be touching them shortly. Your areolae have started to darken and pucker, your nipples hardening; although he's still washing your back, you want him to move on to other parts of you. Other, more intimate parts.

'He's so in tune with your mind that you don't even have to ask him; he knows exactly what you need. He soaps his hands again, and shifts slightly so that he can work on the front of your shoulders. You lean back against the edge of the bath and he lifts your arm, soaping it and paying attention to every inch of skin. Your upper arms, the inside of your elbow, the sensitive pulse at your wrist, your fingers – he doesn't miss anything. All the time, his fingers are moving in tiny erotic circles over your skin; the way he touches you is relaxing you and exciting you at the same time.

'You close your eyes, and he rinses the suds from your skin before taking your other arm and soaping it, working this time from your fingers up to your shoulder. He's still taking it very slowly, very gently and sensually, giving you time to unwind and grow aroused. You can't help making a small murmur of appreciation, and he smiles, moving down to work on your collarbones. His fingers dip into the hollows, then move very slowly downwards, still using those tiny circular movements. His hands glide down over the swell of your breasts and you tip your head back, offering him your throat and willing him to move lower, to cup your breasts properly and touch your nipples in just the way you like.

'He teases you for a while, soaping your skin and sluicing the lather from you; then, at last, he cups your breasts in the way you like best, lifting them slightly and squeezing gently. He flattens his palms again, moving them over your hardened nipples in tiny circles; it's good, but you want something more. Then he cups your breasts again, drawing his fingers very slowly in towards your nipples, almost as though he's moulding your breasts into points; then, at last, he starts to massage your nipples, pulling gently on the rosy tips and making them even harder.

'You arch your ribcage upwards and his hands move lower through the dissolving foam, swishing water over your midriff. Then he moves again, shifting to the other end of the bath and raising your leg. He soaps your foot, paying attention to the sole and massaging it gently; he manages to avoid your ticklish bits, and it feels marvellous. Especially because you know that he's not going to stop there. You smile at him, murmuring with pleasure, and his fingers move upwards.

'He massages the hollows of your ankle, then moves up over your calf, lifting your leg higher and soaping the back of your knee. He soaps your inner thigh, and you think that he's going to touch you more intimately. Your sex feels hot and puffy, and you want him to touch you there, to slide his fingers over your aching quim and massage your intimate folds and clefts; but he merely washes the foam from your skin and starts on your other leg, massaging the sole of your foot and moving upwards again. By the time that he's finished washing the soap from you, you're almost begging him to fuck you. You want him so badly.

'He can see it in your face, and he leans over to kiss you, nibbling at your lower lip until you open your mouth beneath his and slide your hands into his hair, kissing him back. His tongue pushes against you, promising what he's going to do with his cock later. He sucks your tongue, explores the softness of your mouth. Then he breaks the kiss and stands up; you can see how aroused he is, because his old faded denims are so soft and thin from wear that they hide nothing. His cock is swollen to full proportion, straining against the zip.

'He unbuttons his shorts and slides the zip downwards, letting his cock spring free. It's beautiful, the shaft broad and the tip glossy and dark. You can't help licking your lips, knowing that his lovely long thick cock is all yours. You reach out to curl your fingers around the shaft, but he pushes your hands away, blowing you a kiss. He appreciates what you were offering to do, but he wants to pleasure you instead; he knows that you need it more. He removes his shorts, then bends over to guide you onto your hands and knees in the bath. You know exactly what he's going to do next, and it sends a thrill of anticipation through you.

'You move forwards, gripping the edge of the bath, and he climbs in behind you. Again, he massages your back, using those same sweeping motions – thumbs pressing in on either side of your spine as he moves down, and his fingers brushing your sides as he moves up. You close your eyes, concentrating only on the feel of his hands on your body. His hands move lower with each sweep, and he squeezes your buttocks gently. You arch your back, and he slides one hand between your thighs, parting your labia and letting his finger glide through your warm musky furrow. You push back against him, and he inserts one finger into your sex. It feels so good, but you still want more.

'He bends over and you feel his lips tracing the curve of your spine; you push your buttocks back towards him. You can feel his cock against the cleft of your buttocks, and it feels so good. You want him inside you. You want to feel him filling and stretching you. You move your hips in a small circle, rubbing against him. This time he takes the hint, parting your legs and guiding his cock between your thighs. You feel his cocktip sliding across your quim, back and forth; it rubs against your clitoris, and you gasp at the friction against your swollen flesh.

'He pushes, letting just the very tip of his cock enter your sex; then he rocks back and forth, teasing you and pulling almost out of you every time he moves backwards. You can't handle any more of it: you want him inside you now, *now*. You push backwards again so that he slides into you, up to the hilt. Then he rests his hands on your hips and begins to thrust, taking it gently so you don't end up flooding the bathroom with a tidal wave of bath water. He lets one hand drift over your abdomen and inserts it between your thighs, seeking your clitoris and rubbing the hard bud of flesh in the same rhythm that his cock pushes in and out of you.

'You're in heaven; this is exactly what you need. He moves his other hand from your buttocks to your breasts, caressing the soft undersides and squeezing gently. Everything's slow and easy, and your senses are filled with what's happening. The sweet, regular music of Bach, the cello and piano in perfect counterpoint; the warmth of the water as it swishes against your skin; the scent of the bubbles and the oil in the burner; the soft glow of the candlelight on your skin; and the feel of his body against yours, his skin smooth and his cock filling you.

'You can feel your orgasm rising through you, bubbling through your veins; it's a lazy, delicious warmth. Hypnotic, almost; you close your eyes, letting yourself flow with it. Then your climax reaches boiling point, and your internal muscles clutch his cock sharply. You can feel your vagina rippling against the hard rod that fills you, and it's so good. The movement is enough to push him into his own orgasm, and he cries out your name as he comes, filling you completely.

'Gently, he withdraws, and you both shift around so that his back is resting against the end of the bath and you're lying between his thighs, resting your head against his chest. His arms are curved round your waist, his fingers linked together; and you spend the rest of your time in the bath feeding each other chocolates and taking the odd sip of wine, until the water's cooled so much that you're forced to get out.' Sue smiled. 'And then, of course, you both look like prunes, because you've spent so much time in the bath. So you have to oil each other's bodies, moisturizing your skin. And the whole thing begins again, this time on a thick and fluffy bath towel . . .' She spread her hands. 'Now, that's what I call the perfect end to the day.'

'It's a pity that Harry's in Birmingham, isn't it?' Gina asked.

'Mm. There's always tomorrow night, though.' Sue took a sip of wine. 'I don't know about you, Emma, but I always really miss my husband when I'm away. Sometimes I think that a break does us both good – because when we're apart, we stop taking each other for granted. And things are better between us when we're together again.'

Emma nodded. 'I know what you mean. I miss Nigel.' She paused, and looked at Peggy. 'What about you, Peggy?'

'Me, too. I know it's going to sound soppy, but I usually ring Pete every night if I'm away – or if he's away on business, he rings me. I called him last night, after we'd been talking in the library.' Peggy flushed, remembering the content of their call. That was one fantasy that she wasn't going to share with the group.

'Don't tell us that it was an erotic phone call?' Sue teased.

Peggy smiled ruefully. She should have guessed that they'd all pick up on that. 'Yes, but I'm keeping the details to myself!'

'Spoilsport,' Libby said, laughing.

Peggy grinned. 'Even so.'

'I like the idea of having a massage in the bath,' Elaine said, coming to Peggy's rescue. 'Or maybe in a leisure centre. Having a shiatsu practitioner all to myself, straightening out my Qi.'

'Your what?' Emma asked, mystified.

'Qi. It's sometimes spelt with a "ch" instead of a "q", but it's pronounced with a hard "ch".'

'Like Chianti,' Gina said mischievously.

'Mm, but it's more energizing than red wine. I did a feature about shiatsu, and it was really interesting – about how the Chinese believe that there are various meridians in the body, like ley lines, and this energy called Qi flows through all the meridians. I've had a couple of shiatsu massages, actually – and although it's incredibly energizing and it's all done with your clothes on, I bet it's dynamite if your lover does it to you. Touch the right spots, and he'll be able to give you a multiple orgasm.'

'One of my housemates knows someone who does shiatsu,' Libby said thoughtfully. 'Maybe I ought to ask for an introduction.'

'It's definitely the kind of scene that you could put in a novel,' Carolyn said.

'Particularly if it's a fantasy that appeals to you – because you'll write it in a way that makes it appeal to your reader, too.'

'My fantasy would have to include ice cream,' Libby said. 'Top-quality stuff.'

'*9½ Weeks*, eat your heart out?' Elaine teased.

'She has a point,' Emma said, surprising them. 'Strawberries and ice cream.'

'Tell us more,' Elaine invited.

Emma looked slightly doubtful at having the attention focused on her; then she relaxed, taking a sip of wine. 'Okay. Imagine that you're sitting with your lover on a rug. It's a summer day, one of those hot and humid and lazy Sunday afternoons when all you feel like doing is stretching out in the shade under a tree and going to sleep. You've gone on a picnic, and you've found yourself a deserted spot by a willow tree, next to a stream, quite a way away from the road and from other people. It's cool in the shade, and it feels blissful after the blistering heat outside.

'It's just past lunchtime and you've eaten; there's a wicker picnic hamper next to your rug, although it doesn't contain very much now. You've already had the chicken salad sandwiches, and tiny crisp water biscuits with Brie, celery, and black grapes. On the way out to your picnic, you stopped in a field and picked some strawberries; both of you love the taste of strawberries warmed by the sun.

'But your lover has a surprise for you. In the picnic basket he's hidden an icebox, and there's a small tub of ice cream there. Vanilla ice cream. The expensive, creamy sort. The sort you only ever buy as a very special treat, and feel guilty because you've spent a small fortune on something so frivolous. The sort that makes your senses riot – the texture of it in your mouth, the sweet aromatic taste on the tip of your tongue, the scent.

'He's sitting with his back to the tree, and you're lying with your head in his lap. He's feeding you both the ice cream, a spoonful for him and a spoonful for you in turn. There's something so decadent about lying on someone's lap and being fed, bite by bite. Something sensual. You close your eyes, giving yourself up to the taste of the ice cream, the way it melts on your tongue. The fact that he's the one feeding you only makes it better.

'He takes a strawberry and rubs it across your lips. When you open your mouth to taste the fruit, he lifts it away from your lips so that you have to stretch up for it. Your teeth sink into the soft fruit and its juice runs over your lips, trailing over your cheek. He bends down to lick it off; and then you're kissing. His mouth feels warm and firm over yours, and you open your lips, letting him probe the contours of your mouth with his tongue.

'And then he's unbuttoning your loose cotton shirt, pulling it free from your skirt and brushing the swell of your breasts with the backs of his fingers, making you arch against him. The other perfect thing to do on a Sunday afternoon is to make love – and you know that that's exactly what you're going to do, right then and there. Outside, in broad daylight, no matter who might see you. Though it's pretty secluded where you are, so you don't feel at all inhibited. All you feel is pleasure at the thought of your bodies merging, becoming one.

'You raise your upper body then, letting him peel the shirt from you; he undoes your bra, removing that at the same time and revealing your breasts. He takes another strawberry, biting it in half, and squashes the fruit over your nipples. The fruit is warm, the same temperature as your skin, so you don't yelp because it's cold. Though it makes you wriggle when the juice runs between your breasts, sticky and warm. He bends his head and presses his tongue over the soft fruit, squashing it into your nipples before eating the strawberry.

'Then his tongue follows the trail of red juice, licking it from your skin. He nuzzles between your breasts and repeats the action, rubbing the strawberry into your skin and eating it. The difference between the texture of his mouth and the texture of the fruit feels good; you don't care that you're getting messy, or that the strawberry juice might stain your clothes when you dress again. There's always the stream to bathe in first, and then you can dry off under the tree, naked and content, lying on your rug and drowsing in the shade of the willow tree.

'He lifts your buttocks and undoes your skirt, easing it down over your hips and pulling down your knickers at the same time. You're not wearing any shoes, because you kicked them off before lunch; he tosses your clothes aside, and then you're lying naked on the blanket beside him. He takes off his T-shirt and jeans and underpants, throwing his clothes on top of yours, and stretches out on the rug next to you. It's your turn to get your revenge on him with the fruit, so you take a strawberry from the punnet, biting it in half and squashing each half over his nipples, just as he did to you.

'He laughs, and you press the fruit into *his* skin with *your* tongue, letting the juice run over his chest before eating the fruit and lapping at the red stains. Then an idea strikes you, and you take another strawberry, biting it into small pieces and spreading a trail of the red squashy fruit over his abdomen. You nibble your way down it, stopping just short of his erect cock, and he groans, pushing his hips upwards and willing you to take his cock into your mouth.

'You take another strawberry, and rub it lightly up and down his cock. He moans and you split the fruit, squashing it into his skin and masturbating him with it. He closes his eyes and arches up towards you again; you continue to squash the fruit into his skin, rubbing his foreskin back and forth, and then you dip your head to lick the fruity debris from his cock. The sweetness of the fruit is a sharp contrast to the musky tang of the clear fluid that gathers at the tip of his cock; you finish licking him clean, then take him deeper into your mouth, sucking hard.

'You work him just to the edge of coming; then you squeeze just below his frenum to delay him. Then you sit up again and eat a couple of strawberries, taking your time. He opens his eyes, wondering why you've stopped and what you're doing. Then he sees the teasing look on your face and pulls you back on the rug under him. He tickles you until you're squealing, then he kisses you hard and starts anointing your body with strawberries again. As he works his way down over your body, you can't help parting your legs, wanting him to push his hand between your thighs and soothe the ache in your sex.

'He has other ideas. He takes a strawberry without you seeing him, and slides his hand between your legs. Just as you think that he's going to push a finger into you, you feel something warm and bulky pressing against the entrance of your sex. He's pushing a strawberry into you. You freeze, slightly shocked and yet turned on at the same time; he removes the fruit and eats it with relish. He inserts another strawberry, then removes it and rubs it against your lips. "Perfect. Musk and honey and strawberry," he says. You open your mouth, tasting your own arousal on the fruit.

'And then he's kneeling between your thighs, hooking your legs round his waist and pushing the tip of his cock into your sex. You're aroused from the way he's played with you and he slides in easily, right up to the hilt. He leans back on his haunches, lifting your body at the same time and changing the angle of his penetration. Then he thrusts into you, short and sharp and hard; within moments you're coming, your quim rippling round his cock.

'He's not ready yet so he continues, stroking your skin and

kissing your mouth and fucking you hard. You reach another peak, and another; just as you think that you can't take any more, you feel his cock throbbing deep inside you, his climax lengthening your own. And then he shifts so that he's lying on his back, still inside you, and you're lying on top of him. He rubs his nose against yours. "The perfect Sunday afternoon," he says. And it is.'

'Mm, definitely. And then another watery episode,' Gina said, her voice husky. 'When you wash each other in the stream, rinsing the strawberry juice from your skin, and make love again.' She looked at Carolyn. 'Or even in a moat, in the secluded grounds of a country house.'

Carolyn grinned. 'I take it you had a stroll round the gardens here, then?'

Gina nodded. 'This place really is amazing. I could set a book here – although it would have to be an historical erotic novel. About knights coming to a maiden's rescue.' She looked thoughtful. 'I wonder if there's a dungeon here?'

'You mean you fancy writing a whips-and-chains doodah?' Elaine asked.

'Not exactly. But can't you just imagine being held in a dungeon, handcuffed to the wall, with someone like Alan Rickman in his Sheriff of Nottingham role coming to interrogate you?' Gina asked.

'Actually, yes,' Libby said. 'I don't know why, but I found him more attractive than Kevin Costner, even though he was supposed to be the villain. Okay, he hammed it up a lot, but he's a great actor.' She licked her lips. 'My house-mates all really fancied him in *Truly, Madly, Deeply*. Whenever we're all in together at a weekend, we end up watching that film and stuffing our faces with ice cream, before going through a box or so of tissues!'

'Mm, he was pretty gorgeous,' Emma said. 'Actually, I like the idea of erotic ghosts. My story's based on one. It's a bit offbeat, maybe, but . . .' She shrugged. 'It's something different, anyway.'

'I'm looking forward to reading your stories,' Carolyn said. 'Talking of which—' she glanced at her watch '—if I want to mark these before the course tomorrow, I'd better be going.' Not only that. Kit was going to ring her, and she didn't want to have to turn him down for the sake of her work. 'I'll see you all in the Blue Room at ten. I thought that we'd have a later start, as it's a Sunday,' she said with a grin.

'Okay. Happy reading,' Elaine said.

'Cheers. Enjoy the rest of your evening.' Carolyn gathered up her folder and left the dining room. Gina surveyed the empty bottles in the middle of their table. 'How about we order another and go back into the library?' she asked. 'Unless anyone wants coffee?'

'Wine sounds good to me,' Libby said. 'Everyone else up for it?'

'On condition you tell us this dungeon fantasy,' Sue said.

'You're on.' Libby smiled at her.

'You lot go on ahead,' Elaine said. 'I'll sort out the wine.'

Peggy gave her a slightly knowing look, then smiled and scraped her chair back; the others followed her out of the dining room.

FOURTEEN

When Elaine went into the library carrying a tray with two bottles of wine and six glasses, the others had drawn up their chairs by the fire and were sitting down. Elaine joined them, sinking back into the empty chair, and Libby smiled at her. 'I thought I'd wait for you before I started,' she said.

'Thanks.' Elaine smiled back, and poured the wine, handing round the glasses. 'So this is your dungeon fantasy, then . . .'

'Well,' Libby said 'Can you imagine what this place was like when it had just been built? Alongside the Hall, you could see for miles across the flat lands. The fields were full of wheat and barley, with some fields set aside for grazing for cattle and sheep. There were stables in the courtyard, and the moat was stocked with fish. Where the gardens are all flowers now, there was a herb garden and a vegetable plot. Everything they grew in those times was useful, either for food or medicine. They grew roses for scent, of course, and they used the dried petals to strew on the floor among the rushes, to sweeten the air.

'It must have been incredible to live here. Can you imagine being part of a wealthy family, wearing silk gowns that brushed the floor and showed off your breasts to full advantage? You'd spend your time entertaining high-born lords from other areas, feasting and drinking and dancing . . . So that's where my fantasy starts, at a medieval banquet, with all the local gentry invited.

'Though, as always in medieval times, there was always one

rogue among the guests, one who took things he wasn't entitled to. No one opposed him, because they were all afraid of him. He was too strong. And, like all good villains, he always dressed in black. He had a short clipped beard, dark hair and dark eyes, and a sensual mouth. A kind of Black Prince, you might say. He was incredibly handsome, well experienced with women – either he seduced them into agreeing to sleep with him, or he took them anyway and didn't leave them until they were begging for more.

'On that particular evening, he was dancing with me. It was a formal courtly dance, but he made it feel so sensual. The way his fingers touched mine – it was all within convention, well within the bonds of propriety, but I could imagine him touching me more intimately, and it made a shiver run down my spine. A shiver of fear – and of longing. Although I was afraid of him, I was also attracted to him. There was something about him.

'His eyes never left mine for a second. I could see their febrile glitter in the candlelight, and I knew that he wanted me. He told me that he'd come to me later: although he knew that I was about to be betrothed to someone else, he didn't care. He wanted me – and he was going to have me.

'Of course, I resisted him. I bolted my door that night. But still he came, tapping lightly on the door. I told him to go away. He said that if I didn't open the door, he would start banging on it and wake the whole household. I defied him, saying that my father would throw him out if he behaved so boldly; he told me that my father owed him money, lots of money, and wouldn't dare to cross him.

'I knew that we'd had some bad harvests over the past five years and my father had also lost a lot of money at law, so he wasn't lying. When he said that if I didn't open the door quietly he'd remind my father of his debts in front of everyone, I knew what I had to do. It was my duty to give him my body, to save my family name.' Libby rubbed her jaw. 'That sounds more like a scene from a historical romance, I know, but I'm not leaving things at the bedroom door and telling you that the next morning I was madly in love with him and he married me. Love didn't come into it, and neither did marriage. This was something much more . . . well, primeval, I suppose.

'Usually, my maid slept with me but, for some reason, I was sleeping alone that night. I unbolted the door and he pushed me aside, walked into the room. He closed the door and re-bolted it behind him. There was a candle in a holder on the floor by my bed; he stared at it, and then at me. "I want to see you," he said softly.

'I thought that he meant that he wanted me to take off my white shift, so I started to pull the hem upwards – but he had other ideas. He pulled the front of my shift out slightly and I heard a soft hiss; then I realized that he'd slit the material with his dagger and had ripped it all the way down the front. I crossed my hands over my naked breasts, suddenly shy and a little afraid; he shook his head, his eyes dark and demanding. "I said that I want to see you. Drop your hands."

'When I didn't, he picked me up and threw me down on the bed. He was strong, bigger than me; although I struggled, there was nothing I could do about it. He stripped my ruined shift from me and tore two long thin strips from it. He used the strips to tie my wrists to the rail at the head of the bed, then tore two more strips, tying my ankles in the same way. I was spread like a starfish on the bed; I tugged at my bonds, but they wouldn't give.

'It was obvious that he'd done something like this before, because the strips of cotton didn't dig into my flesh: they were firm enough to hold but not tight enough to hurt. My pulse was beating hard. What was he planning to do to me? Was he going to ravish me, take me and not care how I felt? Or was he going to seduce me, make me beg him to let my body melt into his?

'I soon found out. He sat on the bed beside me and looked at me, taking in my creamy skin and the rich russet of my hair in the candlelight. To my shame, I could feel my nipples hardening and my quim moistening as he looked at me. This man had tied me up, lewdly displayed to him. He had threatened my family – and yet I wanted him. I couldn't help myself.

'It was as though he knew, because he smiled at me again. "Well, my lady. Let's see what we have here, shall we?" He drew the middle finger of one hand between my breasts, and I shivered. He licked his lips, and rested his hand on my abdomen. And then he waited. I knew that he was going to go further, touch me more intimately, but I didn't know when or how. The anticipation both scared and thrilled me. He began to stroke my skin again, and then he shifted further down the bed. The way I was tied meant that my sex was open to him, and he could see how puffy it was, my labia swelling with desire and glistening with the sheen of my arousal.

'He raised one eyebrow. "So, my lady. It seems that you're not altogether unwilling, after all."

'I flushed with shame, but I wasn't going to admit that I wanted him. I wasn't going to give him that kind of satisfaction.

'He stroked my inner thighs, and then let one hand drift between my legs. He cupped my sex, pressing his fingers against it, and I shivered. "Cold?" he asked. "But you feel like a furnace here." His fingers pressed harder against my quim and I bit my lower lip, determined not to cry out. "And here," he continued, the tip of the forefinger of his other hand tracing my areolae, "here, you feel hot, too. You'd like to feel my mouth here, wouldn't you? To cool you down – or heat you up to boiling point, giving you your release."

'I refused to answer. He grinned. "Stubborn, are you, Red? Well. By the time I've finished with you, you'll be begging for me to fuck you. You'll ask me to put my cock into you – and you'll ask me the way I want you to ask me. I want to hear all kind of lewd things from your beautiful haughty mouth – and I will."

'He bent down and picked up a reed from the floor. The reed still had a soft fluffy tip; he smiled and drew it down my body, tickling my skin. I closed my eyes, willing myself to stay still and not arch towards him as I wanted to. But I think he knew anyway, because he teased the tips of my breast with the reed, moving it in tiny circles over my areolae until I had to bite my lip to hold back a whimper of desire.

'He drew the reed down my body again and then slid it between my legs. I shuddered, and he laughed softly. "Not so immune to pleasure as you like to pretend, are you, Red? I wonder if your maid's done this to you before. Or did she use her hands and mouth, licking your skin and sucking your nipples, and then crouching between your legs to tongue you?"

'I didn't answer, and he laughed again. "You're blushing, my lady. I've hit on the truth, haven't I? Your maid services you in every way."

' "No," I said fiercely, embarrassed.

' "Or haven't you asked her? Have you just lain in bed beside her and wondered what it would be like if she touched your sex, used her clever hands and mouth until you spent?"

'Again, I ignored him, and he began to slide the tip of the reed up and down my quim. My sex was already slippery, a fact that didn't escape him; he pressed slightly harder, rubbing the end of the reed against my clitoris and teasing the hard bud of flesh from its hood. What he was doing to me was obscene, but I loved every moment of it. I loved the fact that I was in his power, and that he was coaxing a response from my body that my mind refused to give him. It shamed and excited me at the same time.

'He continued to arouse me, until I arched up against him; then he tossed the reed to one side, and drew his fingers along my musky cleft instead. He must have heard me whimper, because he gave a wolfish grin and pressed one finger to my sex. It slid in easily, and he raised one eyebrow. "You like this, don't you, my lady? You like me fingering your cunt. You love what I'm doing to you."

'I remained silent, and he again raised one eyebrow. "You're going to say it, Red." Still he moved his hand back and forth, pistoning his finger in and out of me and rubbing my clitoris with his thumb. I could feel the beginnings of my orgasm rise through me, a warm rolling sensation that made my pale skin mottled. Just as I was about to climax, he withdrew his hand, wiping his finger along my lower lip. "Taste yourself," he commanded. "Taste how aroused you are."

'I fought against it, but I couldn't help licking my lower lip. He smiled again and drew his finger once more along the same lip, pushing its wet length into my mouth as it opened despite my will. He made me suck my own juices from his finger; then he stood up. "Good night, Red. Sleep well."

' "You can't leave me here like this," I gasped, shocked.

' "Can't I?" He stood with his hands on his hips. Too late, I remembered that he took orders from no one.

' "Please," I said softly. "Untie me."

'He shook his head. "A pretty sight like that? No, I'll leave you for your maid in the morning. She'll give you the release you want, I'll be bound. It might even be worth staying to watch you. Unless . . ."

'My sex ached. I was bound too tightly to escape, so I couldn't relieve the ache myself after he'd gone. He was going to leave me here, frustrated, all night – unless I did what he wanted. "Unless what?" I asked.

'He pursed his lips. "Unless you tell me what you want, Red. What your body wants."

'I remembered what he'd said, just after he'd tied me up. *By the time I've finished with you, you'll be begging for me to fuck you. You'll ask me to put my cock into you – and you'll ask me the way I want you to ask me.*

'I swallowed. I couldn't ask him. I couldn't use the words he wanted.

'He waited for a moment, then shrugged. "Well, if you're not going to tell me . . ." He turned as if to go – and I cried out.

' "Wait!"

'He turned round again, his dark eyes glittering. "Was that an order?"

'I shook my head. "A request. Wait – please."

'He nodded. "Ask me, then."

' "I . . ." My throat dried. "I can't."

'He came to sit on the bed again and played with my breasts, squeezing the soft creamy globes and fondling the rosy tips until I arched upwards, closing my eyes and tipping my head back to offer him my throat, my breasts. I wanted to feel his mouth against my skin. I wanted him to suck my nipples, to kiss me hard. I wanted him to touch me and taste me.

' "Tell me," he commanded softly.

' "I want . . ." Still I couldn't say it.

'He inserted one hand between my legs again, brushing my clitoris in a way that made me writhe and try to push towards him, needing greater pressure. I was so near the edge. I needed to come – and he was keeping me right there, in limbo. I couldn't bear it.

' "Tell me," he said again.

' "I want you to . . ." I took a deep breath. "I want you to enter me."

' "No." I opened my eyes in shock, staring at him. "I said that you'll beg me, and I meant it." His face was stern, and his eyes were glittering with a mixture of lust and power.

' "I beg you," I said.

'He shook his head. "You'll say it as I want you to say it, my lady. And you'll mean it."

'He continued to tease my clitoris and my breasts, bringing me right to the point of climaxing and then stopping until the tension had ebbed away again; stopping and starting, stopping and starting. Eventually, I could stand it no longer. "Fuck me," I whispered.

' "I didn't hear you."

' "Fuck me," I said, louder.

' "Louder." He was enjoying his power over me; at the same time, I had power over him. What I was saying turned him on more than anything else.

'The way he was touching me made my control snap. "For God's sake, I beg you – don't leave me here like this. Don't tease me."

' "Then what?"

' "I want you to fuck me. Put your cock into me." The words were shameful, but strangely powerful at the same time.

' "Ask me properly," he said.

'I could stand it no longer. I knew the words he wanted to hear. "Fuck me. I beg you, please – put your cock in my cunt and fuck me."

' "That's all you had to say," he said. He stood up again and stripped swiftly. I watched him; his body almost glowed in the candlelight, his skin so pale and in such sharp contrast to his dark hair. His cock was long and thick, standing proud from the cloud of hair at his groin; I wasn't sure whether I could accommodate him, but he smiled. "Open your mouth," he said softly.

'I frowned, but did as he said. He stood next to me, and fed the very tip of his cock into my mouth. "Lick it," he said. "It'll make things easier."

'I did so, liking his clean male taste as my tongue swirled over his glans; then he withdrew and climbed onto the bed again, kneeling between my thighs. He put his hands under my buttocks, lifting me; but still he didn't untie me. He rubbed the tip of his cock along my satiny cleft, and then pushed, sliding deep inside me.

'This was what I needed, being filled so completely. He held me up and pumped hard, driving deep inside me with each thrust. I couldn't stop a moan of lust spilling out; he bent his head then, jamming his mouth over mine to swallow my cries, pushing his tongue into my mouth in the same way that his cock was inside me. The way he'd aroused me earlier meant that I was close to the edge; I shuddered as I came, and then I felt him come too, his cock throbbing as his seed spilled into me.'

Libby stretched. 'And then, of course, he untied me – and spent the rest of the night making love with me, teaching me all kinds of new and very pleasurable things . . . I almost think I could write a novel based on that. The initiation of a young woman by a debauched knight.'

'Yes, why don't you?' Peggy said, her eyes glittering with encouragement.

'Mm, you'll have to do some research into the period – clothes, food, social life and so on,' Elaine said, 'but I like the idea of it.'

Libby took a sip of wine. 'I might just do that . . .'

Upstairs, Carolyn was lying on her bed, face down, her shoes off and her legs kicked back towards her buttocks, propping herself on her elbows as she read through the manuscripts, a red pen in her hand. She was impressed by the standard of English; on many of the courses she'd taught, she'd spent as much time correcting her students' grammar as she had looking at the content. As she'd suspected, Emma had a very vivid imagination; she was a little coy with the sex scenes, perhaps embarrassed by the explicit nature of what she was writing, but Carolyn knew that she could teach her some coping strategies for that. Like listening to music that turned her on as she wrote, or having a couple of glasses of wine to relax her before she started writing a sex episode. Perhaps all she needed was encouragement; she'd shared her picnic fantasy with the others quite easily, once they'd persuaded her into it.

Gina's half-finished story was raunchy in the extreme – more or less what Carolyn had expected. Elaine's prose was more spare, thanks to her journalist training, but her story was still interesting. Carolyn had just started to read Peggy's story when the phone rang.

She leaned over to pick up the receiver. 'Hello?'

'Hello, Carolyn.'

She smiled as she recognized Kit's voice. 'And what can I do for you, Mr Williams?'

There was a rich chuckle from the other end of the line. 'If I told you that, this would end up as an obscene phone call!'

'Indeed.' Carolyn was already aroused by what she'd been reading; an erotic phone call from Kit was an attractive proposition. Though not as good as being with the man himself.

'What are you doing?'

'Marking my students' short stories. They're very good, actually.'

He sounded slightly disappointed. 'So I won't see you this evening, then?'

'I can always get up early and finish these before breakfast. The course doesn't start until ten, tomorrow morning.' She paused. 'Why don't you come up?'

'I'll be there in five minutes,' Kit promised.

Carolyn replaced the receiver, then stacked the scripts together and replaced them in her folder. She'd just had time to brush her hair when there was a knock on the door. 'Come in,' she called. 'It's open.'

Kit entered, bearing a bottle of sparkling Australian Chardonnay and two glasses. 'Good evening.'

It was the first time that she'd seen him dressed casually, and she was pleased to discover that he looked as good in casual trousers and a shirt as he did in his business clothes. Her eyes widened as she saw what he was carrying. 'Kit, I've already had more than enough to drink this evening. I don't want a hangover.'

'Just one glass,' he said cajolingly.

'All right. But only one,' she warned.

Kit smiled at her and deftly opened the wine without spilling a drop. He poured two glasses, and handed one to her. He raised his own glass in a toast. 'To us,' he said softly. 'And to pleasure.'

Carolyn echoed the toast and sipped the wine before replacing her glass on her bedside table.

'If you really are too busy . . .'

She shook her head. 'Like I said, I can always finish this tomorrow morning.'

'Good.' He sat down on the edge of her bed and pulled her down next to him. He rubbed his thumb over her palm, then raised her hand to his lips and began sucking her fingertips. Carolyn shivered, her pupils dilating. She'd never reacted so strongly with a man as she did with Kit. Although what he was doing was hardly graphic, she could imagine his mouth sucking more intimate parts of her body. The thought made a shiver of pleasure run through her.

'Carolyn.' His voice was soft and husky. 'I have a proposition for you.'

'Oh, yes?'

'Mm.' His eyes met hers. 'I still can't get this picture of you out of my mind. The way you were when I first saw you.'

'Soaked to the skin, muddy, and with my hair in rats' tails?'

He grinned. 'A little later than that. Still wet, but almost glowing with a kind of power. It's like all the energy of the storm was concentrated in you, as you lay on the bonnet of my car. You looked so beautiful, your legs spread wide for me and your breasts thrusting up to the sky.'

She flushed. 'So where does your proposition come into it?'

He raised one eyebrow. 'If I promise to sort your laundry before you leave, tomorrow . . .'

'Yes?'

'I'd like to take a shower with you. Except I'd like to have you fully clothed, and peel your wet clothes from your skin, before I make love to you.'

Just like in the storm. The idea sent a thrill through her. She nodded. 'OK.'

Kit placed his glass next to hers, then drew her to her feet.

He removed her Alice band, placing it on her bedside table, then kicked off his shoes and led her into the bathroom. He switched on the shower, waiting until the temperature of the water had become reasonable, then picked her up and lifted her into the bath. He climbed in beside her, and drew the shower curtain across. The spray beat down on them; Carolyn's lips twitched with amusement. He looked questioningly at her, and she explained, 'It's a bit warm for rain.'

He smiled back. 'Well, if you really want it ice-cold . . .'

She laughed. 'No, I think I can cope with it as it is, thanks very much.'

'Good.'

She noticed that his pupils had expanded and his cornflower-blue eyes had become almost navy. He turned the shower full on her and she tipped her head back, lifting her face to the spray. The water soaked her chiffon shirt, making it cling to her skin; Kit gave a pleased murmur as he saw the material mould itself to her curves, revealing the tell-tale points of her erect nipples. 'Mm, that's just how I remember you.'

Slowly, he unbuttoned her shirt, peeling it from her skin and throwing it to the other end of the bath. 'And then I did this.' He pushed down the cups of her bra to reveal her breasts. 'Except you were wearing a white bra, not a black one. I was going to take this off, but I rather like the contrast between your skin and this.' He took the material between his finger and thumb to emphasize his point. 'You looked incredibly wanton, then. Your breasts so lush, their tips so hard – just waiting for my hands and mouth.'

He cupped her face in his hands and gently kissed her, nibbling at her lower lip. Carolyn couldn't help responding, opening her mouth and pushing her tongue against his. The kiss deepened and Kit pulled her closer to him, stroking her back and her buttocks. Then he broke the kiss and held her at arm's length again. 'I know you believe that you're just ordinary,' he said, 'but I think that you're far from that. There's something about you, something that just drives me insane.' He stooped to nuzzle her collarbones, then bent further so that he could take one rosy nipple peak into his mouth. He made his tongue into a hard point, tracing her areolae; then he bit her skin gently, making her gasp and thrust her hands into his hair. Then he began to suck, all the time caressing her breasts and rolling her other nipple between his finger and thumb.

Carolyn almost thought that she was going to come from the way he was touching her breasts; as if he could feel the sudden tension in her, his hands drifted lower to undo the button and zip of her dark trousers. He pushed the wet material downwards, then straightened up and grinned at her. 'I'm glad you don't wear tights beneath your trousers. I'd feel guilty if I ruined another pair.'

She remembered the way that he'd ripped her tights to give him access to her sex, and shivered. It had been controlled violence, she thought – a violence born from the storm, but which hadn't been directed at her. If anything, she'd incited it, splaying her legs and inviting him to touch her. She coughed. 'And you were intending to remain fully clothed, were you?'

'Not this time.' He blew her a kiss. 'I'm all yours. Do what you like with me.'

She smiled at him and undid the buttons of his shirt, peeling back the sodden cotton and throwing it on top of her own shirt. He was wearing dark casual trousers and she was relieved to find that he wasn't wearing a belt with them. She undid the trousers and peeled them down over his hips.

Kit chuckled. 'I think we need to lean on each other for balance here,' he said, indicating her trousers which, like his, were pushed down nearly to her knees. Carolyn leaned against him and he stooped to remove her trousers properly, peeling the dark material from her skin. Then he stood up and Carolyn bent down to remove his trousers, removing his socks at the same time. The shower was still beating down on then, soaking their underwear; Carolyn's black lacy knickers did nothing to hide the shape of her mons veneris and Kit's cotton underpants clung to him, throwing the outline of his erect cock into sharp relief.

Carolyn put her fingers into the waistband of his underpants and drew them down. Kit stepped out of them and she knelt in front of him, curling her fingers round the thick shaft. 'You did say that I could do what I want with you,' she said. She bent her head and Kit shivered as she made her tongue into a sharp point, tracing the outline of his cock and flicking hard across his frenum, teasing the sensitive groove. He moaned as she opened her lips still further, sliding his glans into her mouth and sucking hard.

She began to masturbate him, pulling the ring made by her forefinger and thumb back and forth as she simultaneously sucked and licked his stiff cock with her eager lips and tongue. Kit groaned and gently pushed her back. 'Carolyn, if you keep doing that, I'm going to come,' he told her hoarsely.

She grinned. 'That was the whole idea.'

His eyes widened. 'Are you sure?'

'Oh, yes,' she breathed. 'I'm sure. I want to do this, Kit. I want to feel your cock come to life in my mouth, and I want to taste you.'

He shivered and closed his eyes, resting his hands on her shoulders and caressing her skin lightly as she bent her head again and took his penis into her mouth. She continued to fellate him, taking it slow and easy; eventually Kit groaned, and she felt his body tense against her. A moment later, her mouth was filled with warm tangy fluid; she swallowed every drop, then stood up again.

Kit pulled her to him, kissing her deeply. 'Thank you,' he told her, his voice cracking slightly.

'Good?' she asked.

He nodded. 'You know it was. And now it's your turn.' He stripped her knickers from her, then reached up to unhook the shower head. 'I hope that you're going to enjoy this as much as I am,' he told her, his eyes glittering.

Carolyn closed her eyes as he directed the spray down her body. He'd left her bra where it was, so that it pushed her breasts up and out; he twisted the nozzle on the shower head, and directed the jet at the tip of her nipples, making her gasp.

Kit smiled, leaning over to rub his nose against hers, then moved the shower head slowly downwards. The water was at the perfect temperature – not too cold, which would have chilled her body, and not painfully hot either. It felt good; and Carolyn leaned back against the tiled wall for balance as Kit smoothed her thighs apart and ran the shower over her mons veneris. He slid one hand between her thighs, parting her labia with his forefinger and middle finger and holding her apart. She felt a dull throb of excitement in her quim: her clitoris was already hard, and she yelped as he directed the shower jet onto the little nub of flesh.

He moved the water away instantly. 'Did I hurt you?' he asked, concerned.

Carolyn shook her head. 'No. I was just surprised, that's all.'

'If you don't like anything I do to you, just tell me and I'll stop,' Kit said. Then he redirected the jet of water at her clitoris, letting the sparkling fluid massage the hard little bud. Carolyn clenched her fists as she felt her orgasm bubble through her;

she opened her mouth, crying out softly as the ripples of her climax became a torrent and then a whirlpool, sucking her down into the vortex.

He reattached the shower head, then took her into his arms, holding her close. She could feel his renewed erection pressing against her and tilted her hips forward slightly, rubbing herself against him. Kit smiled and lifted her up, supporting her weight against the wall; then she wrapped her legs round his waist and he lowered her gently on to his cock, sliding easily into her.

Carolyn bent her head to kiss him, sliding her tongue into his mouth and rocking against him as he thrust into her. Kit grasped her buttocks, squeezing and kneading them and urging her on; at last, he felt her internal muscles rippling round his cock as she reached another climax, pushing him into his own orgasm.

He buried his face in her shoulder, his lips drifting against her skin; then, as he slipped from her, she unwound her legs from his waist and he lowered her to her feet again. He switched off the shower, smiled at her, and climbed out of the bath to fetch a towel, wrapping it round her and then lifting her out of the bath. He tucked a towel round his waist, then dried her skin thoroughly.

Carolyn was touched and amused at the same time when he picked up her bottle of body lotion, poured some into his hands, and smoothed it into her skin. Then he wrapped a towel round her wet hair, turban-style, and kissed the tip of her nose. 'I'll sort out the laundry in the morning,' he told her, drying himself. 'No one's around at this time of night, anyway.'

She gave him a sidelong glance. 'And just how do you propose leaving my room, with your clothes all wet? Or did you bring some spare clothes with you?'

His eyes widened. 'No, I didn't think of that.' He grinned wryly. 'Ah well. Looks like mine will just have to dry out over your heated towel-rail during the night. I hope you weren't planning on sleeping alone.'

'And if I was?' she teased.

'Then you'll be sadly disappointed,' he told her, pulling a face at her and wringing his clothes as dry as possible before spreading them over the towel rail. 'Because I rather like the idea of drinking bubbly in bed with you, and then going to sleep with you in my arms. Not to mention making love with you for breakfast.'

'I have some work to do in the morning,' she reminded him.

He nodded. 'I know. But for now . . . let's just forget the world.' He led her back into the bedroom, pushing the covers back and pulling her down onto the mattress next to him. 'This bed thy centre is, these walls, thy sphere,' he quoted, surprising her.

'Donne, isn't it?'

'Mm. I'm a bit rusty on him now, but I always liked the idea behind *The Sunne Rising* – the lover telling off the sun for interrupting him and his lover, then asking the sun to shine and make their bed part of it.'

She grinned. 'Why do I get the feeling that you learned all the most erotic poems off by heart when you were a student?'

He grinned back. 'You could be right there. Though don't test me on it now. I think I might fail.'

Carolyn curled into his arms, resting her head against his chest. 'I dunno. I think you get a pass mark, from me.'

'Thank you, Madam Teacher,' he quipped.

She grinned. 'The pleasure's mine . . .'

FIFTEEN

The next morning, Kit's clothes were dry; he climbed into them, completely unfussed by their crumpled state, and scooped up Carolyn's still-wet clothing from the bath, wringing it out and hanging it over his arm. 'I'll get some breakfast sent up to you,' he said, 'on my way to the laundry.'

'Aren't you having breakfast with me?' she asked, surprised.

He shook his head. 'You have work to do – and if I stay here you know what will happen. You won't get your work done, and you'll be late for the course.'

'Mm, true.'

'And then I'd feel guilty.' He leaned over to kiss her. 'This lot will be ready by lunchtime, and I'll have it brought back to your room. I'll see you later.'

'Okay.' She smiled at him, then picked up the folder of papers and her red pen, to finish marking her students' stories.

At ten o'clock, she went into the Blue Room. Peggy was waiting there for her; they went through Peggy's story, with Carolyn making suggestions about where Peggy could tighten the plot, change the pace, and correct a few minor continuity errors. They'd already agreed on twenty-minute sessions; while Peggy headed for a sauna in the leisure centre, Gina came in with wet hair to discuss her story. The others followed, one by one; then Carolyn went for a quick swim before lunch.

Following a meal of roast lamb and rhubarb crumble –

which Gina said made her feel more like sprawling out with the Sunday papers and doing nothing, rather than working – they reconvened in the Blue Room.

'Emma, I enjoyed your story very much,' Carolyn said. 'Would you like to read it out for us?'

Emma flushed, but her face showed her pleasure. 'Okay. It's called "The Cat Burglar." The special occasion I chose . . . well, I think it's pretty obvious.' She cleared her throat and began to read.

'*It had been a good night*, Jim thought, surveying the pile of presents before he locked the boot of his car. Mind you, Christmas Eve always was a good night. The amount of rich parents who had dumped a heap of expensive gifts under the Christmas tree and then gone out for the evening to Midnight Mass, trusting that the children would come to no harm while they were away for that short hour . . . He wasn't sure whether to be more amused by their stupidity, or appalled by their ignorance.

'Most of them had forgotten to switch on the burglar alarm in their rush not to be late for church – or maybe it was their way of showing good will to all burglars. The locks on the front or back door were never a problem, with his skeleton key. And even the most savage guard dog usually ended up rolling at Jim's feet, waiting for a fuss to be made of him, rather than seeing Jim smartly off the premises with a snarl. Jim had always been good with animals, and a pocketful of biscuits helped with the more difficult dogs.

'He wasn't sure if he owed more to Saint Francis, Robin Hood, or Santa. Maybe, he thought, it was a bit of all three. Saint Francis tamed the animal, Robin Hood filched a couple of presents from beneath each rich man's tree, and Santa delivered them where they were deserved – to the local children's home and the hospital, with a note attached: *Merry Christmas, with love from Santa.*

'He'd had a fair bit of publicity over it. Everyone was trying to guess his identity – so far without success. This was the third year he'd done it and there were even articles in the local paper, offering rewards for more information about him.

'At first, the local journos had thought that he was some rich man who wanted to give the kiddies a Christmas treat, but didn't want his identity known. Then, when the presents had just happened to fit the descriptions of gifts stolen in minor burglaries in the week before Christmas, some bright spark had nicknamed him Santa Hood – the burglar who robbed the rich and gave to the poor and needy at Christmas.

'Santa Hood. Jim rather liked that.

'Of course, the staff at the children's hospital tried to offer the presents back to their "real" owners. But in the season of good will, who would want to seem mean and demand their presents back when they could so easily afford to replace the gifts themselves? And because he wasn't greedy, only taking a couple of small presents from under each tree, it wasn't worth people's while to claim off their insurance. It was too much hassle for such a small amount.

'Jim smiled to himself. It was just a different way of getting donations, that was all. It cut out the boring bits of charity – selling expensive Christmas cards that people didn't really want to buy when they could get a bumper pack from the supermarket with twice the number of cards at half the price. Or doing the door-to-door rounds, dressed as Father Christmas or Rudolph, singing carols and freezing his balls off for a few miserly pence thrown in his collection tin. He'd done that for two years when he'd first come to the town, and got nowhere for his pains; so he'd decided to take a different tack.

'He knew that what he was doing was illegal – but it was *inspired*. It was for a good cause, so his conscience was completely clear. Besides, the rich householders who'd been burgled still didn't take any more precautions, even though they knew that he was on the prowl and would be visiting their house in the week before Christmas. They still didn't set their burglar alarms – so, in his view, it proved that they didn't really mind what he did. He wouldn't have been surprised if one or two had actually left him a carrier bag of small gifts, addressed to "Santa Hood".

'There was always a chance that someone might see him between jobs and report him to the police – though Jim suspected that the people in the Neighbourhood Watch scheme sympathized with his cause and wouldn't report him even if they did see him. If they did, he had the perfect disguise. If anyone rang up the local station and said what they'd seen, at half past ten that evening . . . Well, who would believe that someone had seen Father Christmas, with his long white beard and red costume, climbing down a drainpipe or easing himself out of a window? The answer of the constable on the desk would simply be "And merry Christmas to you too, sir." End of conversation. And Santa Hood could continue to do his job.

'He climbed in the car and drove down towards the end of the road. It was the richest part of town, and he'd done most of the houses round here tonight. He'd got a good haul, too, from the feel of the parcels. A couple of hand-held computer games, board games, racing cars, dolls and teddy bears, a couple of large tins of sweets . . . The children at the Home and the hospital would be delighted when they opened them tomorrow.

'His smile faded to a frown as he passed the last house. He could have sworn that it hadn't been there before. It was a large house with mullioned windows, a heavy oak door, and what

254

looked like no burglar alarm. Some of the windows were discreetly lit, but some of the curtains were still open – the perfect advertisement to a burglar that someone wanted to make it look like the family was at home, when the place was actually empty.

'It was a big house. No doubt there was a huge tree in the hall, with piles of expensive presents just waiting for him. He glanced at his watch. They'd be about halfway through the service at the church now. He was cutting it a bit fine but – if he was quick – he could do it. He made the decision fast, and it wasn't long before he was in the house.

'No burglar alarm, no dog, not even a lock on the front door ... Whoever lived here really trusted to luck. Jim made a mental note to call round after Christmas and offer some security advice, in his more official capacity. They really ought to fit window locks, a burglar alarm and a decent mortice lock on the front door. Anyone less scrupulous than he was could clean them out.

'Just as he'd suspected, there was a massive tree in the hall, decked with golden tinsel and bright red holly berries and white candles. They were real candles, he saw with surprise. Whoever lived here was taking a fire risk as well. With children in the house, that was unacceptable, he thought, his lips narrowing. He was half tempted to leave the parents a snotty note, warning them to take a bit more care and alerting them to all the dangers in their home.

'He was distracted by the huge pile of presents beneath the tree, wrapped in red and gold paper, with ribbons and bows and traditional-looking cards attached to them. He picked out half a dozen of the most likely-looking ones – Santa Hood wasn't greedy, just exacting small donations – and shoved them in a carrier bag.

'He was just on his way out of the front door when he heard a sound. He scowled. Don't say that he was going to be caught now, after all this time . . . As he saw the door handle turn, he decided to brazen it out. Perhaps whoever it was had had enough Christmas spirit – of the alcoholic kind – to think that Santa Claus was a figure of his drunken imagination.

'His jaw dropped as the door opened and a woman appeared. She was the most beautiful woman he'd ever seen: tall, with long dark hair, high cheekbones, and the most amazing green eyes. And, what was more, she wasn't wearing very much. Merely a wispy white silk-and-lace nightdress and a matching negligée that barely concealed the darkness of her nipples and the mat of her pubic hair. It made his cock harden just to look at her.

'Her eyes widened as she saw the figure in the hall.

' "Who are you?" she asked. She had tried to sound firm and haughty, but he could hear the faint tremor in her voice. She was terrified.

'He was tempted to say "Santa Hood", but he could see the fear in her eyes. He didn't want her to think that he was some kind of outlaw, breaking into her house and intending to hurt her. Rape and murder were definitely not on his agenda. All he wanted were a few toys, for kids who needed them more than the rich brats who were expecting them and probably wouldn't bother playing with them again after the first few minutes. "Father Christmas," Jim said lightly.

'She shook her head. "I'm too old to believe in all that." Too old? She could only be about twenty-one, maybe twenty-two, he thought, looking at her. Five or six years younger than he was. She was probably in her last year at college, home for the Christmas holidays. "Father Christmas doesn't exist," she added, almost as if trying to convince herself, too.

' "Oh, yes, I do," he said, in true Christmas panto tradition. A plan was half-forming in his mind – a crazy plan, and one which could land him in even more trouble than his Santa Hood guise, but he couldn't help himself. This was a case of instant lust – and he had it bad. Not caring about the risk, he removed his long white false beard, and pulled back the hood of his red coat. "I'll prove it to you, if you like."

'The woman smiled at him, her initial fear gone. "Really?"

' "Really," he said, smiling back, leaning his swag carrier bag against the wall, and walking over to her.

'Her skin was very cold, he thought, as he slid his hands under the curtain of dark hair and pulled her mouth towards his. That was the problem with big houses – they cost a fortune to heat, and most of the owners didn't bother. Still, he knew a way to warm her . . .

'All thoughts were wiped from his mind as he kissed her, and discovered that she was kissing him back, her mouth opening under his and her tongue pressing against his. With a shiver of anticipation, he realized that she was undoing his Santa Claus outfit, unbuttoning the heavy red coat. Thank God that he was wearing jeans and a sweater underneath, not his normal working gear. That would have been a disaster – and would have certainly let the cat out of the bag. Though part of him just didn't care, as long as she touched him.

'He groaned into her mouth as she fiddled with the button of his jeans; his erection strained against her as she slowly undid the zip. She curled her fingers round his cock, through the thin cotton of his underpants, and he shivered. God, he wanted to feel her against him properly, skin to skin. He wanted her to rub his cock, to use her mouth on him, and let him slide into her body, in equal measures. If he had his way, she'd do all three with him. And he could do the same with her – touch her beautiful body, kiss her all over, and then use his cock to take her to a screaming orgasm.

'She seemed to sense his feelings and laughed softly, kissing him harder. She pushed his red coat off his shoulders and slid her hands round his neck, stroking his nape and tangling her hands in his hair. Jim could feel the hard peaks of her nipples through the thin nightdress and his shirt, and he shuddered. Part of him wanted to rip the nightdress from her, hear the hissing of the silk as it tore – but he didn't want to scare her. Still kissing her, he began to bunch the thin silk together, gradually drawing up the material until he could slide his hand under the hem.

'She felt good, he thought. Her skin was smooth and soft. She was still freezing cold, but his brain didn't register that. All he could think about was the way she tasted, the way she smelled. She was wearing a sweet and heady perfume that blended with the musky aroma of her arousal. He couldn't quite place it. But whatever it was, he thought, it was expensive. This was a woman with real class.

'He cupped one breast, rubbing his palm in small circles against her nipples; she groaned and pushed her hands under his sweater, stroking his midriff and then moving her hands round to his back. It was his turn to groan as she let her hands drift lower, cupping his buttocks through his jeans and squeezing gently.

'*I don't know who you are, lady*, he thought, *but I bet you're one hell of a lover*. And even better was the knowledge that he'd soon find out for himself. He broke the kiss for long enough to let her to remove his sweater; as she undid the button and zip of his jeans and eased the soft faded denims over his hips, he swallowed hard. She smiled, and took one step backwards; Jim dropped the hem of her nightdress so that the silk fell down in a crumpled mass, sighing softly as it brushed against her skin.

'To his mingled shock and amazement, she dropped to her knees in front of him; she pulled his jeans down to his ankles, and he let her help him out of them, lifting one foot and then the other so that she could remove his trainers. He was half amused to see that she removed his socks at the same time. Obviously this was a woman with definite ideas of what was erotic and what wasn't – and a man clad only in his underpants and socks wasn't her idea of a good time.

'He shivered as she knelt up straight again; her mouth was inches away from his cock. The only thing between them was his underpants. He closed his eyes, willing her to remove them; to his delight, he felt her hook her fingers into the sides of his underpants and draw them down, freeing his cock. He stepped out of the garment so that he was standing naked before her; she looked at him, her head tipped to one side as she surveyed him.

'Jim smiled to himself. He worked out a lot – that, combined with his day job and his Christmas cat-burglar activities, had given him broad shoulders and firm muscles. His stomach was flat, not flabby from drinking too much beer and eating junk food, and his thighs promised staying power. And, from what previous girlfriends had told him, his cock was a little longer and thicker than average, making women want to touch him and taste him.

'His erection seemed to swell even more as he felt her breathe on it. She curled her fingers round his cock, ringing it and cupping his balls gently in her other hand. She touched the tip of her tongue to the eye, licking the clear bead of moisture that had formed there; he couldn't help a soft moan of pleasure escaping him. Go on, he willed her. Do it. Do it. *Do it*.

'She traced the outline with the tip of her tongue, making it into a hard point and flicking it across the sensitive groove at the base of his glans; then she slowly eased her mouth over his cock's swollen tip, taking him deep into her mouth. Jim thought that he was going to pass out, the pleasure was so sharp. The way she moved her head back and forth, sucking and nibbling and licking along the shaft; and the way she caressed his balls at the same time . . . It was too much for him, and he almost sobbed as he came, his cock jerking in her mouth and filling her mouth with salty fluid.

'She waited until his cock had stopped twitching before she got to her feet in one lithe movement. Then she tossed her hair back and let the negligée fall to the floor. Her nightdress followed, falling to the ground in a whisper of silk. She had a beautiful body, all soft rounded curves, and her skin gleamed faintly in the light from the Christmas candles. Jim reached out one shaking hand to trace the curve of her breasts, and was rewarded with a gasp of pleasure from her beautiful mouth, and two dark and very aroused nipples pointing in his direction.

'Jim was very good at following clues and taking hints – thanks to his day job – and wasted no time in bending down to suckle each perfect nipple in turn. He traced her areolae with the tip of his tongue, feeling the way her skin puckered with her arousal; then blew gently onto her spit-wetted skin, making her shiver. He drew sharply on her nipples, sucking one as he fondled the other between his thumb and forefinger. Her head sank back in ecstasy as she offered him her throat; Jim ran his tongue down it before sinking his teeth very lightly into her shoulder.

'She shuddered, and drew him towards the door where she'd first appeared. Jim followed her to her room, his feet sinking into the thick pile carpet of the hall. It was the first time that

Santa Hood had ever had a Christmas present – particularly one like this – and he was looking forward to it.

'It was an incredible room. He'd had her pegged as a student, but there were no posters, either political or trendy, on the walls. Instead, there were drawings – beautiful charcoal sketches.

' "Are they yours?" he asked, looking at them.

'She nodded.

'His eyes widened. God, he could see now how she'd learned to use her mouth like that. On her models, maybe – the sketches weren't complete nudes, but just parts of the body. A curve of a shoulder, the flare of a hip, the softness of a woman's thigh. The sketches were innocuous at first glance – then, at second glance, you realized that the shape or the movement of the part she'd sketched was because the model was aroused. A back arched in pleasure – no doubt the rest of the picture would have shown a man kneeling, on the point of coming in his lover's mouth. The woman's thigh was rigid, as though she were climaxing – the rest of the picture would maybe have shown a woman sitting on a chair, her head thrown back in abandonment and her hand working madly between her thighs.

' "Like them?" she asked softly.

' "You bet." He swallowed. He'd never seen anything that had turned him on as much as that. Bare white walls, with those incredible sketches stuck onto them. A veritable orgy of pictures, as though other lovers were with them, sharing their pent-up need for release.

'And then there was the double bed in the centre of the room. It had a wrought-iron Victorian frame, with a thick mattress and what looked like a feather duvet in a white lace cover. Pictures flashed into Jim's mind – his lover, with her legs spread wide in abandon as he crouched between her thighs, licking her quim. Or himself lying on the bed, his wrists tied to the bedstead with white silk scarves, while she rode him . . .

'He pulled her back into his arms, kissing her hard; then he walked her backwards towards the bed, pushing the duvet cover out of the way. They sank onto the soft mattress; Jim smiled in satisfaction as she lay beneath him, and he began to nuzzle her body, his nose brushing the sensitive undersides of her breasts. He took one hard nipple back into his mouth, sucking gently at first, and then harder, making her groan.

'She arched her back, tangling her fingers in his dark wavy hair; the pads of her fingertips pressed hard against his scalp, urging him on. Jim gave her other nipple the same loving attention, grazing her skin with his teeth very gently, before letting his mouth slide down over her abdomen, licking her skin as sensually as a cat. Her hips arched up towards him and he took the hint, nibbling teasingly down one thigh before lapping upwards again, scenting the warm muskiness of her sex.

'As he parted her thighs and slid one finger between her labia, he discovered that she was already wet with arousal. She felt like warm, wet silk and he desperately wanted to taste her. He bent his head, blowing softly on her quim; she wriggled impatiently, wanting more, and he began to lap at her.

'She tasted sweet-salt, all honey and cream, and Jim enjoyed every stroke of his tongue against her flesh. The heat between her thighs increased as Jim nuzzled the hard peak of her clitoris. He made his tongue into a hard point, circling her clitoris in a figure-of-eight movement that had her jerking uncontrollably; she reached up to grab the rail of the headboard, her knuckles whitening as her grip tightened.

'Jim held her thighs apart and began to lap slowly, his tongue moving from the top to the bottom of her slit in one movement. She cried out, and he changed the rhythm again, alternately licking her slowly and working his tongue swiftly over her clitoris. Her breathing deepened, becoming more ragged; at last, she gave a cry and shuddered under his mouth. He rested his face against her thighs for a moment, until the aftershocks of her orgasm had died down, then moved up to cuddle her.

'Suddenly remembering his Santa Claus costume spread all over the hall, and the carrier bag of stolen presents, he was about to tell her that he had to go, when he felt her hand slide down his thigh towards his cock. It was too much to resist, particularly when her hand started playing along his shaft, rolling his foreskin and slowly masturbating him until he felt ready to burst.

'Christ, he thought. *If I stay, I'll be caught – and the whole Santa Hood thing will be over. I can't do it. But if I go . . . I'll regret it, for the rest of my life.*

'As if she knew what he was thinking, she rolled over to straddle him, the swift movement almost balletic; she let herself sink inch by inch onto his rigid cock, and the decision was made for him. He had never experienced such an exquisite sensation as that slow sliding into her warm moist depths, and he was incapable of saying anything, particularly when she began to move. She was aware of her internal muscles, Jim thought, and she certainly knew how to use them.

'She moved over him in small circles, rocking forward so that the root of his cock rubbed against her already aroused clitoris and then rocking back so that the angle of his penetration changed, became deeper. He shifted his pelvis slightly, moving in counterpoint to her to increase the sensations. He arched up to her as she pushed down to him, so that he filled her to the hilt.

'His hands reached up to cup her generous breasts, pushing them up and together to deepen her cleavage. God, she was so beautiful, he thought. He rubbed his thumbs over her nipples so that she threw her head back, her long dark hair half covering her face. It was the most erotic sight Jim had ever seen; that, combined with the way she rode him, was enough to tip him into an incredible orgasm.

'He cried out, his cock throbbing inside her, and closed his eyes in bliss as she sank down onto him again, her breasts pressed to his chest and her hair draped across his face. She smelled gorgeous, and he took a deep breath of her scent, wrapping his arms round her and holding her close.

'They stayed together like that for a while – and then Jim remembered why he was in the house. Regretfully, he stroked her hair. "I have to go now, lover," he whispered.

' "Now?" Her voice was filled with a mixture of disappointment and hurt.

'He nodded. "Now. Before anyone comes home and catches me here." He dropped a kiss on the tip of her nose. "But I'll be back. Not tomorrow – I have to work – but I'll be back to see you. I promise."

'Her smile was sweet, but piercingly sad, and he found himself almost in tears as he left her. There was something about his beautiful art student, he thought, something that he couldn't pin down, but it made him want to run back to her. Almost like saving a drowning child from the sea . . .

'Then he remembered that he hadn't even asked her name.

'*You stupid bastard, Fisher*, he berated himself. *You've just had the best lay in your entire life, and you didn't even think to ask her name?*

'Still, the day after tomorrow, he'd see her again. He'd take her flowers and chocolates, make amends for his thoughtlessness. Maybe he'd even tell her the truth about Santa Hood. He had a feeling that she'd appreciate it.

'He couldn't actually wait until Boxing Day. Christmas morning saw Constable Jim Fisher driving down the same road, desperate to see his new lover. Maybe it was an imposition, to call on her on Christmas Day, but he couldn't help himself. He had to see her again.

'The expectant light in his eyes faded as he reached the house. The beautiful mansion he'd seen the night before was nothing more than a charred pile of bricks. A very old charred pile of bricks, judging by the ivy sprawling over it. So what the hell had happened, the previous night?

'He frowned. Maybe he'd taken a wrong turning. But no – that was the house with the navy blue Georgian door, the house where he'd taken a racing car and a board game. The house next to the house of his lover . . .

'A look through the police files, when he was back at his desk, sent a shiver down his spine. There had been a fire on Christmas Eve at that house, ten years before, caused by the candles on the tree. Most of the family were all out at Midnight Mass, but there had been one casualty – the eldest daughter, an art student who was home for the holidays. She'd stayed behind with a migraine and had been overcome by smoke before she could escape.

'Jim stared at the photograph of the dead woman. It was black and white, and not particularly well taken, but he recognized her. She was tall, and very beautiful, with dark hair. And her eyes, had it been a colour snap, would definitely have been green.' Emma smiled nervously as she finished reading her story.

The others clapped. 'That's really good, Emma. I hope you're going to submit it to a magazine,' Elaine said. 'Believe me, if the place where I worked had an erotic fiction section, I'd take it in with me tomorrow and put it under the editor's nose.'

'Thank you.' Emma looked embarrassed and pleased, both at the same time. 'I have to admit it's a bit of a cheat. I wrote the story without any sex in it, years ago; I just had him kissing her, and that was it. But the more I thought about it, the more I felt that there was erotic potential in it; so I rewrote it last night, more from memory than anything else.'

'I wish I had your memory,' Sue said. 'Or your ideas!'

'Ideas are easy,' Emma said. 'I just pick a situation, and start thinking "what if" – by the time I'm three jumps away from my original situation, I usually have something I can work with.'

'That's a good method,' Carolyn told her. 'There are quite a few ways you can get ideas, Sue. Try keeping a pen and paper by your bed. If you wake up from a dream, write it down – you may be able to use part of it later, or it might spark off an idea. Or you could talk to your friends and find out what they fantasize about – that's almost like asking your readers what they want. Or if you have some kind of new experience – it might be as simple as visiting the optician, or starting evening classes, or Libby trying out that shiatsu massage – think of its potential as an erotic setting. Who could your characters meet? What could happen?'

'Not forgetting real-life situations and holidays,' Gina added with a grin.

'Or small ads in the local papers,' Elaine said. 'Especially the lonely-hearts section.'

'Exactly,' Carolyn said. 'Now, Libby – I know we always pick on you to read something, but would you like to read your story for us?'

'Mine?' Libby was surprised. 'It's a bit of froth.'

'Mm, and it's great fun. I think you've tapped into the

fantasy of dozens of women, actually,' Carolyn said. 'And you've obeyed the golden rule of writing about something you know about – the theatre.'

Libby grinned. 'Of sorts. All right, then.' She picked up her script, and began to read.

SIXTEEN

'It's called "Private Viewing," ' Libby said. She began to read aloud in her clear, well-modulated actress's tones:

' "Well, they're usually a bit tired after the performance, but I'll go and ask them," Liza said, aware of the envy in the other woman's eyes and taking a sharp dislike to her on the spot. She'd never met the journalist before, but something about the woman made her hackles rise. Maybe it was her pushy smile, the way she'd strutted backstage and *demanded* an interview with the twins, as though it were her right. It was an effort for Liza to remember her manners and act like the professional she was. "Maybe if they don't want to talk tonight they'll meet you tomorrow, before we leave for Nottingham."

' "Thank you," the journalist said.

'Liza smiled ruefully to herself as she walked down the corridor to the twins' dressing room. Landing the job as PR officer for the *I'm Your Man* troupe meant that every day she was surrounded by gorgeous hunks, attractive men at the peak of their fitness who danced like angels, sang raunchy songs, and stripped down to their g-strings to the rapturous screams and cries of their all-female audience. It was a job that plenty of women would have killed for, including the journalist for the local regional paper who'd cornered her during the interval and said that she wanted a quick interview with Jay and Jeff, the two biggest stars of the show.

'The only thing was, the lads hardly ever noticed her. Not

that there was any reason why they should. She was hardly the tall, thin, glamorous type usually found hanging on their arms in nightclubs and bars. If Liza was honest with herself, she was a bit on the dumpy side, with mousy hair and unexceptional grey eyes. Even with make-up, she was passable rather than pretty. She dressed well, but that was all she could really say about herself – and it was true of just about every other woman in PR. No wonder that the tinge of envy in that journalist's eyes had been mingled with rank incomprehension. *I'm Your Man* could have had their pick of anyone and chosen someone a damn' sight more glamorous than Liza Matthews.

'She scowled. She was good at her job; though maybe that was part of the problem. She was just Liza to the boys – the woman who arranged all their interviews and press calls and sessions at the gym, and kept things organized to almost anal-retentive standards. They weren't exactly vain, but they gave her the impression that all they were interested in was in working out to keep their bodies in shape, and being on stage for the evening performance. They certainly weren't interested in *her*. On the occasions when they did pay her some attention, they all just teased her rotten, as though she was their kid sister.

'Tonight was worse than usual. It was her birthday – and they'd all forgotten it. The previous year, at least they had made a fuss of her and taken her out to dinner – all fifteen of them! This year, there had been nothing. Not even a birthday card, or a brief hug and a whispered "Happy birthday, sweetheart". Nothing.

'She forced herself not to brood on it, and knocked on the door. Jeff and Jay were twins, and usually shared a dressing room. "Jeff? Jay?"

' "Yes?" they called in unison.

'So they were both there. "It's Liza. Can I come in?" she asked gingerly, not sure whether anyone was with them. Girls often managed to sweet-talk the bouncers into letting them go backstage after the show, and Liza had walked in on enough steamy clinches to make her wary of going into any of the dressing rooms unannounced.

' "Sure."

'She opened the door and walked in. "There's a journo outside. She wants to know if you'll do an interview tonight."

' "No problems," Jeff said – or was it Jay?

'Even now, Liza found it hard to tell the difference between them. They were both tall, with long dark wavy hair, eyes the colour of cornflowers, and with a physique that earned them jealous scowls from other men and adoring looks from women. For their particular spot on the show, they dressed in black leather, one astride a massive Harley Davidson and the other at the front of the stage, singing the Bad Company standard *Can't get enough*. It was corny, and they knew it, but the audience generally went wild. Particularly when the twins stripped off the clinging trousers and the biker's jackets they wore to reveal matching black leather g-strings . . .

' "You *will* behave yourselves, won't you?" she asked. The twins were fond of making outrageous comments to shock journalists. Though she had a feeling that this particular journalist wouldn't be shocked. Liza could imagine what would happen. They'd start off nice, then make a few suggestions, becoming more and more outrageous as the interview went on. And the reporter would take them up on it, making it clear that she was available to do whatever they wanted her to do . . .

' "When do we ever not behave ourselves?" Jay – or maybe it was Jeff – ruffled her hair.

'She scowled, pulling away. "Do you mind?"

' "Not if you don't, Liza-baby." He undulated his hips.

'Liza rolled her eyes. She was used to them testing out their stage movements on her by now. The first time they'd done it, she'd found it a bit unnerving; but she'd worked with them for so long now that she knew that it didn't mean a thing. They didn't fancy her, and it wasn't a come-on. She was just their PR consultant, and her relationship with them was strictly professional.

' "Hey, you're in a bad mood tonight. What's up, sweetheart?" The other twin came to stand beside her, sandwiching her between them.

' "Nothing." She'd rather die than admit that they had forgotten her birthday and she was upset about it.

' "You're all tense." Jeff drew a finger down her spine.

'She shivered. Anyone would almost think that the twins cared about her. She knew differently. They went for glamorous and slender blondes, not short and slightly overweight mousy women like her. The regional journalist outside was dressed to kill and it was obvious that she would get her prey. Both of them. It hit her with sudden shock that she was jealous; that was why she had reacted so badly when the journalist had demanded an interview with the twins. God. This was impossible. She had to get out of here, right now. "No, I'm not tense," she lied.

' "No?" Jay stroked her cheek.

' "No," she said through gritted teeth.

'The twins looked at each other, then at Liza, then smiled. "We know how to make you relax," Jeff said softly, untying the silk scarf at the nape of her neck and loosening her hair before she realized his intentions.

'She was too surprised to do anything but stand there while

Jeff removed her navy jacket, hanging it over the back of a chair, then did the same with her plain cream blouse. Her tailored skirt followed; Liza couldn't quite believe that this was happening. This sort of thing happened to other women, not to her. And yet she could feel Jeff's fingertips brushing her skin. It wasn't her imagination.

'While Jeff was undressing her Jay turned the lights down and walked over to the stereo in the corner of the dressing room, putting on some music. The sort of music they usually stripped to, she realized with shock as she heard the first few bars.

' "What are you doing?" she managed to ask at last.

' "Giving you a private viewing, Liza-baby," Jay said with a grin. "All for you – for your eyes only." He walked over to her, unfastening her bra while Jeff unclipped her stockings and rolled the navy nylons down her legs, kneeling down and trailing his lips along her skin as he uncovered it.

'Her nipples hardened immediately, a fact that Jay wasn't slow to notice; he cupped her generous breasts and bent his head, licking her creamy skin and blowing gently on it. Liza shivered, her areolae growing darker and more puckered, and Jay pushed her breasts together, nuzzling her cleavage and then taking one nipple into his mouth, sucking gently on the hard peak of flesh.

'Liza closed her eyes, letting the sensations run riot through her body. God, this was so good. The way that Jay's mouth was working on her nipple, and the way that Jeff was stroking the sensitive spot at the back of her knees, lifting one leg and then the other to slip off her shoes so that he could finish removing her stockings . . . It was bliss. *No wonder women would die for the twins,* she thought. They were dynamite.

'They stopped, and she opened her eyes. "I . . ."

' "Ssh," Jay said, pressing his finger to her lips. "Don't say a word, Liza-baby."

'She flushed. What the hell was she doing, letting the twins strip her like this? *At least they'd let her keep her knickers on*, she thought; at the same time, she knew that she wanted Jeff or Jay to remove them, to part her legs and stroke and lick her to a raging climax. Though she wasn't their type. She knew that. So what the hell was going on?

' "Later," Jeff said, as if he could read her thoughts. He kissed the tip of her nose and led her over to a chair. He patted the seat and she sat down; she crossed her arms over her breasts protectively, feeling suddenly shy. This was ridiculous. She'd known the twins for a long while: so why did she feel so embarrassed in front of them? *Probably because you aren't usually almost naked in their presence,* a voice whispered inside her head.

' "Just enjoy the show," Jay said gently, his blue eyes twinkling at her. She recognized kindness in his gaze, and flinched. If the twins were doing this out of pity . . . But why would they do that? Why now, after all the time she'd been working with the troupe?

'Uncomprehending, she gave up and did as they asked, sitting there to watch their private show for her. Jeff was the one with the good voice. He sang along to the CD as he and Jay danced in the middle of the dressing room, swaying to the beat of the music and keeping their eyes very firmly fixed on their audience of one.

'In perfect time, they slid off their black fringed leather jackets, letting them drop to the floor. Liza knew the routine well, but having it done specially for her was something else. Particularly when the twins were smiling at her like that. She began to understand why women screamed for them. This really was the stuff of fantasy, having two very gorgeous men strip for her.

'Their bodies really were perfect, she thought as they grasped the necks of their black vest T-shirts and ripped them right down the front, shrugging off the rags and discarding them casually on the floor. They had such strong biceps and rippling pecs: she knew that they had to work hard at keeping in that kind of shape, but it was more than worth it. The mixture of sweat and baby oil on their bodies made their skin gleam under the dimmed lights of the dressing room; it made her itch to reach out and touch them, run her fingers over their bodies and stroke down towards their cocks . . .

'She shook herself. She really shouldn't let herself think like that. God, it would ruin her professional relationship with them if she did something so stupid. She couldn't afford that. She liked her job, and she didn't want to have to start looking around for another one.

'The leather trousers were next, the special fastenings coming apart in seconds so that the garment could be discarded easily, and the twins danced in front of Liza clad only in their leather g-strings. Very small and very tight black leather g-strings, which only just covered the bulges at their groins. It was obvious that they both had erections; but then again, that was all part of the performance, Liza knew. It was nothing to do with her. It was just the adrenalin and excitement of performing, and it happened to all dancers, actors and entertainers.

'As the track finished, they turned their backs and touched their toes, revealing their perfectly contoured thighs and buttocks, and whipped off their g-strings. Liza, recognizing the end of the show, clapped. This was usually when the lights went out, allowing the twins to leave the stage without compromising their naked bodies – much to the disappointment of the audience, who usually screamed out that they wanted the boys to turn round, show them everything. "Very good," she said.

' "We haven't finished yet," they chorused, standing up and turning round, with the lights still on.

'Liza gasped at the two perfect erect penises that faced her. In all the time she'd spent looking after the troupe, she'd never once seen them naked. She wasn't sure whether to be more embarrassed or thrilled or scared. Embarrassed, because this kind of thing didn't usually happen; thrilled, because it was a beautiful sight; or scared, because she didn't know where this was going to lead.

'The twins made the decision for her. Jay changed the music to something bluesy and soft and they came to stand beside her. Each twin took one of her hands and placed it on his erect penis. Liza made one last attempt at being professional. "What about the interview?" she asked, her voice slightly squeaky.

' "We're a bit too busy, right now," they said with a grin.

'Each twin reached out a hand to touch a breast. Liza gasped, a sharp intake of breath. This wasn't happening. It wasn't Jeff and Jay stroking her skin, each paying attention to a nipple, bending down to lick and suck her skin, then blowing on the erect nubs of flesh in a way that made her moan softly. It wasn't the gorgeous twins kneeling down beside her and feathering caresses up her legs, smoothing over her calves and moving lightly and very purposefully across her thighs, parting her legs wider to give them easier access to her sex.

'She blinked hard. It *was* true. She really *was* naked in the twins' dressing room. Jeff – or was it Jay? – was kneeling to one side, leaning over to kiss her breasts, sucking on one hardened rosy nipple while rotating the other between his finger and thumb, and Jay – or was it Jeff? – was kneeling between her legs, kissing the soft creamy skin of her inner thighs and moving purposefully upwards, breathing on her quim and making her shiver.

'Two skilled pairs of hands were stroking her body, two perfect mouths were creating havoc with her nerve endings, and two pairs of cornflower-blue eyes met hers, sparkling with mischief and affection, as she stared at them in amazement.

'She knew that she ought to stop this. It was totally unprofessional . . . and totally wonderful. *What the hell*, she thought. *It's my birthday, and I'm damn well going to enjoy myself.*

'The twins, sensing her change in mood, picked her up and laid her on a towel that had appeared, as if by magic, in the middle of the floor. The next thing Liza knew, Jay – or Jeff – had picked up a bottle of baby oil and poured some onto her midriff.

'*They really are expert at this*, Liza thought dreamily, as they began to massage the oil into her skin. Though they'd had enough practice at it, oiling themselves before each show. Or maybe they oiled each other . . .

'She closed her eyes in bliss, enjoying the sensation of their fingers stroking her body, from the soft undersides of her breasts to her midriff to her thighs. It was a leisurely massage, designed to relax her, and it did the trick. All the day's tensions drained out of her and she concentrated on the twins' erotic ministrations, the journalist outside forgotten.

'One of the twins was kissing her, his tongue running along her lower lip until she opened her mouth to kiss him back. His fingers teased her nipples, tugging gently at them in a way that made her arch up towards him. The other twin was working from her feet upwards, sucking her toes and nibbling his way over her calves, licking the sensitive spot at the back of her knees and then working up over her thighs. Her solar plexus tightened as she realized that they were both touching her body in perfect time to the music; she allowed Jeff or Jay – she still wasn't sure which one it was – to widen the gap between her thighs.

' "Oh, yes," she sighed into one twin's mouth as the other began to lick at the soft folds of her sex, parting her labia with an expert tongue and circling the erect bud of her clitoris before taking it into his mouth and sucking hard.

'The twin who was kissing her mouth stopped what he was doing, stroking her face; she opened her eyes and looked up at him. He smiled at her. "Lovely Liza. You're so soft and warm – isn't she, Jay?"

'So it was Jeff who was kissing her, and Jay who was working on her sex, making her aroused and languorous at the same time.

' "Mm," the other breathed into her quim. "She tastes sweet, too. Vanilla and honey – like the best ice cream. I could do this all night."

'Jeff ran his forefinger along her lower lip, and she reached up to nibble it. He grinned, and nudged his brother. "My turn, I think."

'Jay gave an exaggeratedly disgruntled sigh, and shifted to kneel beside Liza. He kissed his way up her body, lingering over her navel and finally rubbing his face between her breasts.

'Liza grinned at the twins as Jeff shifted to take Jay's place. From being the worst birthday she'd ever spent, it was fast becoming the best. Particularly as that bitchy journalist was probably standing backstage waiting, wondering what was going on and steaming quietly with fury and jealousy if she'd worked it out. The twins didn't go for bottle blondes after all, it seemed . . .

'Jeff's technique was slightly different from Jay's, more nibbly and less licky, she decided as he crouched between her thighs and began working on her quim, tracing the folds and hollows of her sex and nipping gently at her labia. He pushed his tongue deep into her vagina, making her gasp; then moved his head again to work on her clitoris while his finger replaced his tongue in her warm wet channel.

'He moved his hand back and forth, adding a second finger and a third; Liza shuddered with pleasure as she felt her climax building. All the time, Jay was kissing her deeply, his tongue probing her mouth in exactly the same rhythm as his twin's fingers were probing her quim. Jay stroked her abdomen, moving upwards to caress the soft undersides of her breasts, his fingers moving in tiny erotic brushing movements that made her arch up, wanting more.

'Jeff's skilful mouth continued to play with her clitoris, and he quickened the rhythm of his fingers, pumping in and out of her and driving her to a higher pitch. She writhed beneath his touch, bucking her hips and clenching her fists as her climax rose through her. At last, she cried out into Jay's mouth and came, her internal muscles contracting sharply around Jeff's fingers.

'They waited until her pulse had slowed again, stroking her body and whispering sweet endearments; then they gently turned her over, guiding her onto her hands and knees. They kept in their relative positions, Jeff behind her and Jay kneeling in front of her; Jay bent his head to kiss her again, and Jeff stroked her back and buttocks, widening her stance slightly.

'She became aware that something was pressing against the entrance of her sex. It wasn't Jeff's fingers this time, but the tip of his hard cock. She moved slightly, spreading her legs wider and pushing her bottom upwards and back to give him easier access, and he slid into her, his long thick cock filling her and stretching her.

'Almost at the same time, Jay tipped his pelvis towards her and tangled his hands in her hair; his penis nudged against her lips. Liza opened her mouth and swirled her tongue along his glans, pressing the tip of her tongue against the tiny clear bead of fluid that sat in the eye of his cock. He tasted fresh and male; obviously they'd both had a shower since they'd left the stage. It left her wondering precisely why they'd been oiled and dressed in their stage gear when she'd come into their dressing room; then all coherent thought left her as Jeff began to move, varying the speed and length of his thrusts. She pushed back towards him, arching her back so he could penetrate her more deeply. God, it felt so good, so good; particularly when he curved one hand round her midriff and let it drift down between her thighs, seeking and finding her clitoris. She was thrilled to discover that he was moving in time to the music, his cock and his finger moving in perfect counterpoint.

'Jay, at the same time, was massaging her scalp, urging her on as she fellated him – again, in time to the music. *This could go on all night*, she thought dreamily, *and I still wouldn't want it to end*. She could feel her climax beginning to rise again, a warm bubbling feeling that spread through her veins and made her feel as though she were floating; and then she reached the peak, her internal muscles convulsing hard around Jeff's cock.

'The way that her quim rippled round his was enough to tip him into his own climax; she could feel his cock throbbing deep inside her, and her moan of pleasure bubbled around Jay's cock. At the same instant, she could feel Jay's body tense against her, and he cried out, filling her mouth with warm salty fluid.

'They remained there until the aftershocks of their orgasms had ebbed away; then Jeff bent over to kiss her spine, withdrawing from her, and Jay stroked her face, moving backwards. They guided her over onto her back, then shifted so that they were lying either side of her, curling her into their arms.

' "Happy birthday, sweetheart," they said in unison.

'She kissed them both lightly. "And I thought that you'd forgotten."

'They shook their heads. "We wanted to give you something different for your birthday. And keep it a surprise."

'She grinned. "You succeeded – on both counts!" Her face changed. "Oh God, that journalist . . ."

' "A set-up," they said, surprising her.

' "She's our cousin," Jeff explained. "She's an actress."

' "You always seem to avoid us after the show – you're always too busy sorting out the photo calls, and then by the time it's all over you've disappeared back to your hotel room," Jay said.

' "So it was the only way we could think of to lure you into our dressing room – Ally pretending that she was a journalist," Jeff added. "The type you've always said that you hate – pushy and a bit tarty."

'Liza surprised them both by bursting into giggles. "And there I was, thinking that she was after your body."

' "And all the time, we were after yours." Jay grinned. "By the way, the rest of the guys say happy birthday, too. There's a cake waiting for you in your hotel room."

' "Though they'll have to wait until tomorrow for their share," Jeff said. "Tonight's a private viewing – for just the three of us . . ." '

Libby smiled. 'And that's it.'

'Wow, what a fantasy,' Gina said. 'Two gorgeous young studs at the same time. Yes, please.'

'I went to one of those girly evenings,' Sue said, 'in Birmingham. A crowd of us went. We'd had a few drinks beforehand, like just about every other woman in the theatre. I found it a bit embarrassing, with all these old biddies cackling at the front and yelling to the dancers – "Show us your willy!" – but I could appreciate it, at the same time. There was one who dressed in black leather and peeled it off in the shower that had been installed on the stage; I really could have gone for him. And I love the sound of your twins.'

'Thanks,' Libby said. 'So do I; unfortunately, I don't know any.'

'But you must know some really gorgeous men, being an actress,' Peggy said.

Libby shook her head. 'They usually have an ego to match; that, or they're incredibly ambitious and aren't interested in anything that won't further their career.' She shrugged. 'Ah, well.'

Carolyn could really identify with that. Libby could have been describing Rupert – gorgeous, but with a huge ego. She pushed the thought away. Rupert had no place here. 'Best to stick to the fantasy, then,' she said lightly.

'Indeed.' Libby smiled back at her.

SEVENTEEN

When the group had finished discussing the stories they'd heard, Carolyn switched back to her presentation, displaying another screen. 'You might like to consider giving yourself a set of action points, things you'll follow up from the course, to make the most of what you've learned,' she said. 'Otherwise you're in danger of putting your course notes away and forgetting about it all. I'd suggest that you decide whether you want to write a novel or a short story first, and then pick your market. Once you've decided that, read as many issues as you can of the magazine you want to target, or as many different books by different authors published by the imprint you want to write for, in the case of a novel. You also need to set aside some regular time to write – it doesn't have to be every day as long as it's a regular time. Make yourself write a set number of words in that time, and it'll soon become second nature.'

'What if you get writer's block?' Libby asked.

'Whether it's a novel, a story or an article, the worst thing you can do is to panic about it – right, Elaine?' Carolyn asked.

Elaine nodded. 'I always find that the nearer the deadline gets, the worse the block gets!'

'So how can we break the block?' Gina asked.

Carolyn switched to another slide. 'The most important thing is to go and do something else. It doesn't matter whether it's something you hate doing, like ironing, or something nice like a long deep bath. Call a friend, watch a film, read a book –

anything that's not related to where you're stuck with your novel or story. It might take a day or so, but you'll wake up with some good ideas about what to do with your story. Usually when you're nowhere near your manuscript, and when you don't have time to do anything about it! But if it's a good idea, you'll remember it.'

'Right. So grabbing your partner for a long erotic session won't help, then?' Libby asked.

Carolyn chuckled. 'If it takes your mind off your book, then go for it!' She paused. 'Does anyone else have any questions?'

The others shook their heads.

She switched off the overhead projector and handed them all another pack. 'There's a questionnaire inside it, as well as some useful contact names and numbers,' she told them. 'I'd like you to give me some feedback on the course when you get home. There's a business reply envelope, too, so it won't cost you anything to return it. I'd just like to know how you thought the course went, where we could improve it for the future, and if there's anything you think we didn't cover.'

'I've enjoyed it,' Gina said.

'Me, too,' Peggy said. 'I feel inspired to go home and work on a novel now. I think I know how to structure it, after reading your handouts.'

Carolyn smiled at them. 'Good. But, like I said, if there's anything you think I've missed, just let me know. And if I can be of any help, my number's in the pack.'

They left the room, chatting animatedly; Carolyn returned to her bedroom. Kit had been as good as his word: the clothes that he had peeled so erotically from her body the night before had been laundered and were sitting neatly on the bed. She had half-expected to find a note from him, too, but there was nothing; frowning, she packed her weekend bag, then dialled his extension.

There was no answer; she cleared the line, and dialled zero.

The receptionist answered within two rings. 'Reception. How can I help?'

'Could I speak to Kit Williams, please?' she asked. 'It's Carolyn Saunders in room twelve.'

'I'm afraid that Mr Williams has been called away,' the receptionist said. 'Can I take a message, and ask him to contact you when he returns?'

Carolyn shook her head, then smiled at herself. How ridiculous. Of course the receptionist couldn't see her. 'Thanks, but it's all right. I'll call him later.' She replaced the receiver. Well, in some ways this was easier. No painful goodbyes, no promises that neither of them would be able to keep. The weekend could remain just as a very happy memory.

She took her bags down to her car. Kit's BMW was nowhere to be seen, so he really had been called away. Deep inside, she had wondered if he was perhaps avoiding her, pretending to be unavailable so that he didn't have to face her. But Kit wasn't like that. He was too honest. The complete opposite of Rupert, in fact. For a moment, she contemplated leaving him a note; then she decided against it. He probably wouldn't expect it, and she didn't want to make a fool of herself. The last thing she wanted was for Kit to think that she was some clingy, weak female. Shrugging, she climbed into the car, switched on the ignition, turned the car round, and headed for home.

She switched on the stereo, pushing in the tape and turning up the volume. She hadn't changed the tape from the Bon Jovi tracks she'd been listening to on the Friday night, but this time the music didn't upset her. She was over her broken relationship; instead of making her dwell on her misery, the soft rock made her want to sing along. She smiled and began singing in harmony with Jon Bon Jovi, enjoying herself tremendously. This was real driving music.

It's been quite a weekend, she thought. She had certainly got Rupert out of her system. No one in the group had seemed to regard her as a power-crazy bitch; and Kit had proved beyond doubt that she was not frigid. Far from it. He had probably brought her to more climaxes over the weekend than Rupert had in a month.

Her lips curved as she reached Roudham Heath. When she had had that flat tyre on the way down, she had been angry and upset, thinking that it would set the tone of the weekend and that it would be awful. And yet that flat tyre had actually been the making of her weekend. She would still have met Kit without that incident – but their meetings would have been on a far more formal and professional basis. There certainly wouldn't have been that keenly erotic charge between them.

She pulled into a garage to fill up with petrol. Then, on impulse, she bought a large box of chocolates and a bunch of flowers. She decided to call in to see Mandy on her way home, and tell her about the weekend. Just about the course . . . Or maybe she might confess about what had happened with Kit Williams. She wanted to tell someone about it, and Mandy was the best possible person.

Forty minutes later saw her parked outside Mandy's flat. She rang the doorbell and waited. Mandy took ages to answer, eventually appearing in a dressing gown and clutching a ball of soggy tissues. She smiled wanly as she saw Carolyn. 'Hi. How did it go?'

'Fine.' Carolyn smiled back at her. 'I thought I'd come and see how you were feeling.' She handed Mandy the chocolates and flowers. 'By the look of you, you won't be back at work this week.'

'I can talk now,' Mandy protested.

'Not enough to lecture for a day. If you go back too early,

you'll have a relapse and be off for even longer. Besides, I'm sure your students won't want to catch the lurgy.'

'You're risking it, coming here,' Mandy pointed out.

Carolyn shrugged. 'I'll be fine.' The way she felt after the weekend, she was immune to just about anything awful.

'Well, come and have a drink and tell me all about the course,' Mandy said.

'Sure. But I'll make it. I take it you want a coffee, too?'

'Actually, honey and lemon would be nice,' Mandy said.

Carolyn grinned. 'I should tape this. No one at work would believe that the office caffeine junkie just turned down a coffee.'

Mandy rolled her eyes. 'Huh.'

Carolyn took the flowers from her friend and went into the kitchen. While she was waiting for the kettle to boil, she put the flowers in water. Then she made them both a drink and took the two mugs through into Mandy's sitting room. Mandy was sitting in front of the fire, next to a large box of tissues, with a blanket wrapped round her. Carolyn handed her the mug. 'Mandy, you look dreadful.'

'I'm a hell of a lot better than I was.' She paused. 'So how was Heywood, then?'

'Gorgeous. Even better than the brochure. The food was good, the rooms were comfortable, and it was the kind of place where you wanted to live.' Carolyn grinned at her. 'It was an inspired choice, Mandy. I think we should run other residential courses there in future.'

'Sounds good to me. What were the delegates like?'

'A mixed bunch. A couple of them were very shy at first, but they came out of their shells by the Saturday evening. You'd have liked Gina, the oldest one. She was in her mid-forties, just divorced, and she'd spent the past few months going round Europe and Australia. She fancied writing a book based on her travels.'

Mandy frowned. 'I thought it was erotic writing we were talking about?'

Carolyn nodded. 'Exactly. She'd had a few . . . Well, let's just say that they were interesting experiences. The kind that you would have enjoyed.'

'Sexual experiences with nice men.'

'Oh, yes. Paris, Turkey, the Whitsunday Islands . . . To be honest, next to Gina, I felt really gauche.'

Mandy chuckled. 'Yeah. I think I would have, too. So the course went well, then?'

'Yes. Obviously, I'm waiting for their questionnaires, and then I can work out which topics I should have covered more – or less – but they seemed to enjoy themselves. They came up with some very good work.'

'Good.' Mandy tipped her head on one side. 'And what aren't you telling me?'

Carolyn played dumb. 'How do you mean?'

'Since Mr Obnoxious showed his true colours, you've been moping about like a wet weekend. I really thought that you were going to refuse to teach the course for me and rebook it for later in the year, or tell me to ask someone else to do it. You were so unhappy. Now . . .' Mandy scrutinized her friend. 'Well, I'd say that you're glowing.'

'Maybe I just enjoyed teaching, for a change,' Carolyn said. 'You know that I like working with students; since I started my new role, I've really missed the teaching side of things.'

'And maybe you're not telling me the whole truth,' Mandy said archly. 'Come on, Caro. I've known you for long enough to tell when you're leaving something out.'

Carolyn took a swig of coffee. 'Okay, if you must know, I've had time to think about Rupert – and I've come to the same conclusion that you did. He was a complete arsehole, and he didn't know what he was talking about.'

'So tell me what's made you finally realize that!' Mandy rolled her eyes. 'Honestly, Caro, sometimes you can be so bloody irritating. Don't keep me in suspense.'

Carolyn's lips twitched. 'You wouldn't believe me if I told you.'

'Try me.'

'Well, you know what a foul day it was on Friday. Pouring with rain. Anyway, I got a puncture on the way to Heywood, just by Roudham Heath.'

'Miles from anywhere.' Mandy pulled a face. 'God, what a pain. I hope that one of those nice AA men came out and fixed it for you.'

'They didn't get a chance.' Carolyn wrinkled her nose. 'Guess who forgot to charge her mobile – and the battery was dead?'

'So you're telling me that you had to change a tyre in the rain?'

'I had a go, yes – but I wasn't getting very far. The bloody wheel-nuts wouldn't come off. Then this man stopped to help me.'

'Dangerous,' Mandy said, frowning.

'I know – but he didn't look the deviant type. We're talking new BMW here – a top-spec model. Oh, plus handmade shoes and designer suit.'

'Not all murderers are scruffy oiks.'

'I know, but he just didn't seem the type. I trusted my instincts.'

Mandy was about to make a remark about Carolyn trusting her instincts with Rupert and being way off beam, but the look in her friend's eyes made her decide not to. 'Don't tell me that he was drop-dead gorgeous as well?' she asked lightly.

'Mm, he was the proverbial tall, dark and handsome

stranger; but that's not the best bit. He sorted my tyre for me.'

'And?'

Carolyn's smile broadened. 'This is the bit that you're not going to believe.'

'Well, come on, then, don't keep me in suspense.'

Carolyn inspected the backs of her hands. 'He kissed me.'

Mandy pulled a face. 'Oh. He kissed you. Big deal.'

'I kissed him back.' Carolyn paused. 'And then we made love, over the bonnet of his car.'

Mandy's eyes narrowed. 'Hang on a minute. You're telling me that you made love with a complete stranger, over the bonnet of his car, at the side of the road where anyone could see you?'

Carolyn nodded. 'In a thunderstorm.'

Mandy shook her head. 'No. This is a scene from one of the students, isn't it? Or your version of one of the sample texts I gave you – that one where the couple make love in the middle of a stone circle in a thunderstorm. You're teasing me.'

'No, I'm serious. It happened.'

Mandy thought about it, and shook her head again. 'Carolyn, you're not the type to do that sort of thing.'

Carolyn nodded. 'I know. It was completely out of character. Actually, I thought of you, and what you would have done in the situation,' she added mischievously.

Mandy mopped her nose, then chuckled wryly. 'You're lucky that I'm not feeling up to a row,' she teased, 'if you're saying that I'm a tart!'

'No, I'm not saying that at all. Just that I know your views on sex: maximum pleasure and minimum guilt.'

'So was it good?'

Carolyn nodded. 'Very good. It felt kind of . . . I dunno. This is going to sound so wet.'

'Well, it *did* happen in a thunderstorm,' Mandy said wryly. 'Tell me anyway.'

'It felt kind of elemental.'

'So what happened?'

Carolyn stretched luxuriously. 'You want all the details, do you, Madame Voyeuse?'

'Every last one. This could have happened to me, you know.' Mandy grinned at her. 'I'd quite like to know what I missed!'

'Well, like I said, he kissed me and I kissed him back. Remember that we were both soaked through, and it was cold. My nipples were so hard that they hurt, and I wanted him to touch me. He must have been some kind of mind-reader, because he undid my shirt and pulled the cups of my bra down. He kissed his way down my throat, and sucked my nipples. It felt so good, Mandy. I just wanted him to go further. I . . . Well, I suppose that I just lost control. Like I told you the other week, sex between Rupert and me hadn't been that good for a long while; this man could turn me on with a look, and the way he touched me drove me insane.

'Then he walked me backwards to his car, and moved me so that I was lying across the bonnet. He pushed my skirt up to my waist, and I spread my legs wide. Then he ripped my tights.'

'He ripped your tights?' Mandy's eyes widened. 'Are we talking violence here?'

'Controlled violence,' Carolyn corrected. 'Not aimed at me. If I'd been wearing stockings, it wouldn't have been a problem; as it was, neither of us had the patience to wait for him to roll my tights down. And it really turned me on when he ripped my tights. It made me feel – I dunno, wanton and lewd and incredibly sexy. I spread my thighs for him, and he pushed the gusset of my knickers to one side. He stroked my sex; I was already wet and ready for him. Then he slid one finger into me, and worked on my clitoris. I couldn't help touching my breasts, giving myself up to all the sensations running through my body. I felt like I was almost part of the storm. And then I came.'

'Mm, nice,' Mandy said.

'Then I opened my eyes, and realized that my clothing was all over the place. I looked like a whore, and he – well, his tie wasn't even out of place, let alone anything else. I felt a bit awkward about it, but he drew me up to a sitting position, and encouraged me to undo his shirt. He kissed me again; and although he'd just made me come, I suddenly wanted to come again. I wanted to feel him inside me.

'I undid his trousers; he was big, Mandy, really big. Just the sort you'd like. I lay back on the bonnet again, spreading my legs and just inviting him to slide his cock into me; he pushed the gusset of my knickers to one side again and entered me. I slid my legs round his waist, pulling him in deeper, and he lost control. God, it was so good, Mandy. Better than anything I've had in years.'

'Well, I did tell you that Rupert was BESC.'

'BESC?' Carolyn queried.

'Big ego, small cock,' Mandy enlightened her with a grin. Carolyn chuckled. 'That's cruel.'

'But true. So this guy was good, then?'

'Mm. Like I said, it was the best orgasm I'd had in years. When we'd both calmed down a bit, he was going to say something, but I wouldn't let him speak. We dressed; I thanked him for his help, and got into my car and drove off.'

'You did *what*?' Mandy was shocked. 'Caro, did you switch your brain off or what? This guy's given you the best sex you've had in years, and you just left him there and drove off?'

Carolyn nodded. 'I wanted to keep it as a nice memory. For all I knew, he could have been married, or at least in a long-term relationship. I didn't want any complications. Remember, I've only just split up with Rupert.'

'Even so. You didn't even know his name?'

'Not at that point, no.'

Mandy picked up on Carolyn's comment immediately. 'You saw him again, then?'

Carolyn nodded. 'When I got to Heywood, guess whose car was parked outside?'

Mandy's eyes widened. 'You're kidding!'

'Major coincidence. I didn't see him pass me on the road, but he must have done. It turned out that he was the manager of the conference centre at Heywood,' Carolyn informed her. 'His name was Kit Williams.'

'Kit Williams.' Mandy was thoughtful. 'Hang on. Dark hair, very blue eyes, gorgeous mouth?'

'How do you know? Did you meet him?'

Mandy shook her head. 'I saw his picture in the conference brochure. I have to admit that rather swayed my decision to book Heywood. That, and the fact that the place looked like a Gothic dream.' She paused. 'So what happened? Did you bump into him in reception, or something?'

'No. First off, I had a shower and changed out of my wet clothes.' Carolyn smiled wryly. 'There was ages to go before the reception, so I sprawled on the bed and read some of the stuff you'd given me as handouts. It was good stuff, Mandy – especially the one about the stone circle in Wiltshire. My God, talk about hot!'

'Mm, it had that effect on me, too. I ended up reading it one-handed. And it must have been worse for you, as you'd already more or less enacted it,' Mandy said.

Carolyn nodded. 'Put it this way, I had to take another shower after I'd finished reading. Then I went to the welcoming reception. Kit didn't turn up to that, thank God; I was really worried that he would, and I didn't know what to say to him. I mean, it's hard to play the professional when you've acted so wildly out of character—'

'And let him fuck you over the bonnet of his car,' Mandy finished. 'Mm. Awkward.'

'Anyway, I met the delegates. We broke the ice, and we were all raving about the hotel. I can't remember who said that the place must have been owned by a sensualist, but we ended up looking through the shelves of the library and finding a book of erotic stories. Libby – she was an actress, and nothing like the luvvies that Rupert hung around with – read it out to us, and then we went into dinner. That's when Gina told us a bit about her travels, and Sue told us about something that happened to a friend of hers. We'd had a fair bit of wine, and I think we were all talking quite loudly, because this woman at the next table leaned over to us and asked us what our course was about.'

Mandy whistled. 'Did you end up with extra students, then?'

Carolyn shook her head. 'She was doing needlepoint.'

'Dead exciting, then.'

'Mm. She said that what she'd overheard us talking about reminded her of something that happened to her when she was young – she was in her sixties, I suppose – and then she turned away. After dinner, we went back into the library for our coffee and chatted for a bit. We started speculating about what might have happened to her, so you can imagine the kind of conversation we had. Anyway, when I got back to my room I needed a cold shower to clear my head. Then the phone rang.'

'Kit?' Mandy queried.

Carolyn nodded. 'He said that he wanted to discuss a couple of things with me, about the course. So I pulled on a sweater and a pair of leggings, and went down to his office. I decided to play it cool and professional; so did he, at first. Talk about switched-on – he's the kind of guy I'd like to headhunt for Write Right. I think he'd be great at finding new business opportunities. Anyway, I had the feeling that he was waiting for me to bring up the subject of my car, so I thanked him again for changing my tyre – and the fact that the receptionist was sorting out the spare for me. He persuaded me to have a drink with him – though I stuck to Aqua Libra. I didn't want a hangover in the morning.'

'Chicken,' Mandy teased.

'Even so. We started talking, and the subject of the course came up. Erotica – well, it made us both remember what had happened at Roudham Heath. He said that we needed to talk about it – about us. Anyway, we established that neither of us had a habit of bonking complete strangers.'

'I should think not, in this day and age,' Mandy said with a grin. 'At least, not without precautions.'

'Anyway, he told me that he wanted to make love with me again. He said that it was my choice – no strings, no pressure.'

'And you said yes.'

Carolyn nodded. 'I spent the night with him, in his suite. Would you believe, his rooms are in a tower?'

'Very Gothic – and very sexy, too.'

'Mm. I've always wanted one of those wrought-iron beds.' Carolyn smiled. 'Neither of us got that much sleep. We spent most of the night making love. Just lying next to him made me wet, let alone touching him or kissing him, or feeling his mouth on my skin. He wasn't there when I woke up – he had a meeting somewhere – but he'd left me a note.' She grinned. 'Anyway, that's when I decided that Rupert had been lying. If I'd been frigid, I wouldn't have been able to respond to Kit in the way that I did.'

'Good. I'm glad that that's settled,' Mandy said. 'Because if you'd still had a face like a wet weekend by the time I was feeling a bit less like death warmed up, I would have fixed you up with someone, to prove it.'

'There's no need,' Carolyn said.

'So did you see him again?'

'Yes. I'd set the students a writing exercise that afternoon; so while they were working up a short story, I went to the leisure centre. I had a sauna, though that was a bad move; I started fantasizing about him and the next thing I knew, my hand was between my legs. Luckily for me the place was deserted, so I wasn't caught. So I went for a swim. I'd done a few circuits when I realized that someone else was in the pool, too.'

'Don't tell me that you had sex in the hotel swimming pool.'

Carolyn shook her head. 'I'm not an exhibitionist, Mandy. No, we went into the steam room together.'

'And you made love there?' Mandy's eyes widened. 'Caro, you took a lot of risks.'

'A calculated one,' Carolyn told her. 'It was off-peak time. Like I said, no one else was around: it was just the two of us. And it was good, Mandy. Later that night, when I was marking the stories, he rang me. He came up to my room with a bottle of wine and a proposition.'

Mandy was intrigued. 'What kind of proposition?'

'Repeating what we'd done on Friday.'

'Making love on the bonnet of his car, in the middle of the car park?'

Carolyn shook her head. 'In the shower – fully clothed.'

Mandy whistled. 'God, I'm envious. He sounds like a guy with a hell of an imagination.'

'Mm – and with a good personality, to boot. You'd like him, actually.'

'So when are you seeing him again?'

'That's the point.' Carolyn winced. 'I don't think I will be. The next morning, he said that he'd see me later – but when the course finished he wasn't around.'

'So you left, just like that?'

Carolyn nodded. 'What else was I supposed to do?'

'You could have left him a note.'

'We agreed that it was a short-term thing. It was the end of the weekend, so it obviously meant the end of our affair. I didn't want him to think that I was being clingy.'

Mandy rolled her eyes. 'Caro, you're one of the brightest people I know – but you can be so dense, at times.'

'Look, if he'd wanted to see me again, he would have left me a message. The fact that he wasn't around meant – well, that it was over. At least we didn't have all the hassle of saying goodbye.'

'If you say so.'

Carolyn pulled a face. 'Look, Mandy, I'm not ready for another serious relationship. Not yet.'

'So what are you going to do? Become a nun for the next six months, until you decide that you might be ready to start seeing a man again? Get real.' Mandy took a swig of her honey and lemon. 'It sounds to me like you're missing the chance of a lifetime.'

'If he'd wanted to see me again, he would have left me a message,' Carolyn repeated stubbornly. 'Anyway, I'm not upset about it, or anything like that. I had a really good weekend, and it's put me back on an even keel.'

'I suppose so.' Mandy smiled ruefully. 'Ah, well. Maybe I'll be able to put my matchmaking skills to use in the future, after all.'

They continued chatting for a while; then Carolyn stretched. 'I'd better be going. There are a few things I need to do before work tomorrow – and you look like you could use some sleep.'

'Sleep's about all I have been doing, for the past few days,' Mandy complained. 'But yes, I suppose that you're right.'

'I'll give you a ring tomorrow, to see how you are – and don't you dare come in until you're a hundred per cent fit. I'll make sure that all your classes are sorted,' Carolyn said. 'I'll take some of them myself, if need be.'

'Thanks. I'll speak to you later, then.'

Carolyn left Mandy's flat and drove home, still smiling. *Maybe Mandy was right*, she thought as she unlocked the front door and let herself into the empty house. Maybe she should have left Kit a message. On the other hand, perhaps it was best that she had left things as they were. It was too late to do anything about it now.

She dropped her bag in the hall and went into the sitting room. The light on her answerphone was flashing: she pressed the 'Play' button and sat down to listen to her messages. The first four, as she'd half-expected, were about work. The fifth one was from Kit. 'Carolyn. I'm sorry I missed you this afternoon. I was called away. I have to come to Norwich next weekend, on business; I have this feeling that I might have a flat tyre. Give me a ring if you think that you can help.'

Carolyn grinned. Mandy had a point. Yes, she had just ended a long-term relationship, but she didn't need to spend the next six months living like a nun. Smiling, she stood up and went to fetch her briefcase. She rummaged through her papers until she found the phone number for Heywood Hall; then she picked up the receiver and started dialling. So much for her weekend of lust at Heywood. She had a feeling that next weekend might be even more so . . .